A.E. NALLE

EVERNIGHT PUBLISHING ®

www.evernightpublishing.com

Editor: Lisa Petrocelli

Cover Art: Jay Aheer

ISBN: 978-0-3695-0802-7

A.E. NALLE

DEDICATION

This one is for my husband. Thank you for always
supporting me in ALL of my crazy ventures.
Okay, love you bye!

A.E. NALLE

WICKEDLY BETRAYED

The Wicked Series, 3

A.E. Nalle

Copyright © 2023

Chapter One

The steady beat of hooves pounding on the compacted red dirt road filled Harper's ears. Faster and faster they came, making a mockery of her rapidly beating heart.

She turned from her descent down the front steps of her mother's sprawling estate to gaze down the worn dirt road. Away from the motorwagen, already packed to the brim with her belongings, that was to take her to her uncle's ranch in New Mexico. Half of her thought maybe she was just imagining the sound of those frantic beats. Maybe it was just a cruel trick of her mind making her think Beu was really coming for her.

But as the wind ruffled her long black curls, stringing them around her porcelain face like a wild tumbleweed, she glanced toward that lifting sun and saw what she was hoping for, what she had spent sleepless nights wishing for. Beu, atop his painted prized steed *traveling at breakneck speed.*

"Harper!" she heard him shout her name and her heart leapt from her chest.

As though her feet had a mind of their own, she turned away from the deathly glare her mother was giving her and flew down the steps. The feeling of the hot Texas soil under her bare feet was only an afterthought as she ran for her lover.

"Harper Louise, you get back here this instant!" her mother screamed as she ran. Her normally shrill voice faded in the background as Harper's blood rushed to her ears.

How her mother had found out about her and Beu, she didn't know. Nonetheless, she had discovered Harper's most coveted secret and had all but dragged her out of bed this morning only to shove her into that damned motorwagen. Her mother hadn't even let her dress properly before pushing her toward the door while Harper silently fantasized about Beu coming to take her away from all of it.

But now he was here in real life, to take her from this snooty prison she had been forced to call home for the last twenty years.

He looked like a master of his own rodeo with his long-sleeved, dirt-stained, white work shirt. In his haste to get to Harper, he had missed the top three buttons, letting the fabric flap around his dark cocoa skin as the wind tore at him. His black Stetson hat was only staying on his head by the way he grabbed the top as he galloped toward her. His fitted worn work jeans were just the same as threadbare, so much so that the normally rough fabric looked soft to the touch. A fact Harper knew firsthand.

She knew exactly what that fabric felt like between her delicate fingers as she pulled it down his thighs, revealing his hard length to her for the first time. She also knew that fabric wasn't nearly as soft as the dark skin that lay beneath. The contrast they made together was beautiful, his deep chocolate skin tone all the more vivid when she wrapped her cream-colored hand around him. How could such a hard-looking ranch hand be so velvety smooth under all those layers?

Harper still remembered how she trembled the first time Beu had laid her down. She had been pure as the rising sun before him and now that she'd had him, she couldn't seem to get enough.

He had been everything she had ever fantasized or read about in those books she hid from her momma. She had reveled in the way his calloused hands had roamed the expanse of her soft pale skin. He explored her body for hours up in that hayloft, taking his time as he kissed and licked her most intimate areas. His light-green eyes, so at odds with the rest of him, had gobbled up the sight of her splayed naked beneath him. Nobody had ever loved her so tenderly before him and she feared nobody ever would again.

"Beu!" she screamed as she ran for the wild cowboy. Her momma would kill her for leaving with him, but she didn't care anymore. Her breath left her body in labored heaves as she sprinted toward her future. The thin material of her silk nightdress fluttered behind her in the blazing heat, as if shedding who she once was before Beu.

The galloping of his steed became louder and louder the closer he came to his Southern belle. Finally, he slowed to a trot but didn't stop the horse completely before he leapt from its broad back and stumbled. Regaining his balance under those booted feet, he ran.

"Harper," he breathed before they collided together.

His hands were everywhere as his thick lips crashed onto hers. He stood so much taller than her delicate frame that she had to stand on her tiptoes just to meet him halfway.

He groaned as she opened herself for him to fully devour. His tongue slipped past her parted lips and danced with hers as his hands roamed up her silky torso. He could feel her naked flesh beneath the thin fabric of her nightgown. She was so hot for him she felt as though her skin would melt right off.

Those calloused fingers grazed the underside of her breast as his other hand dipped to grab her behind. He pulled her to him and let her feel the hard length of his manhood through those soft work jeans. She gasped against his lips as he ground into her.

"Don't leave," he begged.

The sound that ripped from her chest was close to a whimper. She shook her head vigorously before pulling him back down to her waiting lips. She was desperate as she climbed his body. She flung her arms around his neck roughly enough to knock his Stetson from his head, exposing his close-cropped black hair.

He held her as close to his body as he could before he pulled his mouth away to speak.

"Harper, I can't go one more day without being near you. I have loved you since the very first day I saw you jump into Granger Creek in nothing but a slip," he admitted and Harper hiccupped a laugh at the memory. "If you leave, I'll follow you. I don't care if I have to go to the ends of this world, I will find you. I will make you my wife. I can't imagine my life without waking up to this wild hair and your soft smile every damned day." He breathed and Harper cried.

Beu smiled down at her while wiping away her tears. "I know I ain't got much, but what I have is yours.

It's always been yours. You have my heart and I don't ever want it back. I want ... no, I need you to keep it," he finished with a shimmer of tears in those light-green eyes.

Harper opened her mouth.
"Beu, I have always—"

"No, I don't like that..." Backspace, backspace, backspace.

Harper looked up at her lover and said, "I will keep your heart as long as—"

"Damnit, no, I don't like that either..." Back, back, back.

She looked up at her cowboy and—

"Goddammit! Come on, Emily!" I scolded myself as I stared at the blinking cursor. I was almost done with this damn book, but I still didn't know how to end it. No matter how much time passed, I still couldn't decide what I wanted Harper to say to Beu.

It was stupid, really. I should just have her say she loves him and wants to spend the rest of her life with him, regardless of what her momma says. But, I couldn't seem to get the words out. The story just didn't seem completed, but I couldn't figure out what it needed.

I should just be happy I was here at all. Six months ago, I was staring at a blank screen while still trying to weave this story. Six months ago when I had gotten that phone call from my crazy-ass mother. I swear, between my mother and Harper's, we could probably write a spin-off book chock-full of all the shit they put us through.

I smiled at my own internal joke. Sometimes I felt like the characters in my books were real people, with real problems.

The smile was quickly whipped off my face as I remembered why Patricia had called in the first place. Tanner. The only other person who had gone through the same childhood as me, who had been my best friend and confidant all my life—my brother—had gone missing. Was *still* missing.

When she had told me all they knew about where Tanner had gone, or more like what they didn't know, my blood had chilled in my veins. Tanner was the only person left in my family I'd actually spoken to since I divorced Chris and left town three years ago.

A pang of guilt rushed through my body as I thought about my lack of communication with him since I moved. It wasn't from lack of trying. We both had ways of dealing with our fucked-up childhood. Mine had been shutting down mentally before marrying Chris as soon as I could to get the hell out of that house. Tanner's had been drugs and partying.

I know that sounds terrible. But, if you had to grow up as we did, you would understand. Sure, we were raised not wanting for much due to the family's wealth, but money couldn't buy the parental love every adolescent craved.

The constant stream of nannies who didn't give a shit about us moved in and out of our lives like they were on a revolving door. Most of them detested us almost as much as our parents did. All they ever saw was the huge dollar sign that came along with raising us. At least there'd only been one who had gotten too aggressive with us.

When I was eight, she'd pulled my arm a little too hard and popped my shoulder out of the socket. Tanner was the only one who believed me when I said she was the one who had done it. My mother and father never took me at my word, always preferring to believe the abusive nanny in all situations. After all, who wants to believe a child over an adult? Sad thing was, that mentality of theirs never vanished, even after I'd grown up.

They even had her take me to the hospital. Can you imagine that? Letting your child's abuser take them to the hospital to fix what she broke.

After that, Tanner had threatened the nanny with bodily harm. I never figured out what he had said to her, as he didn't feel the need to disclose the information to me. He had only been twelve at the time, but whatever he threatened her with had apparently scared her enough she had quit without a resignation shortly after.

As we aged, Tanner started leaving against my parents' wishes more and more. He was constantly sneaking out of the house. Basically saying a big *fuck you* every time he crept out his window in the dead of night.

I receded in on myself further, preferring to shut everyone out even if it went against my every need for human interaction.

Even through it all, Tanner and I always found our way back to one another. When my parents refused to bail him out of jail time and time again, it was me that would come to the rescue. And when shit hit the fan with Chris, Tanner was the only person who took my side. He had stood by me and helped me get out of that house. Even offering to "take care of the problem" for me.

I knew he was serious too. My brother had always been the one to stick up to a bully, especially when it came to me. He was four years older than me and every bit the protective big brother.

He was intimidating to look at until you got to know his sweet teddy bear insides. We were both tall but he was impressively so, with broad shoulders and a thick athletic frame. We shared the same strawberry-blonde hair and hazel eyes. About the only thing we didn't share was the liberal amount of freckles that spanned across my face but not his. He could be considered a very muscular, strong man if only he would lay off the substances that made him less than.

I loved my brother with everything in me and I had a hard time not shutting out the blinding shame that accompanied my thoughts of him lately. I should have been there for him these past couple of years and I hadn't been. I had to think leaving him behind was the cause of him going missing. His constant need to search for something to fill the void left behind from years of neglect always pushed him to wander.

Patricia said Tanner had taken off a couple of months before she thought to call me and they hadn't heard from him since then. We both had access to the family's credit cards and he hadn't used them at all these last six months.

"What the hell do you mean, Tanner is missing?" I had screeched at the woman who had birthed me.

A pregnant pause over the line had blocked any other sound around me while I waited for her response.

"I mean exactly what I said, Emily. Tanner ran off two months ago and we haven't been able to find him since." Her aristocratic tone ground on my last nerve.

"Where the fuck did he go?" I gritted behind clenched teeth.

"I don't appreciate your tone, young lady. We haven't spoken in, what, two years? And this is how you choose to speak to your mother," she scoffed.

I almost laughed out loud at her indignant speech.

"Two and a half years, too little it seems. You still haven't realized I want nothing to do with you. Get to the point of this call, Mother. Where the hell is my brother?"

I could almost see her red face over the phone line that separated us. She was always lousy at hiding her emotions.

Just when I thought she would never tell me where Tanner was, she finally spoke. "The last time he used his card was to withdraw a staggering amount of money and then at the airport to buy two one-way tickets … to Columbia," she spat the word as if it left a nasty taste in her mouth.

When I finally got the info I needed from her, I ended the call happily. It had been decided that she and my father were going to hire a PI to try and track Tanner down and then I would fly down to Columbia and retrieve him. She had told me the whole trip would be at their expense, obviously. When I located him, I was to bring him back to New York and take him to some fancy rehab facility celebrities attended.

That was six months ago. I didn't know what the hell PI firm they hired, but they needed to get their money back. I had spent the last half-year stalled in the same spot I'd been since that phone call. I was fretting over my brother, wondering if he was even alive at this point.

That was until Patricia finally called me last night. They had located where they thought Tanner may be and I was to fly out tomorrow.

The relief I felt from finally finding my brother was quickly overshadowed by the realization that I would have to face my horrible family once again.

Pulling myself from my thoughts, I looked up and across my front room. I didn't know how long I would be out of the country searching for Tanner so I had packed a couple of big suitcases that were neatly stacked by my front door.

I pinched the bridge of my nose and squeezed my eyes closed, warding off the ache that had formed there. When I opened them again, I glanced at the clock and winced.

"Shit," I mumbled to myself. If I didn't leave soon, I would be late.

Chapter Two

Sighing, I saved my work and shut my laptop. It was time for me to get ready for Jill and Damon's barbecue anyway. Or should I say engagement party? That's what it was, but they had wanted to keep it casual, which I loved.

I smiled as I thought of the happy couple. Although their relationship had developed quickly, it was easy to see they were made for each other. Just watching how Jill lit up whenever Damon walked into a room was enough to make anyone believe in happily-ever-afters.

Putting my laptop to the side, I made my way to my room to get dressed for the evening. Mentally going over what I wanted to wear while still mulling over happily-ever-afters.

I was a faithful believer that everybody deserved to find true love, no matter how dark their past was. An image of Chris flashed in my mind's eye and I frowned.

I had been so young and stupid when I had decided he was the one I wanted to spend the rest of my life with. Like Jill and Damon, Chris and I had a fast start at marriage, but I was at fault for that. Maybe if I had dated him longer than three months before asking him to marry me, things would've been different. Yeah, that's right, I asked *him*.

I was desperate to get out of my parents' house, enough to all but beg the first guy who showed me any type of affection to marry me. Pathetic, I know.

Looking back, I should have just moved out on my own, maybe gone to college. Relied on myself to find my own self-worth and not look for confirmation in someone else's arms.

I would have saved myself a lot of mental scars if

I had. I didn't have any physical scars, thank goodness. But, sometimes I think the mental ones hurt more than the physical ones anyway. Chris may have been an abusive prick, but he was always smart enough not to inflict too much damage. No, he liked to make sure his rough treatment could always be covered by a long-sleeved shirt or a little bit of makeup.

I closed my eyes as shame washed over me. The same shame that always accompanied thoughts of my lack of courage when referring to my marriage. It had taken a long time for me to stop blaming myself for his actions.

Chris didn't show his abusive side until after we married, otherwise, I never would have married him in the first place. Even after we got married he took a long time to show me that side of himself. Our marriage was fine for almost five years before he ever showed me the monster that lurked beneath his skin.

It had started small at first. We would go from having an insignificant argument to him ultimately blowing up and throwing things at the nearest wall. Of course, that scared the shit out of me, but he always apologized and blamed it on the stress he was feeling at work. He would ply me with gifts for weeks after the incident to make it up to me. I had been so desperate for the love he showed me I would always forgive him.

Things slowly escalated as the years went by. He went from breaking things by throwing them at the wall to throwing them at me. Never at my face, though. He always made sure to aim low so I could cover up the damage. He didn't start laying hands on me until we had been married for seven years. That ranged from yanking me to him hard enough to bruise my wrists and upper arms, to slapping me with such force that it rattled my teeth.

I had become so used to his sick treatment of me I'd sunk into my old ways of hiding inside of myself and staying out of the way. The only time I showed any kind of life within was when I wrote my books. Each story had been my vise to escape my brutal reality.

We were married for another four years before I decided enough was enough and tried to divorce him. He declined immediately and what he did after that was so bad, I couldn't even leave the house for a week. No amount of makeup was able to cover the damage he inflicted that time.

After that, I shut down completely. I refused to go anywhere or see anyone at all. If it hadn't been for Tanner dragging me out of that house, I would've sunk into a depression so deep I would have never climbed back out again. He had helped me find the courage enough to talk about what was happening. A lot of good it did me, though.

When I say Tanner was the only one who believed me, I mean just that. Although, at first when I told my parents what was happening, they said they believed me. My father told me they would take care of everything and I didn't need to worry about it any longer. I was to act as though nothing had been said, go on with my normal life, and just stay out of the way. So, that's what I did. I went back home, kept out of Chris's way, and waited.

I didn't know at the time my parents had hired a PI to look into some of the dirtier deeds that Chris took part in. It was a closely kept family secret that Chris embezzled money from his company to line his own pockets. I had just wanted a divorce, but my parents were maniacal enough they had other ploys they wanted to cash in on.

I was truly a fool to ever think it was their love

for me that drove them to help me in the first place. I found out after everything that dear ol' Dad had wanted to absorb Chris's company for a long time, and my predicament only proved to work in his favor.

The private investigator they hired was commissioned to follow Chris around for months and find a way into his inner circle. He needed to find hard evidence to put Chris away and open the door for my father to step in.

That PI had been none other than Leonardo Cruz. The bane of my existence and the only man that made me feel truly cherished for the first time in my life. He was also the first man to betray me so completely.

Thoughts of Leo plagued me as I entered my big walk-in closet and thumbed through my sundresses. Jill wasn't wrong when she said I could rival her collection of designer dresses. I had more money in my wardrobe than I did in kitchen appliances. The sad thing was, I didn't care about any of it. It may be childish, but spending huge amounts of money on unnecessary things was just another way I could somehow punish the people who paid the bill each month. Even if I knew my shopping habit barely made a dent in their staggering wealth.

I could wear a dress I bought from Target just as easily as I could wear one from Neiman Marcus.

I grabbed a canary-yellow midi dress with a knee-length scalloped, lace-trimmed skirt. The deep V dipped low, almost to my belly button. I didn't remember the name of the designer but it didn't matter. It looked good on me and that's all I cared about.

As I stood in front of the mirror and stripped out of my graphic t-shirt and cotton shorts that clung to my curves, I couldn't halt the thoughts of Leo as they assaulted my mind.

Up until recently, it had been three years since the last time I'd seen him. Three years to get over the man that had fully consumed every waking thought and every unconscious dream. But three years had not been enough time to forgive him for what he'd done. Seeing him at Jill's all those months ago had proven just that.

But God, he looked good standing there in my friend's living room. He'd seemed to fill out even more since the last time I'd seen him in New York. Those honey-colored eyes had looked at me and I'd watched as they registered surprise then turned molten as they raked me from my head all the way to my toes. His hair was longer and his short beard looked softer. His tattoos were just as alluring on his creamy skin. How I secretly wanted him to take his shirt off so I could again see that tattoo-covered broad chest and ripped abdomen I knew lingered underneath. Would his muscles still flex the way they had all those years ago when I'd grazed my fingers along them? Would his thick cock still jump at the sight of me nude and splayed for his ministrations?

I clenched my thighs together as I felt the familiar coiling in my core. "Don't go there, Em," I mumbled to myself as I slipped my dress past my feet and pulled it up into place. I smoothed the cotton material down my curves and bent to put on my sandals. Straightening, I looked over the image I made in the mirror.

I used to bemoan my overly curvy physique, but as my time away from my abusive ex lengthened, I'd learned to love every inch of my body. It may have blemishes, including a little extra cellulite in some places, but it was mine and I owned that. My thicker frame was complementary to my height so that helped a lot.

I fluffed my curly strawberry-blonde hair and then applied a little gloss to my plump lips. The same lips Leo had worshiped those years ago. I shook my head to try to ward off further thoughts of him. He and I had our chance three years ago but that was over now. I couldn't still be having these lusty thoughts about the man that had so wholly betrayed me.

If it weren't for his lies, I wouldn't be considered a vapid liar and maybe my family and I could have some sort of relationship.

When I was still in the dark about my family's activities regarding Chris, I met Leo at a work function at Chris's company. I remembered how miserable I'd been. It had been months since I'd revealed what was happening behind closed doors and still, nothing had changed.

I'd been in the middle of getting blindly drunk when Leo approached me at the open bar. If he'd known who I was he hadn't let on to it. I just knew I didn't know him at all. But I do know he was the only person to make me truly laugh for the first time in years.

He had been hired to become close to my husband, but in turn, he became close to me. Showing up at the house with Chris, coming to family functions, always finding a way into the inner circle. Always finding a way to get closer to me, it seemed.

Months of casual flirting when Chris was nowhere in sight had led to a short affair. Although brief, he still made me feel better than anyone ever had. He had taught me so much in our short time together. Like how to give over to someone so completely that they could make you feel ways you never thought possible.

When shit hit the fan, Chris revealed to me that he had known all along about my plan to have him tailed by a PI. When I claimed to have no idea what he was talking about, he slapped me across the face so hard I instantly tasted blood as I crashed to the floor. When I held my cheek and looked up at my husband, he threw a pile of pictures at me.

I had laid on the floor in our bedroom and thumbed through the photos with blurry eyes and dread in my stomach. For there was the evidence of my infidelity laid out for me. Candid shots of me and Leo in the throes of blinding passion. The moment I had felt the safest and most cherished was tarnished in just a few moments while my husband towered over me.

"Did you really think I wouldn't find out about everything, Emily? I knew you hired Cruz the moment it happened. You think you can fuck with me?" he had shouted at me like I was the gum beneath his shoe.

I was too blindsided to respond as he continued. "I wasn't about to let you ruin everything I've worked for. It took me no time at all to discover who exactly you hired and change his mind about who he was truly loyal to. If you pay someone enough money, they'll do just about anything. Even fuck your pathetic excuse for a wife to prove she was a cheating whore the whole time," he spat.

Shame washed over me. "I-I don't know what you're talking about, Chris. Leo—" I tried before Chris brought his loafer-clad foot back and kicked me in the gut. All my breath left me in a rush and I was left gasping for air before he gripped my cheeks so hard my teeth sang.

"Leo," he gritted in my face, "has a price tag it seems, honey. I know you hired him to get proof of my less-than-legal activities. Do you know how I know?" he crooned cruelly.

Tears streamed down my cheeks unabashedly as I openly sobbed at the realization of Leo's betrayal that sank into my bones.

Chris smiled down at me but it was a nasty thing.

"When I received the tip that someone was looking into me, I confronted your parents. They admitted you told them I was being a little rough with you. Don't look so shocked, you know they've always had a hard-on for me. They sang like caged birds. They told me all about your little scheme to ruin me. So, I decided to turn the tables on you." He squeezed my jaw one more time, dragging a whimper from me before pushing my face back down roughly.

"Here's what's going to happen." He stood to his full height over me and fixed the cuffs of his designer jacket. He picked up a stack of papers from the bed and tossed them down to me. They hit the floor and scattered around me like some sort of sick confetti surprise.

"I've already signed every place required. You sign under my name and we're done. You are also signing that you get nothing of mine. You leave here the way you came in, with nothing but a good name. If you don't agree to the terms, then I'll release all these photos of you and *my* employee for everyone to see. Then, I take your infidelity to court and take you for your whole inheritance, leaving you with absolutely nothing." He sneered down at me before crouching to my level.

I watched his striking features through tear-blurred eyes. He was handsome in every traditional sense of the word. With his short, blond, elegantly styled hair and strong, clean-shaven jaw, he was a catch. His build was athletic but not overly muscular. Everything about him drew me in when we first met. But if you looked long enough into his dark-green eyes, you were sure to see the monster in his soul. He was the person who proved to me that some of the most beautiful creatures in this world were the most vicious of predators.

He started to drag the back of his knuckles against my busted lip before I flinched away from him.

He smirked before dropping his hand. "It's a real pity, you know. Someone so beautiful has to stoop so low to get someone to fuck her."

It took everything in my being to not spit in his face at that moment. But, I'd been so hurt by everything I'd learned, I just wanted him to leave. I'd called Tanner right after and he came to help me get my things and get out. I hadn't looked back either. Until now.

I had to keep reminding myself that I was doing this for Tanner. Only for him would I face those leeches again.

I tore myself from my thoughts long enough to finish getting ready for the engagement party. I would not let my treacherous memories ruin what should be a happy occasion for everyone. I just had to hope I wouldn't be seeing Leo again tonight.

It had become obvious that he and Damon were friendly. I told myself that maybe it was just a work relationship, though, and he wouldn't be involved in any wedding activities.

Shaking off all thoughts of him, I grabbed my things as well as my gift for the happy couple and left my house. I would let myself dwell in misery later. There was no place for it here at this moment.

Chapter Three

As I pulled up to the impressive cabin by the bay, I was stunned by the sheer amount of people that sprawled the expansive property.

"Jesus, that's a lot of people," I mumbled.

I don't know what I'd been expecting. When I got married it had been so rushed that Chris and I hadn't really invited many people to attend the festivities.

Looking around at the throngs of people coming in and out of the cabin as well as mingling in the backyard, it was clear to see that Jill and Damon had no shortage of people who cared about them.

I craned my neck to see if I recognized anyone when I spotted a familiar mop of dirty-blonde hair and a friendly smile. I waved at Kate as I exited the car and started my way toward her.

"Thank God you're here!" Kate rushed to me quickly and grabbed the envelope I held between my fingers.

We walked arm in arm toward the backyard of the property. My mouth watered as we neared the smoking grill and the delicious aromas coming from it. The sounds of thumping music filled my ears as we came up on the large group of people gathered around the picnic tables. The smile seemed to curl on my lips of its own accord as booming laughter surrounded me. The sound of barking became louder along with the sounds of children giggling as a happy golden retriever bounded past us, three small children chasing after.

As we passed a full table on our way down the hill, I spotted one of Kate's husbands. Heath was talking very animatedly to a group of people I had never seen before. The smile on his face was infectious as the others had no choice but to laugh at whatever he was telling them. Kate reached out as we passed him and gave his back a covert rub with a sultry wink. I wasn't expecting him to stop mid-sentence and grab onto his wife for a heated kiss. I felt my face warm as I watched the public display of obvious affection.

When he released her, she faced me again and fanned herself a little. Heath slapped her on the ass as a way of sending her back on her way. I couldn't help but laugh as we continued our walk.

"Besides anyone you're actively sleeping with,"—I winked—"do you know any of these people?" I asked Kate as we diverted our path toward the dock further down the property.

"I know a few of them, but mostly everyone you see here is part of Damon's family." We smiled at a few handsome Latino men as we deposited my envelope on the gift table before continuing. Reid was among them and glanced at his wife before winking her way. He didn't have to speak to tell her that he saw the exchange between her and Heath and appreciated the show. I nearly had to fan *myself* after that.

"He has a big-ass family." I giggled as I looked down at my friend who returned my laugh.

"You got that right," Kate admitted. "It's a good thing too. Jill is an only child so besides her parents, she only had our little circle to invite to this shindig."

I nodded my acknowledgment as we neared the dock. "So where is the blushing bride?" I paused and glanced around again. "Or the groom for that matter?" I asked.

Kate grinned. "That's the thing. I can't find them. They've been gone for almost an hour now." She winked my way as we stepped onto the wooden decking along the water's edge. A few kids were standing on the rails, looking down into the water and dropping heavy stones just to watch them sink to the bottom.

A smile bloomed on my lips as the giggles fluttered from their little bellies. A bittersweet ache settled in my stomach as I watched them. I'd always wanted kids, but for obvious reasons had opted not to expose them to this cruel world. Maybe one day.

I opened my mouth to ask them if I could play when I heard something falling over in the boathouse, followed by something that sounded vaguely like a groan. I glanced at Kate and she just shook her head with a knowing smile on her lips.

She clapped her hands and squatted in front of the kids. "You guys see that blond guy up there with the dark-blue shirt on?" she asked as she pointed at Reid. When the kids nodded she continued, "He said that the first one to catch him gets to eat all the ice cream they want."

The kids squealed in delight and sprinted toward her unsuspecting husband. When she stood again, she looked back at me mischievously.

"Oh, that was just mean." I laughed as she walked toward the boathouse door.

"It had to be done. They don't need to see this," she admitted before she brought her fist down on the wooden door, giving it three solid thumps before saying, "All right, you perverts, everyone's looking for you!"

I gave her a confused look before I heard it. The sound of a deep muffled voice before a feminine giggle. I held my hand over my mouth to smother a snicker of my own as the door opened, revealing a very rumpled, very satisfied-looking Jill.

She looked between the two of us with a lazy smile on her face as she readjusted her fire-engine-red dress and smoothed her hair. Damon slid up behind her, belt unbuckled, retucking his shirt.

I snorted when I noticed the buttons on his shirt were fastened in the wrong places. He flashed us all his crooked grin before smiling down at his fiancée. Giving her a quick peck, he pushed past her and nodded his head toward Kate and me.

"Ladies," was all he said.

Kate and I glanced at one another before busting up laughing—the kind of laugh that had us doubling over. When we looked up, a very satisfied Damon was sauntering back toward the house and Jill still looked disheveled.

Kate was the first one to quiet her laughs long enough to speak. "Really? In the middle of your own party?"

Jill grinned at us before stepping out from the doorway. She lifted her face toward the sunset and sniffed as if she was above it all.

"It's my party, I'll fuck if I want to." She smiled back at us.

We all dissolved into laughter.

****

The sound of loud feminine laughter filled my ears hours later as all of us sat around a warm fire, a glass of red in each of our hands. The evidence of our fun night could be seen strung out around us in the form of empty wine bottles.

The night had flown by in a blur of good food, better alcohol, and the best conversations. After Kate and I had helped Jill compose herself, we walked around with her and she introduced us to Damon's family and work buddies. I even met Jill's parents.

I had to hide my grin as I watched the older couple try their best to blend with Damon's eccentric family. I smiled fondly at them. They may be from a different class entirely, but at least they made the effort. That's more than my parents would have done.

When I was introduced to Damon's brothers, my jaw almost came unhinged. If it hadn't been for Kate elbowing me in the ribs and telling me to catch my drool, I would have made a complete fool out of myself.

Liam and Oliver looked so much like Damon it was a little unnerving. Oliver introduced us to his gorgeous wife and adorable little girl. She looked just like her momma but was unmistakably the apple of her father's eye. The love they'd shown one another had made my heart flutter.

Liam, it seemed, was a shameless flirt. His dark gaze had taken in every one of my details while we were introduced, and I swear I felt my womb perk up and take notice. Although he looked a lot like his older brother, there were a few differences.

He stood a few inches shorter than Damon but he was just as fit. His face was smooth and free of any scruff, unlike his brother's. The biggest difference was that he was covered in tattoos, from his neck all the way down to his wrists. I found myself mesmerized by the images that swirled in dark ink against his olive-tone skin. What could I say, I was a sucker for ink.

Liam and Damon shared the same dark-brown hair and eyes, but his hair was cut shorter into one of those suave coiffed hairstyles. It looked decadently smooth and I briefly wondered if it would be as soft as it looked. A sudden memory of my fingers threaded through light-brown waves flashed behind my eyes as I spoke with Liam. Honey-colored eyes glanced into mine as he pressed his mouth to my—

I sucked in a sharp breath as images of Leo surfaced. Liam looked me over as if something had struck me. "Are you all right? It sounded like something pained you." The concern in his voice should have made me feel giddy but all it did was embarrass me.

I shook my head to toss away thoughts of the past before I flashed Liam a bright smile. "I'm fine, I … uh, do you want to dance?" I asked around a hard swallow, in hopes of taking my mind off Leo.

Liam's bright smile was enough to do just that as he took my drink from my hand and led me onto the makeshift dance floor. I didn't recognize the music that was playing, but I let the sensual tune flow through me as Liam grabbed my waist. I was on the tall side for a woman, but he made me feel almost delicate as he pressed his body to mine.

We swayed our hips to the beat of the music and I let go of my inhibitions as Liam trailed his hands down my sides. He was respectful, but I felt his hands tighten as they gripped the outside of my hips. His scent of lavender and mint surrounded me, so different from Leo's scent of bourbon and cedar.

I closed my eyes and took a deep breath. *Stop it!* I scolded myself internally. I needed to stop comparing this man to Leo.

It wasn't Leo's hands that were rubbing small circles with his thumb against my hip bone. It wasn't his leg that pressed between mine as he moved me to the thumping music. His breath wasn't the one that brushed over my cheek and still dipped lower toward my neck.

I didn't feel myself bring my arms up around his shoulders and push my hands into the hair at his nape. My eyes were closed as I pushed his face closer to my neck. I didn't notice when I rolled my head to the side, giving him greater access.

He took a deep breath and raked his plump lips against my pulse. My breasts became heavy and my core tightened as he traced my curves until he came to rest under my breasts. My breath hitched as his thumb raked across my peaked nipple just barely.

The music came to a stop and the sounds of joyful talking filtered back in. He didn't pull away from me as he whispered against my neck.

"Damn, I wish my brother wasn't staring us down right now. I would take you somewhere more private if I could, *preciosa.*" Liam's deep voice jolted me back to reality.

My eyes sprung open and sure enough, Jill and Damon were trying to not make it look obvious they had watched our whole exchange.

Fire bloomed across my cheeks as I gently pushed away from Liam. He grinned down at me before kissing the back of my hand with a low bow, only deepening my blush.

"Thank you for the dance, Emily," he murmured before dropping my hand.

I nodded my head, turned, and rushed away from him as though my ass was on fire. Jill caught up with me before I could get too far, looping her arm around mine as we walked toward the open bar.

"We have a spare bedroom if you need to make use of it." She barely contained her snort as I glared at her.

"Oh, hush!" I scolded her with a solid slap to her arm.

She laughed then and I couldn't stop the giggle that bubbled up my throat.

"It's all right, I totally get it. Damon's brothers are fucking hot as hell." She smiled my way before reaching behind the bar and grabbing two bottles of wine. "You don't need to be embarrassed. Anyone could get caught up with any of the Santos men," she said as she thrust the bottles into my arms before grabbing two more for herself.

I felt heat rise to my face again. "I'm not embarrassed because of the dance. Although, that was the most action I've seen in quite a while." I paused to look over at the woman I could call one of my best friends. "I'm embarrassed because I was thinking about another man the entire time," I admitted quietly.

Jill pursed her lips together and nodded her head. "Ah, Cruz, was it? Leo?" she asked and I bulked. My reaction was enough of an answer for her as she continued. "Yeah, I figured. You know, he was invited here tonight. I didn't tell you because he said he would be out of town and wouldn't be able to make it anyway," she admitted.

"I don't know much about your past, Em. But, seeing the way you reacted to him being at my old house last year, I could guess it was a lover's scorn type of reaction." She shrugged. "Judging by the intense sexual chemistry, I would also say there's a little bit of unfinished business between you two."

I sighed and looked toward the sunset. "There's a lot of fucked-up history to unpack regarding Leo." I flashed her a sad smile, hoping she wouldn't push. I wasn't ready for my friends to know just how pathetic I used to be.

She pointed her index fingers at herself around the bottles she held. "Hey, you're talking to the queen of keeping secrets. You can talk to me whenever you're ready," she offered. "In the meantime, if you want to get a little piece of Latino tail on the side, I can hook my bitch up." She grinned so proudly at me I couldn't stop the laugh that rose.

Maybe it was because of my shitty past that I had such a great group of friends now. Maybe this was my reward. Either way, I gave Jill a quick hug as a thank you before we headed toward the water.

Three hours later, I looked around our circle with a grin that had been plastered on my face for most of the evening. Kate sat next to me telling a very animated tale of her and Jill growing up together while the rest of us listened intently, laughing at the story.

Next to Kate sat her daughter Lindsey. Her dark-brown curls almost looked black against the waning sun. She also held a glass of wine in her hand, even though she wouldn't be of age for another month. She giggled against her glass as she watched her mother.

Jill sat across from me, face flushed red from the alcohol rather than the embarrassing story Kate was reminiscing about. Jill leaned forward in her seat and pointed a finger at her best friend. "I still swear to this day he was trying to kill me!" She laughed.

Kate's belly laugh was infectious as she cackled. "Imagine a seven-year-old Jill, riding her bike without training wheels for the first time down our street. She was screaming her ass off that her dad was trying to kill her!" She heaved in a breath around her giggles.

Jill rolled her eyes but smiled widely at the newcomer to our little group. The younger beautiful Latina was wiping away tears of laughter. Her short inky-black curls framed her round face so well I could swear the hairstyle was invented just for her. Her dark-brown eyes matched that of her brother's, as did her smile. She was a short thing, standing at least five inches shorter than my 5'8'' frame. She was on the thicker side, like many of us, but her soft curves only added to the feminine confidence that surrounded her. Sofee was Damon's little sister, and she fit right in with the rest of us perfectly.

"My father thought it was a grand idea to take my training wheels off and throw them away. After he promised he wouldn't let me go, the old bastard pushed me away from him. That wouldn't have been so bad if we hadn't been going downhill!" Jill sounded outraged but the fond smile on her lips said otherwise.

I was gasping for air as I gripped my stomach. Maybe it was the wine, but we all found Kate's story extremely hilarious.

Kate continued around her humorous laughs. "The only thing that made it all the funnier was when she crashed into Mrs. O'Malley's peonies! Man, was she pissed!" she hollered before she slapped her knee and howled.

Jill shook her head and dissolved into another fit of giggles with the rest of us. "I still don't know how to ride a damn bike!" she screeched.

The wine and the stories kept coming for the next hour until the sun had fully sunk behind the horizon. Most of the party had dissolved and it was just our group, Kate's husbands, Damon, and Liam. I tried not to dwell on the thought that Liam was still here and he kept glancing at me now and again.

I watched as Reid strutted up to a very inebriated Kate and knelt behind her chair. I tried not to blush as he leaned in to whisper in her ear. I could only imagine what was being said. Kate giggled and turned her head to face him. She gave him a quick kiss before speaking to us. My heart seemed to sputter at the obvious love they shared.

"Well, girls, it's getting late so I think we're gonna get going," she said, trying to hide her smirk.

"You just want to get laid." I snorted.

"I already offered Em the spare room, do you need to borrow it instead?" Jill grinned behind her nearly empty glass.

Kate scowled playfully at us. "Not all of us had

the chance to sneak off in the middle of the party to get a quickie."

"Okay, I don't want to hear any of this." Sofee plugged her ears but had a smile on her lips.

"Same here!" Lindsey waved her hand desperately.

Jill snorted loudly. "I make no apologies."

We all laughed at the playful banter before we stood and made our way back up to the house. The moment I took a step, my legs felt a little wobbly and I giggled.

"I think the wine finally hit me," I admitted with a loopy grin.

Jill wrapped her arm around mine. I wasn't drunk but I definitely shouldn't drive. "The offer stands to use the spare room tonight," she said and I glared at her. "Alone if you want, although that's boring." The mischief in her grin made me snort again.

We waved at Kate, Lindsey, and the boys as they climbed into their car.

"No, my flight is super early so I need to go home. Do you mind if I leave my car here and I'll just call an Uber? If Damon wouldn't mind driving it to my house while I'm gone and just parking it, that would be awesome," I asked.

"I can drive you home."

I jerked around to the sound of Liam's voice and flushed. Jill squeezed my arm and seemed to bounce up and down with excitement. I gripped her tighter in silent warning.

"No, I couldn't put you out like that," I tried.

He shook his head. "Nonsense. Come on, I can drive you in your car and Sofee can drive my bike behind us. She only had one glass so she's fine to drive." His smile bloomed across those sensual lips. Sofee stood behind him and gave me an encouraging nod as if confirming that she was indeed fine to drive.

"I—"

"She would love to." Jill cut me off and all but pushed me into Liam's arms.

I stumbled but Liam steadied me against his chest as I sucked in a sharp breath. I whipped my head back to my so-called friend and scowled at the smirk she had on her lips.

"Thanks," I gritted behind clenched teeth and gave her a tight smile. Jill just winked at me before sauntering off toward a grinning Damon. *Bunch of traitors.*

I took a deep breath and faced Liam with a soft smile before letting him lead me to my car. I watched as Sofee strapped a helmet over those thick curls before slipping on an overly big leather jacket. Judging by the sheer size of the garment, I assumed it was Liam's.

I became mesmerized by the design sprawled across the back of the weathered black leather. *The Insidious Seven,* I mouthed to myself. The intricate letters surrounded an extravagant design that depicted a wicked-looking skull sitting in what I could only assume was hellfire. At the bottom of the picture, it read "New Orleans Chapter."

Was Liam in a motorcycle gang?

I watched almost dumbly as Sofee straddled a metallic purple chopper sitting in the driveway. She didn't seem to care as her white sundress rode up her smooth caramel-toned thighs. She looked like this wasn't her first time on the sleek machine as she started the engine with the proficiency of an expert. The deep rumble of the bike was enough to make every last morsel of feminism leave my body. The sleek metal seemed to shimmer, even under the dim moonlight. The black leather seat looked well used but still in pristine shape. The shiny chrome wheels even looked as if they were brand new.

"That's your bike?" I asked almost dumbly.

Liam smiled at the lustrous machine proudly before looking back toward me. "Boy, I hope so. Otherwise, Sofee is getting ready to steal someone else's bike," he teased.

I puffed a laugh before rolling my eyes and smiling at the handsome Latino as he opened the passenger door of my car. Once seated inside, I mouthed a thank you before he closed the door. When I looked up toward the house, Jill and Damon were blatantly staring at me with huge shit-eating grins on their faces.

I gave them a flamboyant smile before flashing them both my happy middle finger.

Chapter Four

"So where are you flying tomorrow?" Liam gripped the steering wheel of my car in a relaxed way while he drove with practiced precision along the dark back roads. I couldn't help but feel something as I watched his muscles flex when he turned the car along the windy roads.

I swallowed to bring moisture back to my suddenly parched mouth. God, what was wrong with me? I'd been acting like some hormone-riddled teenager since the moment I'd met him. I knew it had been a hot minute since the last time I'd had sex but this was ridiculous. I shouldn't be feeling this way just by watching the man drive my car.

I cleared my throat before speaking. "Cartagena." I rasped as though I hadn't used my voice all night. "Columbia."

The city lights made an appearance as we came closer to my home.

Liam took his eyes off the road and looked over at me. The flare of heat in his dark eyes had me curling my toes in my sandals.

"It's a little early for spring break, don't you think?" he teased.

I snorted and then flushed. I had to stop doing that. The noise was the last thing men found sexy.

"I'm actually meeting my brother. I'm supposed to bring him back to New York." I shook my head. "It's a long story, I won't bore you with the details," I said as I pointed out the window. "Up here on the right." He nodded at my direction and pulled onto my street.

When we first got into the car a thread of worry flashed through my gut. After all, I'd just met this man for the first time tonight. Now, he would know where I lived. Besides the fact that I was pretty sure he was part of some motorcycle club, he was a virtual stranger to me. That thought alone should have made me push harder to just get an Uber. But, the fact that he was Damon's brother and Jill didn't seem to think I was in any danger, made me feel better about getting in the car with this mysterious man.

I told him which driveway was mine and he pulled in. After placing the vehicle in "park," he twisted in his seat and handed me his phone. I looked at it in my hand dumbly before glancing back up at him. His eyes sparkled with humor before he boldly cupped my chin. He stared as he rubbed his thumb against my lower lip. I nearly shivered at the sensation.

"I need you to put your number in there." He nodded toward the device in my hand. "I say *need* because it's not a want at this point. I need to get to know you, Emily."

I flushed again as I diverted my eyes. It had been so long since I'd gotten any kind of male attention, I didn't know how to react. I quickly put my number in his phone and texted myself so I would have his too before handing it back to him. He pocketed it before looking back in my direction.

"So, when will you be back from Columbia?" he asked. He licked his lips and my eyes followed the motion of his tongue.

"I … uh…" I swallowed thickly. "I'm not sure."

My nervousness must've been palpable as he grinned at me. He knew exactly what he was doing. "Do you need a translator to go with you? *Estoy a tu servicio,*" he finished with a wide grin. *I'm at your service.*

I returned his smile. "*Apuesto a que lo eres,*" I

responded with a wink. *I'll bet you are.*

The slight shock on his face was enough to make me chuckle.

"You know Spanish?" he asked as his smile broadened and he leaned closer to me.

"I know enough to get by," I offered with a shrug.

His smile dimmed as he looked between my lips and my eyes again. When he reached for the side of my face I leaned into him. His dark gaze seemed to pull me in as my breath became slightly labored.

"*Puedo besarte, preciosa,*" he whispered as he leaned in closer, his fingers once again cupping my chin. I felt heat flash through my body under his hooded gaze. A shiver ran down my spine as I nodded. He was asking for permission.

"*Si,*" I breathed.

He pulled in a deep breath before closing the gap between us. His lips were as soft as they looked and he was far more tender than I figured he would be. His smooth skin was soft but I swear I could almost feel the rough drag of a short beard against me.

He slid his tongue along the seam of my lips and I opened for him. He tasted sweet as his tongue danced with mine. The sound of his deep groan reverberated through my core as he pulled me closer to him.

I panted for my breath as we parted, just to dive back in. I never opened my eyes but I could see molten honey as his free hand slid to my side and pulled me closer to him. My chest thrust toward his at the angle I was being pulled. His other hand left my face and trailed a blazing path toward the V of my dress. I hissed as his calloused fingers grazed my exposed cleavage. I dug my fingers into his short hair and felt a pang of disappointment when I didn't feel the shaggy curls I still craved.

The sound of a motorcycle revving behind us seemed to break the moment. He kissed me softly one last time before pulling his lips away just far enough to graze them against mine. "If I don't stop now, I don't think I'll be able to at all," he murmured against me.

He pulled away and exited the car. Before I could open my door, he was there opening it for me. I smiled up at him before saying a quick thank you and reaching for my keys in his outthrust hand. He walked me to the door with a hand on my lower back. After I opened the door I looked back up into those chocolate eyes. He leaned down like he would kiss me again, but paused.

"I'll be texting you soon," he promised before he pushed my hair back from my face.

I nodded my acknowledgment before I stepped through the threshold of my home and he walked back down to his sister waiting at the end of the drive. I watched through the window as they pulled away and contemplated to myself.

That was the first kiss I'd had in years. The first time I had wanted to kiss anyone since Leo. I grazed my fingers against my swollen lips and sighed.

Liam was interesting and funny. Obviously, I found him attractive as I'd had such a strong reaction to him. He'd been the first man in three long years that had sparked that place deep down inside of me that had by far been neglected. I could easily see myself being more than just friends with him.

So why didn't I get that feeling you're supposed to get in your stomach when you realize a guy likes you? Why didn't I feel excited about the prospect of something new? He was overly interested in me and yet I couldn't stir that same feeling for him.

I can't say when he kissed me I hadn't liked it. I had. He was a really good kisser and I'm sure he would be equally as good a lover. But, for whatever reason, I couldn't stop thinking about the one man who had single-handedly ruined me for all others.

I couldn't stop thinking about Leo.

****

"*Now boarding first class on flight 708 to Cartagena, Columbia. Again, that is first class on flight 708 to Cartagena, Columbia. Thank you.*" The monotone voice screeched over the intercom in the terminal where I sat with my laptop on my legs.

I closed the screen and placed the device back into my carry-on before standing. I sighed to myself. I didn't even know why I bothered bringing my computer. I was no closer to finding the perfect ending for Harper than I'd been yesterday.

Quickly, I dug into my bag and retrieved the only thing that would get me through this flight. I popped the pills, to prevent motion sickness, into my mouth and swallowed them with a big gulp of water. What that really meant was, it was guaranteed to knock my ass out for the five-hour flight.

I watched as a few people stood around me in the first-class lounge and started to make their way to the gate in our terminal.

I looked almost homely compared to these first-class citizens. I wore a simple pair of cut-off jean shorts and a faded graphic tee with one of my favorite bands plastered on the front.

I grabbed my phone to pull up my ticket when I saw I had a text waiting for me.

Not sure what time your flight leaves, so I just wanted to say I hope you have a safe trip and I would like to see you again when you get back. – Li

I bit my lip as I stared down at the screen. I couldn't help the flush that overtook my neck as I read and reread his text while walking to the gate, carry-on slung over my shoulder.

I didn't know why, but I didn't expect to hear from him for a while. That's not to say I thought he wasn't interested in me. It was obvious there had been some attraction between the two of us. I just figured a guy like him would have so many different options for female companionship that he really wouldn't miss me, of all people. I wasn't dogging on myself by any means. I wasn't completely oblivious, I knew I was pretty. It wasn't being conceited, it was just a simple fact. I just thought maybe he would've gotten a small taste last night and then waited for me to come around to him. Men that looked like him didn't have any shortage of options.

Regardless, he *was* texting me. I should text back, right? Even if I was still hung up on a different guy? I rolled my eyes before opening my keyboard on the screen. I needed to move on from Leo. Why I was still under his spell after what he had done was beyond me.

What better way to get over one man than to get under another?

"Pfff," I snorted at my own attempt at humor.

I quickly typed back

Just boarding now… I would like that too. – Em

I swiped out of the message and presented my electronic ticket to the worker standing by the gate. She waved me on as my phone dinged again. I read his text as I walked down the carpeted hall.

Can't wait. I should start planning where I'm going to take you now. Will you be up for some Mexican food by the time you get back? – Li

I boarded the plane and quickly found my seat before replying. I mindlessly tossed my bag into the oversized seat next to mine as I grinned mischievously. I felt a strange boldness develop. Maybe it was the sudden male attention I was receiving. Whatever it was, I was feeling flirty as I typed.

I'm always down for some Mexican... Food that is. – Em

I added a winky emoji while still smiling like a crazy person. I watched the screen as it flashed from being delivered to being read. I looked on eagerly as three little dots appeared, indicating he was typing. God, I felt like a teenager with her first crush.

Even though I couldn't stop myself from comparing Liam to Leo last night, I had the feeling that maybe this is exactly what I needed to get over the past. I had laid in bed for the better part of last night pondering what it would be like to try again. When I said Liam was the first person in three years to spark any type of feeling, I meant just that. Sure, other men had approached me in the past, but I hadn't been interested in any of them. I couldn't help but think that maybe if I gave it the ol' college try with Liam, I could finally forget about Leo.

I nearly squealed with excitement as my phone dinged again.

Is that so? Maybe I will just skip the restaurant altogether and cook for you then. That way I don't have to rush you home for some ... South of the Border dessert. – Li

I covered my smile with my fingers as I read his text. Huffing a laugh through my nose as I typed back.

You, sir, are shameless – Em

The reply was instantaneous.

You have no idea, preciosa. – Li

I felt myself flush as I started to type back when the flight attendant came over the intercom, asking everyone to put away devices as we were readying for takeoff. I quickly typed back to Liam, saying I would text him when I landed. He responded almost immediately.

If you decide to visit any topless beaches while in Cartagena, don't be afraid to facetime me. ;) – Li

I snorted loudly at that. Barely able to contain my laughter, I typed back.

Like I said, shameless! – Em

I was still smiling unabashedly at my phone when I heard a deep voice next to me.

"I believe they already said to put away your devices, Princess."

Chapter Five

All the blood drained from my face as I forgot about the phone in my hand, and dropped it to my bare thighs. It was a trick of my ears. There was no way that deep voice that sent shivers down my spine was who I thought it was. It was too cruel to truly be him.

I winced and squeezed my eyes closed, willing it away. It was a bad dream, that was all. I heard the soft chuckle I knew so well.

"You gonna move your bag so I can sit down, or are you gonna make that nice stewardess yell at me for clogging the aisle?" Leo's sultry voice filled my ears once more and my eyes sprung open.

I turned my head in his direction so fast my neck nearly popped at the motion. It was real. He *was* really here.

He stood with his bulky body leaning nonchalantly against the opposite seat from me. His tattooed hands were crossed in front of him as were his ankles, as if he had all the time in the world.

The worn work boots on his feet looked like they had seen better days with the number of scuffs that marred the toes and sides. His holey faded jeans had also been well worn. I swallowed hard as I gazed at those powerful thighs hidden away under the tautly stretched light-blue denim. I diverted my eyes from the slight bulge at his fly as I continued my trail north.

His maroon-and-blue flannel, long-sleeved button-up was left open to expose the white shirt underneath. His sleeves were rolled up to his elbow, revealing corded forearms and thick dark ink that traveled up under the fabric. Those biceps were thick under the soft fabric, a testament to his physical fitness. His beard was little more than overgrown stubble, but it was well-maintained and still looked just as luscious as the last time I'd been forced to interact with him.

His hair still tickled the tops of his ears in wavy, light-brown locks with threads of sun-bleached highlights throughout. His longer hair partially covered the tops of those honey-colored eyes that were taking in my every detail, as I did his.

I watched as he pulled a plump lip behind his teeth and sucked it slightly before releasing it with a small *tsk*. The movement reverberated straight to my core and I felt a distant throbbing form down low. I squeezed my thighs together to ward off the sudden ache and that bright gaze shot right to my exposed limbs as his nostrils flared slightly. A lazy grin creased his lips as he met my eyes again.

As if his smirk had broken the spell he had captured me under, I scowled at him. I sucked in a large breath and turned in my seat to face him.

"What the fu—"

A small little slip of a woman came up to the two of us and interrupted me. The short brunette smiled at Leo with dazzled eyes and I nearly vomited on the spot. Of course, she thought he was hot. Anyone who wasn't blind would say the same thing. I tried not to snarl as he returned her smile with a soft grin of his own.

"Excuse me, sir, the captain has put on the "Fasten Seatbelt" sign. I'm going to have to ask you to take your seat." She blushed, actually *blushed* at the fucker.

His stupid grin widened as he regarded the delicate female. "Yes, ma'am. I was just asking my traveling companion if she wouldn't mind moving her bag." His slight Brooklyn accent drawled from his lips before he winked at her. I swear she sighed before turning her eyes to me.

She squinted as if sizing me up before speaking. "Ma'am, it's the airline's policy you stow all carry-ons in the overhead bin. If you need assis—"

"I got it," I said from behind my clenched teeth, cutting her off.

She hardened her stare at me before returning her attention to Leo, who happened to be grinning back at me. I nearly saw a tinge of red when she grabbed his biceps in an overly friendly gesture before telling him to let her know if he needed anything further. He never took his eyes off me when he nodded. With one last scowl in my direction, Ms. Skanky Stewardess walked back toward the front of the plane.

Leo and I locked eyes again as I continued to throw daggers at him. If looks could kill, he would be dead a hundred times over.

He smirked at me again before finally moving. He extended his hand toward me before he spoke. "Give it here, I'll put it u—"

"I said, I got it," I repeated.

He held his hands up in defeat but otherwise didn't move.

I huffed loudly as I moved my phone from my lap into my seat and stood. I grabbed my heavy bag before I turned my back to the solid slab of muscle in front of me.

Even though we were technically in first-class, like most airplanes, space was cramped. I managed to get the overhead bin open without touching Leo, but when I raised my bag above my head to shove it in the tiny cubby, I felt my overly curvy backside graze against the front of his jeans. I heard Leo's sharp intake of breath and couldn't help the smile that formed on my lips.

Paybacks were always a bitch.

I may have wiggled my ass more than necessary as I tried to shove my bag into the tiny space above my head. I stood on my tiptoes as I pushed it a little further, making sure to expose a little of my midriff as my shirt rose with my stretch.

Leo didn't attempt to move at all but I could feel the tension rolling off him in thick palpable waves as I moved against his crotch. Not a lot, just enough he could feel. The surge of feminine power that rushed through my body was giving me a crazy high. That was until I felt his hands circle my hips, halting my wiggling.

I sucked in a sharp breath of my own as he stepped closer to me. His calloused fingers touched my bare flesh at my hips as I felt his breath fan across the hair that draped down the back of my neck. I just barely stalled the shiver that tried to wrack my body as he spoke softly.

"Careful, Princess. Wouldn't want to get something started you're not ready to finish," he whispered as one of his hands trailed from my hip up my side.

I nearly closed my eyes at the sensation of his fingers grazing up the side of my stomach, across the side of my breast. He kept up his slow ascent to the ticklish flesh of my arm up to my hand, where he grabbed my bag and pushed it the rest of the way into the bin.

I could feel his aroused length against the curve of my ass as he closed the cubby and inhaled deeply at my hair. His voice seemed hoarse when he spoke again.

"You still use that coconut shampoo," he rasped before his fingers tightened briefly on my hip.

My breath hitched. He remembered what shampoo I liked to use?

My phone dinged again and just like that the spell was broken. Permanently this time. I inhaled sharply as I pushed out of his embrace and stepped to the side. I didn't look back up at him as I gestured my arm in front of me. I praying he would just take his seat and not speak again. That was evidently too much to ask for.

He bent slightly so he wouldn't hit his head as he took his seat by the window. He grabbed my phone so quickly, I didn't even have time to reach for it. He glanced at the screen and his jaw clenched ever so slightly, if I hadn't been watching him I would have never seen it.

"Who's Liam?" He glanced between me and the phone as he said his name.

I plopped down into my seat and snatched the phone out of his hand, pocketing it quickly before hastily gripping my seatbelt. I snapped it into place angrily and then faced the imposing male who sat so close to me.

"None of your damn business, that's who he is," I scowled. "Mind telling me what the fuck you're doing here, Leo?"

His stupid smirk made another appearance before he answered me. "What do you think?" he asked. When I didn't grace him with an answer he continued, "My job, Princess."

I had to remind myself I was on an airplane with witnesses as I thought about strangling the cocky asshole.

"Stop calling me that!" I hissed. "What do you mean by your job? You mean to tell me out of all the airlines and all the flights, you just so happened to get on this one for some *job*?" I used air quotes when I said "job."

He said nothing as he met my stare, letting me figure out the puzzle that was sitting between us like the elephant in the room. Dread curled in my stomach as I realized. "You're the private investigator my parents hired to find Tanner, aren't you?" It wasn't really a question but I still waited for him to nod in confirmation. When he did, I turned back in my seat and let my head fall back against the cushion. The plane lurched forward down the runway and so did my stomach. I closed my eyes at the burning sensation I felt there.

Why would my parents be so cruel to do this to me? They knew exactly who Leo was to me and still hired him … again! Sometimes it felt as though Patricia and Frank Donaleigh had only been put on this earth to torment me until my last day.

"Emy, I—" Leo started but I cut him off as my head snapped forward. I was seeing red as I faced him.

"Don't!" I snapped. "Whatever you're about to say, just don't. I refuse to hear it," I growled. "I may not have had any choice of who my goddamned parents hired to do their dirty work, but I do have a choice to not speak to you unless absolutely necessary. Let's just hope this time you're better at doing your fucking job than you were three years ago. Maybe this time you won't lie through your fucking teeth." My chest heaved as I finished speaking.

A look of confusion crossed his beautiful face as I turned away from him. He opened his mouth but before he could try to speak again the flight attendant's perky voice came over the intercom. I felt my heart beating wildly in my chest as I sensed Leo's attention on my profile.

I adamantly ignored him as I dug my headphones out of my pocket and quickly put them in my ears. Ignoring the text from Liam, I turned on my music full blast and leaned back in my seat. I could still feel his gaze on me as I closed my eyes, shutting everything out.

As we ascended into the air, I felt intense

exhaustion take root behind my eyes. I swallowed thickly, willing the rising emotions back down.

What had I done to deserve such cruel treatment from the people who brought me into this world? Chris had told them exactly what I had done with Leo after everything was said and finished between us. My father at least had the balls to tell me he was the one that had hired Leo in the first place. I remembered screeching at him so loud over the phone my voice broke.

They had told me to sit tight and they would deal with everything, I didn't know that included hiring a PI. I still didn't know why they had decided to flip the script and act as though I'd hired him when Chris found out. And I couldn't fathom why Leo had flipped on me so easily either.

I'd been such a stupid little girl for ever believing anything Leo had told me. I guess in my defense, he'd been a good liar. I never once guessed he was being paid to fuck me. The sad thing is, I could have moved past the lie if any of it had truthfully been real for him. I thought he cared for me as much as I did him. That's what hurt the most—the realization that I fell for someone who hadn't felt the same way at all. He had been paid to fake that feeling for me.

I took a deep breath as my limbs became heavy. The motion sickness pills were kicking in just like I knew they would. I had traveled enough to know when exactly I should take them to where they would be the most effective. I wasn't sure if I should be relieved or concerned about falling asleep next to my current company. On one hand, I wouldn't have to talk to him if I was unconscious. But, on the other, I would be completely vulnerable next to him for long hours.

Either way, it seemed I didn't have a choice in the matter. I took another deep breath and leaned my seat back as the captain gave the all-clear. Trying to ignore the smell of bourbon and cedar that surrounded me like a warm blanket as sleep took me against my will.

Chapter Six

The giggle that sprung from my belly was completely involuntary as Leo pushed me against the door of the run-down motel we frequented more often than not these days.

I'd done that so often lately. Laugh and smile, that is. More than I ever had in the last eleven years. I knew it had everything to do with the man in front of me.

I smiled up into those molten honey eyes I spent way too much time pondering. His smile mirrored mine, so wide I could almost see those dimples that lurked under his thick beard. I pushed up on my tiptoes and put my arms around those broad shoulders. I leaned in like I was going to kiss him but stopped just as my lips grazed his.

"Now that you have me here, what do you plan on doing with me?" I teased against him. Reveling in the way his facial hair tickled my lips, I flicked my tongue out and swiped it between his lips ever so slightly.

His hands tightened around my ribs as a growl rumbled deep in his chest. I smiled against his lips before he crashed into me. My arms tightened around his neck of their own accord as he pressed our bodies tighter together. No space or air between us.

His tongue demanded entrance and I gladly opened under him. He groaned and pushed his thick erection against my core. Heat rushed up my body and flooded my senses.

Leo never pulled away from me as he unlocked the door and pushed it open. Rather than letting me walk away from him, he picked me up. I wrapped my legs around his muscular hips and nearly moaned when his big hands gripped the globes of my ass.

He walked us into the room and kicked the door closed with a solid slam. We were so lost in our own world that we couldn't be bothered to be good motel neighbors and keep the noise down.

I'd lost count of how many times we had snuck off to this very room. Our little private oasis from the rest of the world. It may be a shabby little motel you could pay for by the hour, but it was clean enough.

Although, the pale-yellow colored carpet and matching drapes left a lot to be desired. As did the full-sized bed as the focal point with its lime-green, floral-print bedspread. At least the linens always smelled like laundry soap. The bed was smaller than I was used to, but we didn't come here to be apart from each other so the size of the bed didn't matter. The biggest thing it offered was anonymity.

If Chris ever thought I was cheating on him, this would be the last place he would look. I winced at the thought of what he would do if he ever found out. I pushed thoughts of my abusive husband aside in favor of living in the now. The now with Leo.

His strong legs carried us to the bed at the center of the room where he deposited me hastily. I screeched but it quickly became a giggle as he dropped me to my back. I bounced slightly as I looked up at the bulking man at the foot of the bed. He looked down at me with such heat in his eyes that I thought I might melt right then and there.

His gaze ate up the sight of me. My simple cotton, white body-con dress was low-cut on my breasts so an almost indecent amount of cleavage peaked over the top. The tight material clung to me like a second skin, stopping mid-thigh. One of the thin spaghetti straps slipped down my shoulder as I sat back on my elbows to look up at the leading star of all my fantasies.

He stood before me in his usual faded jeans with his thick work boots. The fact that he never wore a suit around Chris or any of his other business partners had been strange at first. But when I learned that he was a sort of bodyguard, his choice of attire made more sense.

I watched as he pulled his tight olive-green tee over his head, revealing that cut chest I had traced with my tongue the last time we were here. His skin from his hands to his chest was covered in intricately detailed depictions in the form of black ink. I tried to count the number of different images one night and promptly got distracted by the sensual man beneath them.

When I'd asked him about the odd-shaped lettering along his left pec, he told me it was written in Greek. He wanted to honor his heritage as well as remind himself to stay strong in hard times.

Learn from yesterday, live for today, and hope for tomorrow.

It was beautiful. He *was beautiful.*

He had been out of town with Chris so it'd been a long two weeks since the last time I had seen him and now was the only time we could sneak away. I didn't know what he did for my husband in exact detail, but as a bodyguard, he definitely fit the bill.

He was taller than me by at least six inches. His biceps were larger than most of the men I had ever encountered. Thickly corded muscles rippled along his torso in a way that was intimidating but also extremely alluring. His waist was lean with those sexy indents along his hips. I'd discovered he really enjoyed being licked and nipped there as I'd traveled farther south.

He had been the only man I thoroughly enjoyed worshiping in that way. The noises he made and the words of praise from his lips alone were enough to have me wet and ready to take him when I finished.

My breath hitched in my chest as Leo gripped my ankles and pulled me to him. My dress rode up my hips, exposing my naked flesh for his scorching gaze to devour. I had foregone any undergarments when he'd asked me to meet him. I wouldn't be needing them in the foreseeable future.

I felt thick, languid heat rush to my pussy as he knelt between my legs. He lifted my legs and placed my feet, still encased in my Jimmy Choos, onto the edge of the bed. Splaying me wider for him to see all of me.

"Leave them right here." His deep voice seemed to reverberate through my core and I shivered.

Letting go of my ankles, he gripped my inner thighs and pushed them down toward the mattress. When he blew lightly against my drenched folds I nearly came off the bed. His chuckle of approval was all I received as he looked up into my eyes.

"I missed you, Princess," he admitted seriously.

I stared back into those honey eyes as I said, "I missed you too." My voice was shaky. It wasn't from fear, but from the emotion that accompanied the words. I had never felt like this for any man. Even Chris.

Leo made me feel things I'd never thought possible before. He made me want to cut myself open just so I could bleed out every single detail of my past with him. It wasn't just about the way he worshiped my body, but rather how he treated me. He was the first person to truly treat me as a man should treat a woman—with mutual respect and love. And he was the first man I had ever allowed myself to fully trust.

"I love hearing those words," he rumbled and closed his eyes as if immortalizing this moment.

I clamped my mouth closed before the words could surface. "I love you," was what I wanted to say, what I wanted to scream from the rooftop.

Instead, I watched silently as his mouth descended on me. The sight of his thick mop of brown and blond waves had been permanently etched into the recesses of my mind. I didn't even need to watch to know what I would see. But I did anyway.

His eyes seemed to dance with a smile as his tongue swiped at me with that firm pressure I loved as much as the man gifting it to me. My back arched as his mouth latched onto me and sucked. I moaned as he groaned his own pleasure for what he was doing to me. The sound, only increasing my pleasure.

His tongue rapidly flicked at me and I was shaking within moments. The rough drag of his beard against my tender flesh was just another sensation I indulged in unabashedly. My arms wobbled so much I could no longer hold myself up as I let my back drop to the bed. My hips swiveled against him of their own volition.

Leo's hand left my thigh and descended to my wet channel. He thrust two big fingers into me and groaned again at the wetness he found there. I had no control over my own body as I threaded my fingers through his soft waves and pulled him closer to me. The growl he emitted at my rough handling had me all the hotter.

He pushed into me slowly at first before picking up speed as he licked and sucked at me. I was shaking and moaning so loudly I was surprised the neighbors hadn't knocked on the thin wall.

The orgasm built and built until I was wound so tightly, I was sure to break. His other hand left my thigh before he placed it on my mound. His bent arm lay against my inner thigh, keeping me spread wide for his ministrations. He used his thumb to pull up the hood that covered my clit, exposing it further, before he sucked it into his mouth and I went flying.

I bucked against him as I screamed my release but he never relented. He fucked his fingers into me harder and flicked his tongue against that exposed nerve wildly. I felt him watch me with those molten eyes as I crumbled in his arms, just to be pushed back over the edge once again.

My voice broke as he curled his fingers inside of me as I shattered into a million pieces. I saw stars that time as I plummeted to the bottom of my orgasm.

When the aftershocks wrecked my body, Leo took his time licking me up and down. He closed his eyes and groaned against me as if savoring my taste. He licked his fingers clean before he gave my pussy one last kiss and stood.

I watched with lazy eyes as he unbuttoned his jeans and slid them down his lean hips. His thick cock sprang free and my mouth watered. He was, by far, the biggest I'd ever had. The thick long appendage jutted almost straight out toward me as if it knew exactly where it wanted to go. The intricate veining along his impressive shaft was like a piece of fine art. My tongue still carried the memory of what those heavy veins felt like as I'd tasted him for the first time.

Seeing the bead of pre-cum at the tip made a deep hunger form in my stomach. Without second-guessing, I lunged into action. I sat up with my ass still on the edge of the bed and grabbed him with a firm grip, my fingers not quite touching each other around his huge member. He jerked against me and tensed, not from pain but pure ecstasy.

I swiped my tongue against him and he groaned before pushing his hand into my short strawberry-blonde locks. Emboldened by his touch, I sucked his bulbous head past my lips and swirled my tongue before pulling him back out. Just to dive back in.

I worked him into my mouth, going deeper with each pull. I gripped him tightly and used my saliva to lubricate what my mouth couldn't reach. I worked his whole shaft with my hand and mouth.

I looked up to face him and the sight of his heaving chest and hot eyes urged me on.

"Fuck, yes," he cursed as he gripped my hair in his fist. "You suck me so good, Emy. Can you take all of me? I want to feel your throat swallow around my cock, Princess."

He guided me further onto him and I moaned at the salty taste of him. He was getting close and it was turning me on further. I pulled him in until there was hardly any space between his pelvis and my nose.

"That's my girl," he praised me. "Cup my balls," he ordered

Eager to please, I did as I was told. While still working him with my mouth and hand, I grabbed his heavy balls and rolled them. I wasn't gentle as I knew he liked it when I was a bit rough with him. He hissed and jerked in my mouth. I had a hard time not smiling around his cock as he growled his appreciation.

I bobbed my head back and forth vigorously and sucked at him harder. His thick head knocked the back of my throat and I gagged but still pushed on. Tears pricked my eyes as I swallowed him down.

"Oh, fuck!" he roared as his cock jerked. I felt a small stream of semen flow down my throat before he pulled away from me. His eyes were wild as he reached down and yanked my dress over my head roughly. My breasts sprang free from the thin material and I sat naked in front of him.

"Missed you so fucking much," he spoke in broken sentences. "Don't want to come in your mouth," he finished before he crashed onto my body.

His hands were frantic as he grabbed and pulled me where he needed me. His mouth wrapped around my achy nipple as he spread my legs, making room for himself. I arched my back as I felt the head of his erection nudge my drenched pussy.

I reached between us to guide him where I needed him most. He groaned and released my breast with a smack before slamming into me. I screamed at the sudden invasion but pushed against him all the same. He leaned over me and fucked into me ruthlessly as he took my mouth. His tongue mimicked what he was doing to my pussy.

"This is mine. My fucking home!" he growled against me as he fucked me hard.

"Yours. All of me is yours!" I screamed.

He twisted his hips with each plunge, grinding into my engorged clit with every movement. The sounds of wet skin slapping together turned me on more than words could describe. He gripped my breast again and nipped the peaked flesh he found there.

"Come for me, Emy. I need to feel you squeeze my cock with that little cunt," he growled before he sat back. He hooked my legs around his hips and changed the angle at which he fucked me. He gripped my hips and pulled me up to his every thrust.

"Come, now!" he commanded as his thick cock rubbed against the bundle of nerves inside of me and I tumbled over the edge again.

I screamed my release as he groaned deep in his chest.

"Fuck!" he roared above me as I clamped down on him.

He fucked me so hard I thought my body would never be able to remember a time when he hadn't been inside of me. The ghost of his cock would always be *there. I felt my own flood of arousal coat him as his release joined mine in hot jets inside of me.*

Eventually, he slowed his grueling pace. But he didn't stop his long, languid thrusts after we'd found our bliss. Both of us panting in the aftermath. I watched him as he looked down to where we were connected. I knew he was seeing the evidence of both of our releases along his still-hard length.

He closed his eyes for a moment and when he looked back up into my eyes he smiled lazily at me. I felt his cock twitch with new life as he picked his pace back up, lighting me up from within.

He made love to me slowly that time as he released my hips and leaned down. He let me have his full weight as he thrust into me over and over again. Kissing and nipping at my lips just as tenderly.

It was as though something had been riding him in those first few moments and he wanted—no, needed—*to remind himself that I was his. Even if I was still technically married, I would always be his. My body and soul would always belong to him.*

Chapter Seven

I awoke with a start as the plane jolted forward and we landed. Peeling my tongue from the roof of my mouth, I surveyed my surroundings. I stifled my yawn before frowning when I noticed the blanket that had been draped over my body to my shoulders.

I was cozy under the warm blanket and drowsy enough I almost didn't notice the warmth under my cheek. That was until I realized the warmth had a steady heartbeat and an even breath. I jerked upright and sucked in a sharp breath. Embarrassment washed over me as I shoved the blanket off me as if it burned me.

"You looked cold." Leo's deep voice washed over me as my dream came to the forefront of my memory. I was definitely not cold now as heat flushed threw my entire body. I nearly moaned at the throbbing between my legs as I glanced over at my once lover.

He had that stupid half-grin on his face as he looked me over. Could he see how hard my nipples were from beneath my bra and tee? I nearly panted as he readjusted himself as if his pants were too tight.

Don't fucking look, don't fucking look, don't you dare fucking look, I chanted in my head over and over again as I strained to keep eye contact and not look at the bulge I knew was just out of sight.

It was like my stupid eyes had a mind of their own when they glanced down. His hand was dangerously close to that bulging zipper. He caught my glance in that direction and his hand clenched down on the tightened denim. I sucked in a sharp breath as I diverted my eyes.

I forced myself to face forward as the plane slowed further and we approached our gate. I heard his chuckle as if he knew exactly the type of reaction he was having on me. Then the creak of the armrest between us as he leaned into my space.

"Sorry, I couldn't stop it from the moment you laid your head on my shoulder. Then you started making all those moaning sounds and I almost exploded right here in my pants. Like a fucking teenager the first time they touch breasts. Almost scared the flight attendant." His teasing voice flowed right over my ear, sending shivers down my spine.

The sound that left my throat was somewhere between an indignant screech and a choking cough. His chuckle as he receded into his seat made me violent.

"Oh," I grumbled as I balled up the blanket still in my lap and chucked it in his face. "Shut up!" I hissed.

He let the blanket hit him in the face before throwing his head back and laughing. I could feel that deep laugh reverberate through me. So much that I had to bite my lower lip to keep from grinning.

What was wrong with me? I just had a sex dream about the last time Leo and I had been together. While snuggled up to him! Maybe it had been the smell of him that brought back all those memories. Or maybe it was just being so close to him in general.

"I'm sorry," Leo howled as he held his stomach. Like I was the punchline to his own personal little joke.

I felt my face redden as he continued laughing. He hadn't known the dream was about him. A wicked thought struck me and it was out of my mouth before I could think to reel it back in.

"No, I'm sorry. I should have tried to stop the dream about Liam from turning me on so much. I guess it was just fresh in my memory." I shrugged as if I didn't have a care in the world.

I should've left Liam out of it, but he just happened to be the only man I could think of. My list of love interests was sadly lacking.

Being with Leo those years ago had sexually awoken me. I hadn't known sex could feel that good until him. The sad thing was, even though I had been shown this whole new way to enjoy someone else's body, I hadn't wanted to since that last time.

My mentioning of another man quieted his laughs quickly enough. I didn't have to be looking at him to know he was staring at the side of my head with heat in his eyes. I risked a glance in his direction and I learned I wasn't wrong. Although, there was something more than just heat in that gaze. There was also jealousy swirling in those creamy eyes.

His jaw clenched as he stared at me. When he leaned in toward me again I didn't back down. We were almost nose to nose when he spoke. "Careful, Princess. You shouldn't tease me like that if you don't want to get reacquainted with my cock." His breath brushed over my lips as he whispered the words.

I swallowed heavily as I held his gaze. I would not back down. He had been the one to fuck up, not me. I *tsked* as I pressed my breasts out a little further than necessary. I nearly smiled as I watched his gaze divert there.

"Pity, you already had your chance to *keep* me acquainted with your cock. But, you fucked that up. You don't get a say in who I decide to spread my legs for anymore." I tried to turn away from him at that but he gripped my neck too quickly for me to move.

He wrapped that tattooed hand around me and squeezed ever so slightly. My eyes nearly rolled back into my head as I saw the fire lit deep within his own. He brazenly licked my lower lip before speaking. My panties were officially toast as I felt the flood of arousal there.

"The things I plan on doing to that foul mouth of

yours," he rumbled against my lips as he spoke. I felt a whimper rise from within me as his hand started to lower to my breast when someone cleared their throat.

I jerked away but Leo still leaned toward me. He couldn't even be bothered to look at the flight attendant. The skank from earlier scowled down at me with a crease between her perfect eyebrows.

"The captain announced first-class could now deboard. Do you need help with your carry-on … again?" she asked almost bitterly.

I opened my mouth to say something snarky about where she could shove my carry-on when Leo gripped my upper thigh with his big hand. My lips tightened but I didn't look at him. Instead, I watched the woman's gaze follow his hand, jealousy flaring in her eyes. I almost grinned at that.

"We have it handled. Thanks," Leo said from beside me before unbuckling my belt. His fingers grazed against the part of me that was still throbbing as he did. My sharp inhale did not go unnoticed.

When the flight attendant gave a fast nod and walked off toward the economy seating I hissed and quickly stood. I grabbed my bag from the overhead bin and tried to bolt toward my freedom when Leo gripped my upper arm, forcing me to meet his hard gaze.

"You may not like the fact that I'm the one you're here with, but you're going to listen to me. We are now in a different country, a more dangerous one at that. You will listen to me at all times in regard to your safety. I don't give a fuck how mad you are at me. Shit could go wrong at the drop of a hat and I need to know you will take my direction, for your own safety. You do not go off by yourself for any reason. Always wait for me, call me and I will come for you. I can't have anything happen to you. Do you understand?" he finished with a calm voice that raked on my nerves.

I rolled my eyes, but rather than answer him, I gave him a flamboyant salute. I watched his jaw tick before I showed him my backside once again.

I didn't fake myself into thinking he actually cared about me. He had been hired by my parents to find my brother. They had probably paid him a little extra to watch out for me as well. That's all I was to him—a payday. All I had ever been to him.

****

I looked down at the little paper I'd scrawled the address hastily on. Looking back up at the run-down apartment building in front of Leo and me, I frowned. This was the place Tanner had last been tracked to.

We rented a car right out of the airport and drove here in silence. Leo navigated the clustered streets of Cartagena like he could do it in his sleep. I had never been to Columbia before so the drive had been enlightening, to say the least. It was like a completely different world.

Most of the homes we passed were little more than run-down shacks. The homeless littered the streets enough to rival the stray dogs. I couldn't help but feel sad for these people.

"You're sure this is the right place?" I asked quietly, not bothering to look away from the window.

Leo shuffled a few papers before pushing them back into the center console. When he didn't answer immediately I risked a glance in his direction. He gripped one of the pistols he'd kept in his checked bag before slipping it into the holster under his shirt. He clicked the safety off the other gun and primed it to fire before he put it in the glove compartment. When his gaze met mine there was nothing of the playful lover I once knew. Now there was only a cold professional.

"My contact down here seems to think so. I'm going to go up and talk to whoever is in that apartment and find out when they last saw Tanner. Isabelle seems to think he hasn't been here for a few days but we'll see what this guy says," he explained in a calculating way.

I assumed Isabelle was his contact here in Columbia. I tried to ignore the spike of resentment at the mention of the other woman's name. I didn't know this woman from Eve, but that didn't stop that stupid bitterness from climbing up my throat and taking root.

It was ridiculous, this reaction I was having to Leo. I couldn't understand the sudden need to mark my territory like an animal. He wasn't mine to claim and he never had been. I needed to get over the silly notion that he'd been as celibate as I had these last three years. A guy like him had probably left a string of satisfied women in his wake everywhere he went.

Nodding, I gripped the door handle and started to open it. Leo immediately lunged for the door and slammed it back into place. I scowled at him. "What are you doing? Let's go." I gripped his wrist to pull him away from the door handle but he didn't budge.

"You're staying in the car," was all he said before he locked my door.

"The hell if I am," I seethed as I glared harder at him. He gave me a serious look before he spoke again.

"We don't even know what we'll find up there. Tanner more than likely isn't even here. I'm just going to ask this guy a few questions and then we will head to the resort," he offered by way of explanation. I continued to stare at him, my grip still firm on his wrist.

He sighed. "Look, I know what Tanner means to you, Emy. We're going to find him and I promise when we do, you will come with me. But right now, I'm not going to be able to do my job if I'm worried about you.

Just … stay in the car this time. Please." His eyes softened for the first time since the airport and so did a little of my resolve.

I released his wrist and slumped back into my seat. He seemed to drop some of the tension in his shoulders as well.

"Fine," I said, "but if you're gone for more than ten minutes, I'm coming up there," I threatened.

His half-smile caused me to look away from him. Every time I saw it, he broke the cast around my heart a little more.

"I wouldn't expect anything less, Princess." He chuckled before he opened his door. "Stay put and use it if you need to," he said as he pointed to the glove compartment. He shut the door behind him and walked toward the building that had seen better days.

I locked the doors before my gaze followed his receding form as he entered the building. I watched people in my surroundings eye me warily. They seemed just as leery of me as I was of them. I knew Leo left that gun for me, but I prayed I wouldn't have to use it. Just as much as I prayed that Tanner was here and he was okay.

Chapter Eight

"Bienvenidas! Bienvenidas!" The elderly woman behind the resort check-in desk waved to us overenthusiastically. She was a short little thing, with deep cocoa skin and a thick speckling of white in her otherwise midnight-dark hair. *Gloria,* her name tag read. Her smile was contagious. I smiled back at her as Leo and I approached the desk.

It was an amazing thing I even wanted to smile at all now. The apartment complex had been a bust. Leo had come back to the car within the ten minutes I had allowed him, as sober as I'd ever seen him. When I'd asked what he found up there, all he said was that Tanner was nowhere in sight.

I had the feeling he was keeping the contents of that apartment a secret to spare me. I'd allowed him the small courtesy of dropping the subject. I could guess it was probably an immense amount of cocaine that kept his mouth closed.

I knew my brother enough to know he'd always dealt with some shady characters.

Even though I had expected nothing less, I'd still deflated at not finding my brother right away. Leo had told me on the way to the resort that we would hunker down and he would use all his resources to find him. The look in his eyes as he promised was that of a professional who always got the job done. I simply nodded and looked back out the window.

I, of all people, knew he always did what he was paid to do. That was until someone came along to pay him more not to. I refused to talk to him for the rest of the ride. Even though he never stopped trying to gain my attention in one way or another.

It was late evening when we pulled up in front of the luxury resort. I was ready to eat something and crash. The day had been an emotional roller coaster ride and I was ready to get off.

"*Hola,*" I answered the elderly woman. "Reservation for Schafer,"—the annoying man behind me cleared his throat loudly. I rolled my eyes—"and Cruz," I mumbled.

Gloria tapped her nose like she recognized my annoyance with the overwhelming presence at my back. I could feel his scalding stare as I dutifully ignored him.

"Hmm," she hummed to herself. "I have a Cruz and a Donaleigh. No Schafer?" she asked with confusion in her voice.

I nearly rolled my eyes. Of course, my parents had made the reservation under their last name and not mine. I changed it from Hasting to Schafer, my grandma's maiden name, after Chris and I divorced. I would be damned if I went crawling back to the same name that was just as bad as my ex-husband's.

I gritted my teeth as I nodded. "That's the one," I mumbled.

She smiled brightly. "We have you in the two joining private terrace suites with a private pool." She smiled up at me. "Javier here will take your luggage and escort you to your rooms." She pointed to the man standing in the corner next to my large amount of baggage compared to Leo's one suitcase.

"*Grac—*wait, did you say joint?" My eyes widened at the realization of my predicament. I couldn't have a joint room with Leo. I wouldn't be able to exist for the unforeseeable future knowing I shared a wall with this man. I shook my head vigorously. "No, we need to change th—"

Leo's thick arm wrapped around my waist, hauled me up, and faced me in the opposite direction. I yelped before I could realize what was happening.

"*Gracias!*" I heard him say to Gloria as he held me firm. I felt like a wayward child as he held me with my feet off the ground. He started walking after Javier as I heard a cheerful, "*De nada!*" I could hear the laughter in her voice while Leo carried me away as if I weighed nothing at all. *Traitor.*

I smacked him on his forearm and tried to wiggle out of his embrace. "Let me go!" I seethed and thrashed like a wildcat.

His chuckle pissed me off further as he only continued to walk toward our *joint* suite. How the hell was I going to get out of this? I was fully aware I was making a scene in front of all the other resort guests but I didn't give a shit. I dug my nails into his arm and kicked my feet out wildly. When my heel landed a blow on his shin and he grunted, I felt a surge of victory course through me.

"Hold still," he groused at me.

I could see ahead of us that Javier was already putting our luggage in our rooms as we approached.

"This is fucking ridiculous, Leo. Let me down," I gritted between clenched teeth.

"I don't think I will. I prefer you right where you are." I could hear the smile in his voice that only served to grate on every nerve.

I thrashed even more now. Somehow he had twisted me around so my back was to his front but kept that steel vise that was his arm firmly wrapped around my middle. I felt the deep rumble in his chest as he thanked an unconcerned Javier and sent him on his way with a hefty tip.

What the hell did a girl have to do to get a little

help around here?

I kicked behind me again and smiled when I connected with his knee that time. Though my victory was short-lived as Leo pushed me against the wall that separated the doors to our suites.

There was barely any room to breathe as he crowded me. His thick front was pressed tightly against my back. I tried to wriggle away from him as I bared my teeth. He pushed me further into the wall as he seemed to growl in my ear.

"You are the most difficult woman I have ever met in my entire life, Princess," was all the warning I got as he bit down on my earlobe. The yelp on my lips nearly turned to a moan as he ground his erection into my backside. I bit my lip as the explosion of heat flooded my core.

He chuckled against me. "I told you to hold still." He licked the shell of my ear. His hot breath against my ear zapped a sharp yearning straight to my sex. "You caused this." He thrust against my ass again, letting his body tell me what I was doing to him. My body fully betrayed me as I felt my ass push back against him. God, it had been too long.

"Fuck," he rasped before he gripped my hips. He spun me in place to where I faced his looming figure.

I scowled up at him as he crowded me again. I was still so angry with him, but he smelled so fucking good. I hated the way I longed for him as he pressed against me.

He leaned down toward me and buried his face against my neck. I felt myself turn my head to give him greater access. When his hot tongue licked across my pulse point I shivered. He groaned against me before he kissed his way up to my jaw. The feel of his facial hair against me lit me up like a live wire.

When he reached my lips he paused and pulled away from me just long enough to look into my eyes. He searched them as if solving a puzzle before lightly brushing his plump lips against mine. My breath hitched in my throat.

I don't know if it had been the stress of the last few months finally coming to a head. It could have been the frustration that we weren't any closer to finding Tanner. Maybe it was because this was Leo. Or maybe it was the fact that it had been so incredibly long since the last time I'd been touched like this. But, at that moment, I didn't want to stop him.

I wanted to feel like I had in that motel three years ago with him. Even if it had never been real in the first place. I wanted to go back to the past just so I could be the same Emily that experienced love for the first time. To experience *being* loved by someone again.

I brought my hands up and pushed them into the hair at the back of his head. His eyes flared as I pulled the silky strands lightly before pulling him to me.

As soon as our lips met, *really* met, it was as if the entire world fell away. The sound that came from his chest was like a release of his own stress. I sighed against him as I sank into the kiss. He stood still as I explored. I kissed softly against his lips. Slipping my tongue out to rub at the seam of his. He opened for me to continue. His tongue joined in the slow sensual dance I provoked from him.

My breasts became heavy and my nipples tightened into painful peaks as I ate at him. My core felt like a tangle of unhashed yearning. The deep throbbing in my sex matched the twitches I could feel from his hard length against my lower belly.

I tugged his hair as I licked into his mouth. Through it all, he let me move the way I wanted to. He let me take the lead as he kept his hands on my hips. The only sign that he wanted more from me was the slight squeezing of his fingers against me.

When I pulled away, his eyes held all the promises I had wanted to be fulfilled three years ago. The need I saw there was almost palpable. I'm sure my eyes reflected the exact same thing as I lunged for him. I nipped his lower lip hard enough it would definitely be sore later. That seemed to break his ironclad restraint.

His sharp inhale was the only warning I got before he moved. His hand came up to the back of my head before he dug into my hair. He pulled a handful down, lighting my scalp up and craning my neck back so I had no choice but to take what he offered.

His mouth fully devoured mine as he took control of the kiss. I moved my hands then, trailing them down his torso, to the front of his jeans. When I rubbed the flat of my palm against his impressive length he jerked against me with a deep masculine groan.

He moved his mouth away from my swollen lips in favor of traveling lower. His hands were everywhere at once it seemed. He kissed, licked, and nipped down the side of my neck as he lifted my shirt to one side, exposing my bra. He held me still by my hair as he explored. With deft fingers, he pulled my bra cup down and released the tightened peak.

I fumbled with his belt and loosened it enough to shove my hand between him and the denim. He was hot and heavy in my hand as I stroked him as best I could.

"Oh, fuck," he growled before he pinched my achy nipple with his fingers. The moan that ripped from my throat was so loud, I should have been embarrassed. But I wouldn't have even cared if someone happened to walk by us at that moment. I had been pent up for so long, I needed this. For closure if nothing else.

"I thought I would never get to feel your hands on me ever again," his admission was muffled against my collarbone.

I kept stroking him as he pinched and pulled at me. Working me up into such a tizzy I didn't know how I would ever come back down.

Suddenly, he pulled away from me, forcing my hand away from his cock. He slid down to his knees in front of me. I nearly shouted as he lifted my naked breast and sucked the achy nub past his kiss-swollen lips. When I say the sensation of his soft lips paired with the roughness of his beard was enough to make me see stars, I mean just that.

I shoved my hands into his hair, desperate to hold him to me. He groaned against me as he released my other breast from the fabric that restrained it for his ministrations. I hissed as he plucked my other nipple and nipped the one in his mouth. My head hit the wall behind me as I arched into him.

He released me long enough to look into my eyes. Molten honey stared back at me as he continued to pluck me with his fingers.

"God, I missed you so fucking much, Emy." His words slammed into me like a blast from the past.

One minute I was standing in the walkway being groped within an inch of my life and the next I was back in that shitty motel with him between my legs. The echoes of the past assaulted me.

"My fucking home."

The sudden burning in the back of my eyes had me pulling my hands out of his hair. He continued to kiss my breasts as if he didn't notice I'd stopped moving.

"I love hearing those words."

Memories of laying together. Laughing as we explored one another lazily. All the promises that were made but never fulfilled.

Unholy anger replaced that tight coiling in my gut. He had been nothing but a fucking liar. And here he was, using those same damn words on me again. As if I didn't remember how he had betrayed me so thoroughly. Shame washed over me as I realized how desperate I must've looked to him at that moment. I closed my eyes as I hardened my resolve to not let it get this far ever again.

He made to pull me away from the wall before I pushed at his chest. He dislodged himself and looked up at me with such confusion on his face, he almost had me fooled. He didn't give a shit about me. He never did.

I said nothing as I glared down at him. Rage I'd never experienced flooded my every movement as I pushed him again. This time he sat back on his heels as he looked up at me. That was where he needed to be. On his knees begging for my forgiveness.

That's the part that hurt the most—he never even told me he was sorry for what he'd done. It was as if he had stepped back into my life and just expected me to get over all the shit from the past.

Not this time. I had way too much self-respect for myself to allow this to go any further. I huffed a heavy breath before pushing him again. I allowed him to stand after that, even though all I wanted to do was beat him into the ground for doing this to me.

"Emy," his voice was small as though that would calm me down.

I sucked in a shaky breath as that burning in the back of my eyes intensified. The sound that left me as I shoved him again was tortured. I felt dampness flow down my cheeks as I pushed him again. He held his hands to his sides and let me move him further away from me.

I roared my anger at him with a scattered breath as I pushed and pushed and pushed. He yielded step after step to me. I hit his chest with such force, I knew it had to hurt. The solid thump of my palms against his pecs became a steady beat inside my head.

I gritted my teeth as I wore down. The sympathy in his eyes was too much to take as I heaved air in and out of my parted lips. It was that horrible shrieking breath you heard when someone was completely losing it.

When I couldn't shove him anymore, I leaned heavily against his chest as my body shook with heaving sobs. He raised his hands to my outstretched arms and gripped my wrists. His thumbs moved in soothing circles against the skin there.

"I'm sorry if I took it too far, Emy. It's just been so long and I've missed you and now you're here but I don't know why you won't talk to me. Why you won't look at me?" His voice sounded smaller than I had ever heard it before.

I looked up from his chest into those concerned honey eyes before I shook my head and ripped my arms away from him.

"I know about everything, Leo. So you can stop pretending," I relayed to him much more calmly than I felt. His eyebrows furrowed as I continued. "It was a lie, all of it." I backed away from him toward my room. "Chris told me all about your little employment opportunity with him. He showed me the proof *you* collected for him so he could prove I was a cheater and a liar. So you won." I splayed my arms wide open and bared my teeth in a snarl. "You got the easiest job in the world. You were able to fuck a lonely, pathetic housewife and got paid to do it. Congratulations!" I shouted.

"Emily, I have no idea wh—"

"Save the fucking explanation for someone who gives a shit, Cruz! I'm done!" I yelled over my shoulder as I walked over the threshold to my suite. I turned as he started for me.

"Emily, please," he said as I slammed the door.

Chapter Nine

I still remembered what it was like to meet Leo for the very first time. I'd lost count of the number of useless work functions Chris had dragged me to over the years. The endless monotony that came with all his work events blended together like an ad from an antidepression pill commercial. More often than not, those were the only times I was allowed to leave the house.

As my years with Chris dragged on, I had lost all will to even want to pretend to enjoy myself during those outings. Most of the time, I didn't even know what the event was for. It always seemed to be some kind of award show for his company or a Christmas party or some other sorry excuse for his employees to spend lewd amounts of company money.

But the night I met Leo would forever be ingrained in my memory. Even if I didn't want it to exist anymore, it would always be there.

That particular event had been the company's annual New Year's Eve party. I still remember I had taken up residence at the open bar like it was my right to do so. I was on my fourth dirty martini for the night and I was trying desperately to find the bottom of that bottle. It had been months since I told my parents what had happened to me and yet there I was. Still stuck in an abusive marriage.

I gulped down the last of my martini and scarfed down the olives. I placed the empty glass on the bar and tapped my nose toward the bartender. She gave me what seemed to be a sad smile as she grabbed the glass and started to refill it.

"Extra olives this time, please." The pretty female raised a regal eyebrow at me and I shrugged. "I skipped dinner." I smirked.

"You know, if you just wanted a jar of olives, I'm sure they'd be able to give them to you," a deep sensual voice raked over me as if I were an exposed nerve.

I turned in my seat and assessed the bulking form that stood behind me. I was probably a little tipsy at that point as his good looks didn't even really sink in until later that evening. I think the fact that I was so far past my limit of putting up with people's bullshit made me roll my eyes at him and turn back around.

"Better yet, we could go raid the vending machines I saw down the hall," he said. He slid into the seat next to mine and faced me fully. The first thing to seep through my liquor-soaked brain was his scent of bourbon and cedar. If I had been in a better mood I would have said his scent invited me in. But I wasn't in the mood to deal with anyone that night.

The bartender placed my glass in front of me, this time with three olives instead of two. *How generous of her.* "I'm not in the mood to deal with yet another one of the almighty Christopher Hasting's lackeys. Kindly fuck off," I said as I brought my glass back to my lips. When I heard his booming laughter I turned back toward him in shock.

I was used to Chris's friends always making passes at me. It was like they had a running bet to see which one would be able to sway me toward them. I always shut them down. Chris never so much as blinked when it happened. It was as if he knew I would always be faithful to him for fear of what would happen if he found out I was less than the compliant, devoted housewife he married.

Even though none of this was new to me, this time was different. This *one* was different. The man that sat next to me didn't call me a bitch and stalk away like all the rest. This one laughed and smiled at me like I was the most intriguing creature he'd ever come across. This guy was the complete opposite of the rest.

Now that I really looked at him, I mean *truly* looked at him, I became curious myself. He wasn't dressed like the other business partners and employees were. He wore a simple fitted t-shirt and faded jeans. His hair was an unruly mop and his face was covered in a thick beard. His eyes sparkled with laughter as he looked me up and down with an appreciative gaze.

"So, the princess has claws." He chuckled.

For the first time in a long time, I felt a grin tug at my lips. I slowly turned in my seat and crossed my legs. I held my glass between my thumb and forefinger and twirled it around and around as I stared at him. He looked at me with no small amount of heat in his gaze. I felt the urge to clench my thighs together as an unfamiliar feeling took root in my core.

"I'm far from a pampered princess," I scoffed before nodding in Chris's direction. He stood proudly in the middle of his friends looking like the King of Shit Mountain. His three-piece designer suit had been tailored to his exact measurements making him appear immaculate. If you didn't know the narcissist that lived beneath those fancy distractions, you would say he was everything you wanted or wanted to be. His inner circle surrounded him like they were fighting for the right to be the first to kiss his ass tonight. "You're not like the others." I eyed them wearily.

Mr. Casual shook his head without taking his eyes off me. "I'll take that as a compliment. If I ever become half as needy as any of those poor fuckers, I would hope someone would put me out of my misery." He finally glanced over at the group and pointed to the tall lanky man next to Chris. "That one with the pained expression, Clark I think. He's so desperate for Chris's attention it looks like the poor guy has a pole shoved directly up his ass," he joked.

I laughed at that. It was refreshing to speak to someone in a place like this who was so … real. I kept the smile on my lips as I played with the toothpick that held my three olives in my drink. Picking it up and tapping it against the side of my glass before slowly bringing the garnish to my lips. I watched his eyes follow the movement of my tongue darting out to grab the olive and slide it off the stick. I'd gone from being miserable to having fun with this stranger.

"So what do you do?" I asked him as I placed the remaining olives back into the liquid.

He seemed to think about his answer as he leaned forward in his seat. I don't know what possessed me to lean forward as well. "You could say I'm a bodyguard of sorts." He smiled a secret smile I didn't quite understand.

I placed my drink on the bar and forgot about my mission to get drunk for the rest of the night. I faced the bodyguard again and held out my hand. He grinned and chuckled as he grabbed it and made a show of shaking it with fake seriousness.

"Emily," I said.

"Leo," he said and smiled. We stopped our handshake and he held onto me for longer than necessary.

I thought he'd introduced himself because he was overcome with the need to talk to me. Maybe he had seen the lonely person I had become and wanted to help me. I was so wrong.

When I remembered that night and how he had only approached me because I was a job to him, it made it easier to come to terms with my present predicament.

I hadn't left my room for the last three days. I had

all my meals delivered to my suite and hadn't left once. Opting to be in solitude rather than face the man that had once again wrecked me.

The evening we arrived here, after the heavy petting in the walkway, I slammed the door in Leo's face and then promptly ignored his muffled voice on the other side. I had all but plugged my ears as I walked into the massive bathroom in my suite, started the shower, and walked in without caring if it was warm. I was so emotionally spent I didn't even take my clothes off until I'd sat under the stream for a few minutes.

Even over the water's spray, I'd still been able to hear Leo's pleas through that damn door. He had begged me to open it, to talk to him about the past. He claimed he had no idea what I was talking about.

I had only exited the shower when the pleas stopped. I'd wrapped myself in the big fluffy robe provided by the resort and exited the steam-filled room. Turning out all the lights on my way to the massive bed before curling up on top of the pillowy duvet.

I was all dried up from my earlier explosion but I was still just as miserable. I'd lay and stared toward the door that separated the interior of our suites. I had to assume the door connected families who wanted to stay close to one another. But, right now that door only served as a reminder of all my mistakes

In the dark of my room, I'd heard a rustle outside that door before light flooded under the crack. I'd watched more intently than I liked to admit, waiting for a glimmer or a shadow of the man that occupied the other side.

When two shadows of legs crept along the bottom, my stupid heart leapt into my throat. He stood on the other side of the door for a long time after that. Never knocked. Never spoke. Just stood there. If I listened closely, I could almost hear him breathing.

I had stared for so long my eyes started to wane before I could stop them. They only sprung open when I heard a slight thump against the door. When I looked back in that direction, those two shadows had turned into one big one. Then another thump had sounded. As if he was leaning against the door and laid his head back a little too forcefully.

I'd fallen into a deep, dreamless sleep while Leo sat on the other side of that door.

When I woke, his shadow was gone.

The next few days had been spent in solitude. I didn't speak to anyone but the room service workers. I ate in silence, hearing movement from Leo's room now and again. The only sign he was even still there was the sound of his door opening and closing. Whether he was going to get food or meeting with his contacts, I didn't know.

He'd only knocked on my door a few times, trying to get me to talk to him. Trying to see if I was still alive. I never answered him.

I would sit in front of my computer day in and day out. Staring at the damned blinking cursor until I would get so mad at myself, I'd slam the screen closed and push it further down the bed.

Liam had texted me a few times over the last couple of days. I'd ignored him at first and then realized he deserved better than that. It wasn't his fault I was in a bad mood. I'd gone through the motions of talking with him but nothing sparked as I did. I had the feeling this was how my life would be from now on. Anytime a man would show interest in me, I wouldn't be able to move past the one I shouldn't want.

When I wasn't trying to write or texting Liam, I spent most of my time soaking in the bathtub with only my thoughts to keep me company. Wishing I wasn't such a fucking coward. I was in this beautiful place with all these areas to survey and explore, but I refused to leave my room because of the man next door.

The only time I'd seen him was when he would emerge to his terrace. I would cower onto the huge bed and watch him from a distance at first. The windows along the sliding glass patio doors were tinted on the outside. Allowing whoever was inside to look out, but if you were outside you couldn't see in.

I'd watched him every day these last three days as he stripped his shirt over his head before plunging into our private pool in nothing but his swim trunks. I couldn't even lie to myself, I had sat there and drank in every one of his details like he was a bottle of water and I was in the desert.

The way his hair slicked back when he got it wet reminded me of all the times we had showered together in that tiny stall at the motel. The water along his tan, inked skin, gracefully glided over all those bulges and crevices. I watched those powerful muscles flex and pull as he swam laps in our tiny pool. And every day, without fail, he would stand up out of that pool and look straight in my direction.

At first, I had squealed before ducking behind the massive bed, as if he could see me. It took me several minutes to realize that hadn't been the case. He would keep his eyes trained on my door as he hooked his thumbs in those swim trunks before pulling them down to his ankles. I had swallowed thickly as I'd watched him shamefully. I eventually came up from my hiding spot and walked to the door.

Our joint suites were closed off from prying eyes but I had the feeling even if others could see him, he still wouldn't care. I knew he was putting on a show just for me and that thought alone made me want to run out that glass door and take him right then and there. Damn the consequences.

I would gobble up every detail as he stood in front of me with a ravenous gaze. Every day, he stood there in all his glory as if saying he would lay himself bare for me. *Only for me.* I would watch the water bead on his skin as he let his wet hair fall in front of his face. Water droplets dripped to the ground. He held a towel in his hand but never made a move to cover himself as he continued to stare. His thick muscular legs held up that impressive form and I would become hypnotized just watching the way his muscles worked under his skin. Especially that thick cock my mouth watered for each time I saw it.

The way it would bob between his legs as if it was telling him which way it longed to go. I felt the flood of arousal soak my inner thighs, preparing for something that would never come. After long-drawn-out moments, he would wrap the towel around his waist, taking away my view but never leaving. Then we both just stood there and stared.

He never said anything and I never opened the door. His honey eyes searched the outside of that glass as if he could see straight through to me. To my soul. The longer we stood there, the hotter I would become. Even if all I wore most days was that plush white robe and the room was chilled, I would always melt while watching him.

As the days went on, I couldn't help but feel as though I was being cruel to him. I hadn't ever given him a chance to explain himself. I kept replaying the pain in his eyes as I slammed the door in his face over and over in my mind. Hell, I hadn't even dared to go outside since we'd gotten here for fear of having to face him.

Truth be told, I didn't even want to hear his side of the story. I just wanted to move on with my life, but being around him just kept me in the same spot I'd been three years ago. Not in that shitty little motel with him. But instead, I was still on the floor of my bedroom, being kicked like a dog. The sad thing was, that kick had been mild compared to the pain I felt regarding Leo's betrayal.

When he would finally divert his eyes, it seemed like all the air would leave my lungs in a rush. As if I had been holding it and hadn't realized it.

I watched him back away from my glass door and head back over to his side of the connected terrace. I would stand rooted in that same spot as he would place his towel on one of the hooks to dry before he returned to his suite. Sometimes I stood there until I heard him leave his room to go roam the resort or do whatever he did.

That's exactly what I did now. I stood in that same spot, stared out the glass door, and waited for him to leave his room. It was so quiet in my room you could hear a pin drop. So it was easy to hear the rustle of clothing in the other suite. I listened as he got dressed, grabbed his room key, and then left his suite with a muffled clink of the door.

I stood stock still in the same spot for a few more minutes before I stepped toward the terrace. I didn't let myself think about what I was doing as I unlocked the sliding glass door. I slid it open and was immediately accosted by the sultry heat of the early afternoon.

Chapter Ten

My bare feet touched the hot concrete as I stepped outside and surveyed my surroundings.

This little private pool area was everything you would expect from a luxury resort. Lush greenery climbed up the walls surrounding me, adding to the solitude of the area. There was a mesh hammock hanging beyond the far side of the pool that looked like it would be a good place to snuggle down with a book. The water in the private pool was blue as the sky and looked cool in comparison to the humid heat outside. On my side of the terrace were two white lounge chairs away from the walk-in pool. One of them faced the pool and the other was at an angle so you could see over to the other joint terrace. There was also a little bistro table that sat between our two areas, obviously meant to be shared between the suites.

The glass wall that divided the two areas was there more for decoration than privacy. Leo's side showcased the same furniture as mine. The plants and loungers were in the same spot.

I glanced down at the water spots from where Leo had stood moments ago. I could still see the outline of his naked feet as he'd walked back to his side of the enclosure. Stark nude. I clenched my thighs together to ward off the achiness that filled my sex.

My gaze followed the water trail. I felt my feet moving but genuinely had no control over them. When I looked up where the trail had ended, I saw his towel hanging from the hook to dry. I reached out and grabbed the soft material. Rubbing the damp plush fabric between my fingers.

Glancing around at his terrace door to see if I

could detect any movement before I pulled the towel down. I walked back to my side and sat on the lounger facing his side. I sat with that towel in my lap as I leaned back, propping my feet up in front of me.

Maybe I was perverted for it, but I brought that towel up to my nose and inhaled deeply. Leo's scent coated every fiber of the material. The slight smell of chlorine was overshadowed by the man that had been drenched in it.

His smell seemed to overwhelm all my senses at once. I couldn't stop myself as I spread my legs apart. I took one last deep breath of that towel before gripping it in my hand and lowering it to my side.

I was so ungodly turned on. It could have been from the fact that I was still riding the high from my flashback dream. Or maybe it was from being so close to the only man to bring me any kind of sexual pleasure. Whatever it was, I didn't stop myself as I unbelted my robe and let it fall to the side.

My nipples pebbled into painful peaks the moment they were exposed, despite the hot temperature. I raked my hands down my torso, making sure to let my fingers trail over the sensitive flesh there. I plucked at myself firmly, drawing a breathy moan from my own lips.

Somewhere in the back of my mind, I knew what I was doing was wrong, but I didn't care. I had deprived myself of my most basic need for far too long and I needed to feel it again. Even if it was my own hands that had to do it.

I continued to tweak my nipples with my left hand as my right continued its descent. It would have been so easy to picture that it was Leo's fingers blazing a scorching path straight to my pussy. When my fingers grazed over my mound and delved into my folds, I wanted nothing more than to have it be his hands that spread my thighs apart further. The vision could have been so clear behind my eyes, but I didn't allow it to come to fruition.

I needed this to be just me, not Leo. I needed to learn to let go of the fantasies that were likely never to be true. To learn I didn't have to have Leo's hands, or anyone else's for that matter, to bring me to ecstasy

I was so wet, there was no resistance as I swirled my middle and ring finger around the thumping bundle of nerves at my center. I gasped as I spread myself with my fingers, letting the fresh air flow against the normally hidden flesh.

The moan that left my lips as I pushed my fingers into myself made my throat feel raw. I gathered more moisture from the weeping entrance before bringing my fingers back up. I spread my arousal around my clit as I continued to pluck at my nipples. My breath left me in a rapid release as I worked myself into a frenzy.

The snap of a door being unlocked registered in my brain but I didn't stop. I was winding up to crash back down and I didn't want the pleasure to end. Then a sharp intake of breath had me opening my eyes.

Leo stood on his side of the glass partition blatantly staring. His eyes widened with shock but the look was quickly replaced with something else entirely. Something darker.

I halted my movements but didn't remove my fingers from myself as we stared at one another. He didn't move as though he was grounded to that spot, his hand still on the glass door. Neither of us spoke. His eyes flickered from where my hands lay against my pussy and breast, to the towel beside me. His nostrils flared as did recognition in those honey eyes. He knew it was his towel from earlier.

Something unspoken seemed to pass between us. Most men, I'm sure, would have either done one of two things: 1) turned around and went back inside, too embarrassed to stay; 2) tried to join in.

But, as Leo stood there it was as if he knew I needed something different from him. He knew I needed this for myself. To take back some of the power that had been ripped away from me.

He seemed to struggle to tear his dark gaze from me as he turned away. I thought for a moment he would go back into his suite, but he turned the opposite way. He took a few long steps to his lounge. My breath hitched in my chest as he folded himself onto the white seat.

As he sat, he readjusted himself by thrusting his hips in the air and tugging on his shorts. My gaze flew straight to the bulge at his zipper and nearly whimpered. My fingers twitched against my throbbing clit as if it was begging me to continue.

Leo's eyes met mine as he rubbed his hand down the front of his shorts. I bit my lip as I watched the lust that visibly filled his body. I swirled my fingers ever so slightly around myself and gasped. He groaned as he pushed up into his own hand before moving it. He unbuttoned the restraining fabric so quickly I almost missed it. Pulling the zipper down before releasing himself from the garment. His head lulled against the back of his lounger as he gripped himself in his big hand.

My lips parted as I watched him stroke himself once from tip to root. I plucked my nipple again as I panted. My fingers dipped in and out of my drenched pussy. He groaned again as he watched me before pushing his shirt up his torso, revealing those corded muscles along his abdomen.

I moaned as I finger-fucked myself faster now. The wet squelching noises filled the terrace. Leo jacked himself roughly, keeping up with my hastened pace. His lips parted as he panted. He cupped his heavy balls as he continued to slide up and down that thick shaft.

I wanted nothing more at that moment than to be the one touching that cock. I wanted to taste him along my tongue as I played with my cunt. The thought of swallowing him down released a fresh gush of arousal from me.

I gripped my breast hard as I undulated my hips.

"Fuck." I breathed, my desperation plain. My fingers worked faster and faster against my sopping sex.

I watched myself for a moment before returning my eyes to Leo. His muscles along his abdomen flexed and released rapidly as he worked himself fast. I knew he was close by the way his legs started twitching. I was at the top of my mountain ready to fall off, just waiting for him. He stared at what I was doing before glancing into my eyes one last time. He was waiting for me too

"Come!" I screamed as I exploded.

His long groan spurred on my own orgasm. My hips lifted off the lounger as I rubbed my fingers in and out of myself, up and down my whole pussy. My release coated my fingers thoroughly.

"Oh, God!" he groaned as he watched me.

Long thick jets of cum spewed out from his cock and landed on his stomach. He never took his eyes off me as he continued to grunt his release all over himself.

We were both panting as we came down from our highs. I twitched in the aftershocks as he lightly stroked his still-hard length. He had completely emptied himself but his eyes told me he was still ready for more.

I removed my fingers from myself and grabbed his towel. I held his gaze as I cleaned myself up, gently wiping away my release from my still needy sex along with each of my fingers. When I was done, I stood on weak legs. Not bothering to close my robe, I gripped the used towel in my hand.

I should have just walked back into my suite and closed the door. I should've left him there to clean up his own mess. It would have been no less than he deserved. But instead, I sauntered over to him. I let him soak up every detail I had on display. Feeling his gaze scorch me as I came closer with each step. When I stood within reaching distance, I saw his cock twitch in his palm. I licked my dry lips, bringing moisture back to my suddenly parched mouth. He looked up at me slowly as if he would eat me alive at any moment. *Was I terrible for wanting him to do just that?*

I was so close to him, there was no way he couldn't smell my arousal. But, he held still, not moving a single muscle to grab onto me. His eyes were the only thing that moved. I held his towel out for him almost as a peace offering. He looked between it and me before he grabbed it with his free hand. Slowly he pulled it away from me and toward his nose. When he inhaled against the soft material I felt my knees almost buckle. I backed up from him as he brought the towel down to his cum-covered belly. He held eye contact but said nothing as he cleaned his mess from himself.

I blinked quickly to release the spell we seemed to be in before spinning on my heel. Walking hastily to my side of the partition, I felt his eyes on me the whole time as I walked back into my suite and closed the door. The giggle that bubbled up from me was almost erratic. My lips had a genuine grin on them, the first one I'd had since we checked into the resort.

I didn't know if I'd consider the moment on the terrace purifying as it was anything but pure. But I felt a huge weight lifted off my shoulders at that moment. Something about us not speaking and just being with one another without touching, had felt respectful. Like him not trying to take over what I was doing, was him somehow saying he saw me. *Really* saw me, down to my core. He had known I needed to take back something others had stolen from me, inadvertently or not.

I covered my smile as I pushed away from the glass. I was suddenly feeling the need to get out of this room and explore the resort. Humming to myself as I stepped into the shower, I found myself looking forward to something for the first time in days.

Chapter Eleven

I smiled at the elderly couple that passed me on the way to the beach. The older woman that reminded me of my nana gave me a bright smile as she wrapped her hand around her husband's arm. The feeling of love that surrounded them pinched my heart.

I walked on until I came to the edge where the sand met the concrete. I slipped my sandals off my feet and held them between my fingers. As I walked onto the sandy shore, I glanced around at all the other beachgoers. They were few and far between this time of day. I had spent most of the day wandering around by myself, even participating in a few resort activities along the way.

I'd spent most of my time at the main pool surrounded by strangers. I'd allowed myself to relax in the cool water and sip on some strong mixed drinks. When I decided to explore the beach, I realized just how late it had become.

Most people were going back to their rooms to prepare for dinner, so I thought it was the appropriate time to come here. The fewer people blocking the view of the water the better.

I found an empty lounger and placed my sandals down next to it. Taking my big sun hat from the top of my head, I placed it on the seat. The bright-white, sheer material of my bathing suit cover left little to the imagination as I shed it as well. The tankini I wore was simple and seemed to mimic the sunset. The top was bright yellow but slowly faded to burnt orange the further it went down. The top stopped just below my belly button, leaving my midriff on display before reaching my deep orange bottoms.

It had always been a struggle to find the correct-fitting bottoms to cover my curvy ass. Eventually, I'd given up my search and just wore what was comfortable. Even if they always showed more skin than necessary.

I walked to the water's edge and let my feet sink into the sand there. The clear liquid looked so clean I could see the sand beneath. It was colder here than anywhere else. The water lapped at my ankles as I stepped forward. I walked until the water covered my hips, allowing my body to become used to the chilled temperature. My nipples puckered as a shiver snaked up my body from the sudden change. Before I could talk myself out of it further, I dove into the clear water, letting it wash away any stress left in me.

I stayed under that water longer than necessary. Waiting until the last possible moment before my lungs felt like they would burn up. At last, I emerged with a long gasp and shrieked at the brisk breeze that flowed over my sodden skin. I giggled to myself as I wiped the water from my eyes and gently wrung my hair out. I felt refreshed, I didn't know if it was the water or my earlier *me time.* Whatever it was, I embraced the feeling.

"I wasn't sure if I needed to come under and save you." Leo's deep voice startled me.

There goes my stress-free evening.

I rolled my shoulders back and braced myself as I faced him. He stood at least ten feet away from me with the water up to his knees. I tried not to blush as I saw the same swim trunks from his earlier swim. The dark tattoos along his exposed skin looked stark compared to the rest of our surroundings. His hair was mussed as if he had run his fingers through it multiple times since I'd last seen him.

"I don't need you to save me from anything," I muttered dryly.

He smiled under that overgrown stubble.

"Clearly," he said.

I turned away from him and walked further into the water, stopping as it reached my breasts. I wasn't foolish enough to think that Leo hadn't followed.

Long moments passed as I stared at the waning sun before he spoke again.

"I've been looking for you." His voice seemed hesitant, as though he were trying to gauge how I would react before he even spoke the words.

I puffed a humorless laugh. "Well, you found me." I turned to face him again. "What do you want, Leo?" The harshness in my voice wasn't dulled by the peace I'd found.

Though I had taken something for myself earlier, that didn't mean I had forgiven Leo for anything. All it had done was let me come to terms with myself. To rediscover that part of myself I associated with this man. I had needed to disengage that part of myself that had thought he was the only one I could link my sexuality to.

I owned my sexuality. No one else but me. I had just chosen to share that part of myself with him, and it had been a mistake.

"I want to talk," he replied as he held my gaze.

I snorted, not caring how unsexy the sound was. "You want to talk?" I asked. At his nod, I continued, "The time for talking was three years ago." I tried to hold back the anger I felt coiling in my gut.

"Emy, you left me. Not the other way around." His hard voice only increased my anger.

"Excuse me?" I screeched as I stepped closer to him.

"How was I supposed to talk to you about anything when you just ran? I didn't even know where you went." He held his arms out like he had every right to be angry with me.

I would be damned if he thought he could turn this around on me.

"What the fuck was I supposed to do, Leo? Was I supposed to go to you and let you fix the problem *you* created? You sold me out!" I yelled as I stepped closer to him. He was within arm's reach now and I vaguely thought about strangling him.

His smirk did nothing to cool the boiling rage in my gut. "See, you keep saying that and I have no fucking clue what you're talking about. Were you angry with me for not telling you I was working for your father? I didn't really see it relevant to tell you any of that because I thought you already knew. He hired me to dig up dirt on *your* husband after all," he seethed.

I snapped at the mention of *my* husband. As though all of this was *my* fault. I took the last step in separating us and slapped him right across the cheek. The loud crack felt like it split my ears as I felt a deep throbbing start in my palm. Leo's face snapped to the side and I gave him no time to recover as I pointed my finger at him.

"How dare you!" I screamed. "Like you, my parents left me in the fucking dark the entire time. I didn't even know they had hired you until Chris threw his evidence of my infidelity in my face. All because they told him that I was the one that hired you. Why they lied to him, I still don't know." I knew my face was red and my voice was wobbly but I kept berating a very shocked-looking Leo.

"All I ever knew was that you were his goddamn bodyguard. But don't worry, Chris told me everything right after he kicked the shit out of me!" Leo's eyes flickered with rage. Good. I needed a good fight to release this monster that lurked beneath the surface.

"He told me how he flipped you. Paid you to fuck

me. Just so he could blackmail me into a divorce that I'd already asked for. He just wanted to make sure I couldn't take any of his goddamn money." My breath left me in heaving gasps now.

"All I wanted was a fucking divorce!" I screamed at Leo like the last fourteen years had been his fault alone. "Not a single person told me the truth! Chris … my parents … you!" I pointed an angry finger at him. "Everyone saw what that fucker was doing to me and nobody would help me." Tears of anger flowed down my face. I shook my head as I tried to step around him.

He grabbed my wrist before I could brush past him. "Emily, I didn't know he was hitting y—"

"Don't you dare try to make yourself look better with more lies." I cut him off as I tried to jerk my wrist from his grasp.

Leo's eyes darkened as he went deathly still. "If you think for one moment I had any idea what he was doing to you that I wouldn't have ripped his goddamn throat out, you're dead wrong."

I stilled as he spoke. He sounded like he was being completely honest.

"Be that as it may, you still took his money and betrayed me." I pulled myself from his grasp and walked out of the water.

I quickly grabbed my things as I walked back toward my room. I knew I'd made a scene but I didn't give a shit. I walked past multiple people that were outright staring at me.

When I hit the concrete, I heard Leo shout after me. I didn't slow as I kept walking. I was done. He could report to me about anything related to Tanner but otherwise, I never wanted to see him again.

When I reached the walkway that led to my door he finally caught up to me. He gripped my hand and twisted me around.

"You're going to listen to me," he growled as he crowded me.

"I'm not going to do anything that concerns you ever again," I seethed.

"Goddamnit, just listen!" he shouted. "Chris never paid me to do anything, Princess. Your parents are the only ones who gave me a job. I was hired to find dirt on your ex-husband and that's exactly what I did. I fucked you because you are the sexiest, most interesting, smart-ass, infuriating woman I have ever met. I was never paid to get you into bed. I did that all on my own, baby." He was so close that it was making me dizzy.

"And when you left you took a piece of me with you that I have never been able to replace." His breath came out in rapid pants as he confessed. "Everything that happened between us was real, Emy." It was as though he was begging me to believe him.

"Don't," I said as I looked away from him. I couldn't hear anymore.

"If I had known what Chris was doing, I would've killed him," he rasped as he inched closer to me.

"Don't," I begged again as tears washed down my cheeks.

He reached out and swiped my tears away before he grabbed both sides of my face, crowding me further.

"I would never willingly let another man abuse the woman I loved." His voice was small.

I huffed as I tried to pull away from him but he held me firm.

"*Don't*!" I shouted.

"I love you, Emily. I fell for you all those years ago and I haven't been able to stop since then." His voice was hoarse.

I couldn't take it anymore. I thrashed away from him and slapped him again. He released me and stood still as he rubbed his cheek. We both stared at each other as the emotion in my gut bubbled over. I could take the lies. I could be angry at him for what he did to me. But I couldn't take it if he started saying things like that.

The wounded sound that came out of me was nothing I'd ever heard before as I tried to slap him again. This time, he caught my hand before it could connect. I brought my other hand up to hit him and he caught that one too. He stepped into me, making me back up until I stood against the wall.

He held my hands over my head as he stared down into my eyes. My chest heaved in and out heavily. Neither of us spoke. The tension built around us until my skin felt so tight I could hardly stand it. The string of pressure formed between us, becoming thinner with each passing second. Then, all at once, it snapped.

Chapter Twelve

When Leo's lips crashed down onto mine I didn't try to stop him. I opened under him like a flower at the first sign of spring. He groaned against me as he released my arms from where he held them against the wall. I wrapped them around his shoulders before he picked me up.

He held onto the globes of my ass as he pushed me flush against that brick wall. I pushed my hands into that mop on top of his head and kissed him back as wholly as he did me. Our tongues intertwined in a delicate dance of their own making.

I could feel his erection prodding at my sex through my swim bottoms. I wiggled against him, silently telling him exactly what I wanted.

I shoved everything from my mind. Past and future. I was going to live in the right now with him. Three years ago didn't matter anymore, nor did what we would be after this. All that mattered was my need for him and his for me.

Leo used one strong arm to hold me as he pushed us toward his door. Somehow he managed to get the door open without ever taking his mouth from mine. One minute, we were pawing each other in the sultry heat and the next cool A/C was washing over my damp swimsuit. Gooseflesh raced across my skin as he kicked the door closed behind him.

I didn't let myself think about the similarities to the last time he had taken me. This was now. We were here in this nice resort, not a shitty motel. I was no longer the cheating wife and he wasn't my husband's bodyguard. I wasn't the same person as I was then and neither was he. I wasn't looking for an escape from my brutal reality like I had been all that time ago.

This was happening just because I wanted it.

My feet touched the floor and I felt the edge of the bed against the back of my knees. Leo ripped his lips away from mine before he dropped to his knees in front of me. He said absolutely nothing as he yanked my bottoms down in one harsh tug. The still-damp fabric pulled roughly at my skin as he did, but it was just another sensation to be had.

I hissed at his urgency when he gripped onto my ass and drew me closer to him at the same time he buried his face in my cleft. The first swipe of his hot tongue had me moaning so loudly, I was sure others would no doubt hear me. I honestly didn't care if they could. I was finally remembering what it felt like to be wanted, it felt as though he would die if he didn't get his mouth on me.

"I didn't think I would ever get to taste this sweet cunt ever again," Leo murmured as he pulled away from me just to dive back in. He groaned against my clit as he hoisted my leg up and over his shoulder, opening me up to him further.

I gasped as he sucked my engorged bud between his teeth and nipped it before swirling his tongue around it to soothe the ache. I bucked into his mouth as he continued his unique brand of torture.

Nip, swirl, nip, swirl, nip, swirl…

When he pulled his mouth away again he replaced it with his fingers. He watched what he was doing to me as he spread me wide before sinking two fingers in deep. The resounding groan that came from him was almost as satisfying as what he was doing to me.

He looked up at me then, hot lust swimming in those molten eyes. "You taste like fucking sunshine, Princess." His endearment always annoyed me until he used it like this. This turned me on more than I liked to admit.

"You're going to cream all over my tongue, aren't you?" It wasn't a question but I stared down at him as I breathed my answer.

"Yes."

He was pumping up into my pussy and raking those digits across my G-spot with each pass. I could feel my wetness coating his fingers more and more with each second.

"That's right. Can you hear how wet this tight little cunt is, baby?" His dirty talk always did this to me.

I nodded as my legs started to shake. I was going to explode. The only choice I could make was to squinch my eyes closed under all of the sensations I was experiencing, it was too much. His fingers moved faster as he kept speaking.

"You look me in the eyes when you come. Scream my fucking name." He smacked my ass with his free hand to accentuate his point. My eyes sprang open.

"Be a good little princess and come all over me, Emy," he ordered harshly.

His command was the knife that cut the last thread holding my sanity.

"Leo!" I screamed as the first wave of my orgasm crashed over me.

"That's it, Emy. Fuck yes," he groaned right before he latched those perfect lips onto me again.

I gripped his hair as he sucked my clit into his mouth and started my orgasm anew. I screamed so loudly my voice cracked. My hips undulated themselves as I rode out my bliss roughly against his mouth, but he didn't seem to mind. In fact, his face had a look of pure euphoria along it.

I collapsed in a heap against him on the floor. His hands ripped at my top, pulling my breasts from the material hastily. It was like if he didn't get his hands on my skin he would burn up. When my already hardened nipples were free from their constraint, the chill of the room puckered them further almost painfully. Until his mouth descended on me and he sucked the achy flesh in with a growl. He bit down roughly as I arched into him. His harsh treatment was something I didn't even know I had needed until right now.

My fingers fumbled with the strings on his shorts, trying desperately to unleash that cock I had only been able to dream about filling me. By the grace of God, I finally pulled the damp fabric down far enough to draw him out. He landed heavily in my palm and hissed as if just my touch completely unmanned him. He pulled away from my breast to look down at what I was doing to him.

I watched him watch me as I stroked his length from tip to root. The pearly liquid that gathered at the tip of his head made my mouth water to taste him once again. I collected the liquid with my index finger and lifted my hand from him. Leo's eyes followed that hand up, up, up. Until I reached my mouth and sucked the digit inside. His eyes flared as I savored his unique flavor with a long moan.

Whatever tight restraint he had left snapped at that. He gripped my hips and lifted me. My back was against the edge of the bed as he sat back on his calves. Then he positioned me right above his huge cock and lowered me until he breached my entrance.

I gasped at the slick invasion and watched his face contort almost painfully as he filled me. Inch by inch, I sank onto him. He stretched me so tightly I could hardly take it. It had been so fucking long.

"I don't know if I can!" I panted.

His naked chest heaved under my palms as he

slowly bobbed me up and down his long erection. I was maybe halfway down his entire length and I wasn't sure I could take much more.

"You were made for me, Emy. You're going to take this cock like the good girl I know you are. Put your feet on either side of me, flat on the floor. Hold yourself up with my shoulders and lean against the bed," he ground between clenched teeth.

I did as I was told and helped him bounce me slightly. He gained a little more with each slow movement. My chest swelled as I realized he was going slow so he wouldn't hurt me.

He moved his hands from my hips then. One hand went around to my ass and the other went to my front. The one at my back slid down my crack until he circled the backside of my pussy. He gathered moisture there and traveled back up until his long middle finger pressed against my puckered hole there. He watched my reaction the entire time.

I felt myself clench around him as he pushed in just slightly. I gasped at the sensation and was surprised when I pushed back for more. His cock twitched inside of me as he groaned.

"Fuck, you're going to kill me, Princess," he rasped.

His other hand slid to my pussy. His finger splayed around his cock, slowly moving in and out of my opening, before sliding to my clit. I bucked against him and slid further down him as he rubbed my arousal around.

"Oh, God!" I exclaimed.

Everything he was doing lit me up like a torch. The sensation of him thumping that finger against my ass, his thick erection slowly fucking me, and now his fingers against my clit were too much.

"That's it, Emy. Take everything I give you. All of it is for you, Princess," he gritted harshly.

He moved me with his hands. I was wound like a coil about to pop loose. I started shaking as he continued to rub me in tight circles. Gripping his shoulders so hard, I'm sure he would wear my marks for a few days. Lower and lower I bounced until I no longer knew where he began and I ended.

When I finally sank all the way we both released harsh breaths. He continued to sink the tip of his finger in and out of my ass while rubbing my clit. I felt his cock twitching as if begging me to move. I was so impossibly stretched but in the best way possible.

When he started to lift me, I squeezed down on his cock. It was like my body was afraid to lose him. He groaned deep in his chest as he watched where we were connected. My shaking intensified as all my nerves lit up.

When he spread me wide and pinched my clit with his splayed fingers I went off like the Fourth of July. I screamed as my release exploded from me. My arousal rushed from me like a flash flood and drowned his cock. I clamped down on him with such force that I saw the moment the rest of his control snapped.

"Fuck!" he roared right before he slammed up into me with all his might.

He moved his hands back to my hips and pushed himself to his knees. I had no choice but to hold onto the edge of the mattress as he thrust into me roughly. I was so fucking full but I loved every moment of it. He kept me on the right side of pain.

He pulled me to him before he stood. Never pulling out of me as he laid my upper body on the foot of the bed. He kicked his shorts off from around his ankles as he wrapped my legs around his muscular hips. My breasts were still poked out the top of my swimsuit but that wasn't good enough for Leo as he gripped the fabric and ripped it down the middle.

"Nothing between us," he breathed as he leaned down to suck on my heavy breasts.

He fucked me with hurried thrusts. The sound of wet slapping skin spurred us on. I could feel his balls slap the curve of my ass with each of his powerful slams.

"You. Are. Mine. Do you hear me?" he growled as he pulled his mouth from me.

"Yes!" I screamed. It was only the truth after all.

He kept up his brutal thrusts as he put his thumb down on my clit once again. He pushed down as he tweaked my nipple and I went flying again.

"Yes, Emy, soak my fucking cock. Oh, shit!" he roared as he slammed into me one last time. His long groan above me released something primal in my soul. He was coming in long hot jets inside of my pussy as I reached between us and grabbed him. His mouth fell open in a surprised gasp as I pulled him from me and stroked him firmly.

"Fuck!" he breathed as he jerked in my hand.

His cum covered my hand, mound, and lower belly. I stared up at him and watched his face contort as he finished all over me. We were both panting and sweating when he collapsed on top of me. He didn't care that we were both now covered in his release.

He kissed his way up my jaw until he captured my lips. He ran his fingers through my hair as he gently kissed me. Only pulling away to whisper right against my lips.

"I was so scared I'd never get to do this again, Emily. I need you to believe that I would never do anything to hurt you. I looked for you for so long, baby." His quiet words were so hushed you could barely hear them.

He didn't wait for me to respond before he pulled me to him and carried me to the bathroom. He sat me on the edge of the tub before starting the hot water. He knelt between my legs and tongued me again while the water level raised. If he cared that I was covered in his release, he didn't show it as he brought me to another earth-shattering orgasm.

It was as though he couldn't stop himself as he took me again in the bath. I rode him in the hot water, surrounded by all of those bubbles while he touched and worshiped every inch of my body.

We'd talk later, I told myself. *Now, I needed to make up for the lost time.* Maybe we couldn't go back and rewrite the past, but we could change the future right now.

Chapter Thirteen

We'd stayed in that bath long after the water ran cold. Taking our time relearning one another's bodies. Never speaking more than dirty, filthy things that turned us both on.

Now, hours later, I watched from my spot on the bed as Leo hung the phone up. He ordered our room service meal, never once asking what I wanted to eat. I tried not to dwell on the fact that he already knew exactly what I wanted.

It was surprisingly late in the evening when we emerged from the bathroom. Neither of us spoke about our sleeping arrangements. I had just wrapped my robe tightly around my naked body and climbed in under the plush white blanket on his bed.

He had opted to just wear one of the big white towels wrapped around his muscular hips. The soft fabric hung low on those hips and effectively short-circuited my brain every time I looked at him. It really was unfair how dangerously attractive this man was.

Leo climbed under the blanket with me and pulled me to his side immediately. It was like he thought if he didn't keep his hands on me I would disappear. We were both content to lay like that for a long while. My head was draped on his chest, my leg over his. I felt warm and safe and ... I felt like I was home. Like I was exactly where I was supposed to be. That was until he decided to open that wicked mouth and bring me back to a screeching reality.

"We need to talk," he murmured against my hair.

"We already talked. I don't want to fight anymore today, Leo," I said.

He was quiet for a few beats but I could tell

something was eating at him. I knew we would need to hammer everything out eventually. I just wasn't ready to break the bubble I had fully encased us in yet.

I winced at my own selfishness. It wasn't fair to not let the man say his peace just because I was completely content not rehashing the past right now.

What is it they say about ripping a bandage off? Better to just get it over with.

I sighed as I pushed away from him. I adjusted myself until I was sitting cross-legged on the bed facing him. I made sure all of my naughty bits were fully covered. Wouldn't want anyone to get distracted.

"Talk." My voice held none of its usual animation as I spoke the one word.

Leo looked me up and down before he moved as well. Soon, we were both sitting on the bed, cross-legged, facing one another. I stifled my smile as I thought about how we were sitting. We looked like a couple of college girls at a slumber party. You know, if there was extreme sexual tension at slumber parties.

If I thought about it hard enough, I could write the scene beautifully. I had never written a girl-on-girl book but the idea did spark that feeling in my mind when I felt the urge to write. Sometimes it was impossible to quell the creativity I felt when inspiration hit.

"I would like to know what goes on behind those beautiful eyes, Princess." He smiled my way as if he was trying to read my mind.

I smiled then. "Trust me, no, you don't." I was a creative writer. The things that flashed behind my eyes daily were not always for the faint of heart.

Leo returned my smile before sobering again. "I know the last person you want to talk about is Chris," he said coldly and I shivered. I stayed silent though, willing him to continue.

"I already told you I never worked for him. Everything between you and me is and always has been real. I was never paid by anyone other than your parents, I swear on everything I am, Emy. And I know I don't have anything solid to prove my innocence besides my word. But, I have been trying to work this out in my head and I think I figured it out."

I nodded my head for him to continue. I was going to let him say what he needed to say, even if I was still doubtful.

"I was hired to dig up concrete evidence that Chris was embezzling from his own company. I'm still not sure how he found out that I was hired but my guess would be he had someone watching your parents. He was a very paranoid son of a bitch, and for good reason." Leo's face dulled its usual playfulness as the professional in him slid into place.

He was right, though. Chris had always taken every security measure he possibly could. He had hired a security firm to cover every square inch of our home with cameras. There were alarms set at every door and window as well. I felt like I lived in Fort Knox most days. And that was exactly why Leo and I always had to sneak off to that motel. Even if Chris was gone a lot on business, he would know if anyone came or went from that house.

"From the time he opened his company to the time I came into the picture, Chris had stolen over five million from his investors and nobody was the wiser." I shook my head in disbelief. I'd known he was taking money from his investors, but I never knew how much.

"I think when he was tipped off about your parents hiring me, he confronted your father. I think Chris knew he was fucked when he saw the evidence I had given to your dad. He knew there was no way he could get out of trouble other than making Frank a deal. I think he offered him a way to make millions by joining him and getting rid of all the evidence." Leo studied me carefully as he dropped the bomb between us as if he were talking about the weather. I openly gaped at him.

"That's an awful tangled web you're weaving, Leo," I said. I didn't quite believe everything he said, but I couldn't say some of it wasn't ringing a familiar bell.

"I do the same research on my clients as I do the people they hire me to follow, Princess. Daddy was in the red in a bad way. He was less than a year away from bankruptcy." His words cut through me like a knife to the gut. I had no clue the family's money well was running dry. I nearly laughed to myself. Why would I know? Patricia and Frank never felt it necessary to tell me anything.

"Of course," Leo continued, "when Chris confronted him, Frank had to save his own ass and blame the whole thing on someone else. I would guess your father saw a dollar sign and looked for the easiest way to cash in. What better way to get on your husband's good side than by lying and telling him his wife was the one that betrayed him?" Leo was starting to sound more and more convincing the longer we sat there.

Restless energy had me moving away from him. Panic laced his eyes as he watched me stand from the bed. He thought I was going to run. I *wanted* to run. Even though I didn't want to hear anymore about how I was just a pawn used by everyone, I forced myself to stay in the room with him. I watched my feet as I paced back and forth next to the bed. When I nodded at Leo, he continued.

"That was his way into the business. An easy payday, Emy. He told Chris you were the one to hire me in hopes that he would throw him off his trail. After that was settled, Chris hired another PI to follow you. That's how he got the pictures of us in that motel. And Chris lied too, just to hurt you. He told you he hired me when he really hadn't, just to get back at you for trying to ruin him, Emily."

Leo finished with such sympathy in his eyes that I couldn't take it. Hurt and rage mixed in my gut like a ball of tangled yarn. I didn't know who to be mad at but I needed to scream and thrash and let the world know that I'd been wronged. Nothing about the last fourteen years had been fair.

"That's a whole lot of lies, Leo. You don't have to try and be so creative. Just tell me the fucking truth for once!" I screamed at the only man to treat me like an actual human being. I knew it wasn't fair to him. I knew he was trying to be honest with me but it felt too good to lash out right now.

Leo stood too. He rounded the bed and for a moment I thought he was going to grab me and shake sense into me. He walked right past me and grabbed the shorts he had been wearing earlier in the day. *Was he going to leave? Did I want him to leave?*

"I'm telling you the truth, you stubborn woman. I'm telling you the truth now, just like I was telling you the truth back then. I wasn't lying when I said I wanted to take you away from it all, Emily. And if this is the only way I can prove to you how real everything was for me, then so be it," he beseeched me before holding up his shorts.

Flashbacks of spoken promises as we lay in the motel assaulted my memory. I squeezed my eyes closed as the old pain resurfaced. A lot of things were said and a lot of promises were made that were never followed through on. It still hurt just as badly as it did back then.

Confusion creased my brows as I watched him

dig out his wallet and fish out two pieces of paper that looked like they had been unfolded and refolded thousands of times.

The memory assaulted me full force. The image of us laying in that crappy motel room, limbs tangled together. Laughing so much, my cheeks ached.

As if something was tickling the back of my brain, it clicked together all at once.

****

"I'm going to take you away, Emy." Leo's voice rumbled across my neck as he leaned over my naked body. I'd lost count of how many hours we'd been here. I smiled as I threaded my fingers through his hair, loving the feeling of those silky locks caressing my skin.

"Is that right?" I could hear the smile in my voice. I felt him return my smile against my skin.

"Where do you want to go? If you could pick one place in the entire world, where would it be?" he asked as he kissed my collarbone.

I turned my head around to his face and smiled widely as I stared into his honey eyes. Trailing my fingers along the smooth lines of ink that scattered across his chest.

I thought about his question for a beat, even though I already knew the answer. When most people would say something exotic like Hawaii or the Bahamas, my place was much simpler than that.

"When I was a kid, we took a family vacation to Montana. We were way up in the mountains for a couple of weeks." My smile wobbled as I became lost in the memory. "I was twelve at the time, I think. Tanner just turned sixteen. My parents spent the entire week working." I huffed a laugh. "Big shocker, I know."

I let my fingers trail down Leo's chest to his lower belly. I grinned at the way his abdomen flexed when I circled his navel lightly. We had just spent our bodies to the point of exhaustion but I still hadn't had my fill of him.

"Even though they ignored us the whole time, that was the best vacation I have ever been on." I snorted despite myself. Leo's perfect teeth made an appearance as he smiled down at me. He always said he loved my little sniffles when I laughed. I thought the sound was less than attractive, but he would always give me that look when I did it.

"Tanner and I explored the mountain around our small cabin and the tiny town at the base. We hiked and fished and just enjoyed each other's company without any distractions. We found a waterfall tucked back in a small cove of the mountain that we played in for hours. Until it was past dark and it was hard to find our way back home." I grinned as I remembered the carefree smile on my brother's face as we jumped into the freezing water. That was the happiest I'd ever seen him. It was as if we had gotten to take a break from our normal awful lives and just be kids for once.

I rolled over on top of my lover, letting the sheet slip away from my body. The way his scalding eyes ate up my naked flesh had me shivering before I leaned down to take his lips with mine. His hand grazed up my thighs and came to rest on my behind before squeezing me there. I felt his cock start to stir back to life beneath me.

I pulled away from his lips long enough to speak. "Montana," I mumbled. "That's where I would like to go." I smiled.

He returned my grin with one of his own before flipping me beneath him. I squealed at the sudden movement before it turned into an unabashed giggle.

He rubbed his parted lips against mine. "Montana it is," was all he said before he slipped inside of me with one smooth thrust.

****

As I looked down at the three-year-old airline tickets in my hands, I realized he had been telling the truth all along. The top of the tickets read out the evidence in bold letters. He had bought two tickets to Montana.

Chapter Fourteen

"I bought them after that last night we were together." His voice seemed far off in the distance as I read that one word over and over again.

Montana. Montana. Montana

That night we were last together was the same night he told me he wanted to take me away. I had thought he was frantic to get inside of me that night. To claim me as his own. I thought he had just missed me and that's why he wanted to take me away from it all. I still didn't know what had been riding him that night.

As if he was reading my thoughts, he stepped closer to me and answered my unvoiced question.

"While we were out of town, I think Chris had secured your father completely into his criminal activities. He knew about our affair already and I think he was trying to punish me as much as he was going to punish you." I could hear the tension in his voice as he told me his story.

"He made sure to talk to me a lot while we were gone. Looking back now I see how odd it had been. I was supposed to be his bodyguard but we never really spoke more than necessary." He huffed a humorless laugh at the thought. "I couldn't stand the little prick so I always tried to keep our interactions to a minimum."

My eyes became watery as I continued to stare at those tickets. I ran my fingers over the indented folds and crinkled edges. *How many times had he taken these out of his wallet to think about the what-ifs? To think about me?*

"I think I hated him, not only because he was a snooty asshole, but I hated him because he had you." His swallow was so thick I could hear it as if it came from my own body.

"The whole two weeks we were out of town I came closer and closer to killing him. He made sure to sit right next to me when he spoke about you. He would brag to all his coworkers about his hot wife waiting on him to come home and fuck her." I didn't have to look into Leo's eyes to tell there was an intense rage in them.

"He would brag about the little noises you made right before you would come. And the demeaning things he claimed you liked. I knew none of it was true. I believed you when you told me you stopped sleeping with him years before. But he always would nudge me on the arm while he would say things about you. Like it was his way of rubbing it in that he was the one that owned you." He stepped into my space now.

He grabbed my chin in his fingers and pulled my face up to look at him. He was blurry through the tears gathered in my eyes. The look on his face was full of so much emotion it was almost painful for me to look at him.

"When I came back to you that night in the motel, I had to remind myself you were mine, not his. After I left you that night I drove to the airport and bought the first available tickets to Montana. I had planned on telling you about them the next time we went to the motel. I was going to steal you away from him." The desperation in his eyes was so thick I felt as though I would drown in it.

"But, I was too late. You left without a word. I had no idea where you went. You changed your number and your last name. I used every single one of my resources and I still couldn't find you. I even begged your parents to tell me where you went but they wouldn't tell me." His story made my chest ache.

"I didn't tell anyone besides Tanner." When I

finally spoke my throat felt raw.

"I didn't realize Chris had fooled us all until today. He played his cards extremely well, I'll give him that. He wanted to punish you as much as he did me. He knew if he made it seem like I was the one to betray you, it would shatter you and you wouldn't want anything to do with me. Neither of us would walk away happy."

All the pieces of the puzzle fit together so nicely. I was disgusted with myself for ever believing anything Chris had said in the first place. If I hadn't been such a fucking coward, I would have confronted Leo immediately. Maybe we wouldn't have lost so much time.

Leo shook his head. "I never asked why you didn't leave him for me. I was honestly so in love with you, it didn't matter. I thought you wanted the life he could give you so you didn't want to leave. It's pathetic, but I would have been your lap dog for the rest of my life just to have a slice of your attention. I would have waited for you forever." He searched my eyes for, what, I wasn't sure. I choked on the emotion clogging my throat as I tried to calm the storm that brewed beneath my skin.

"I tried." My hushed voice seemed so loud to my ears. "I tried to leave him before I ever even knew you. He wouldn't let me." I closed my eyes as my shame washed over me. I'd been so weak. "He … hurt … me so bad after I asked for a divorce that I never tried again. I couldn't even leave the house after what he'd done to me," I finally admitted.

The look of pure unadulterated rage flickered in his eyes at my admission.

"One of my biggest regrets is that I was too blind to see what he was doing to you. I would have strangled the life out of him if I knew. I still might," he promised, his voice deathly calm. I believed him.

Even though I had moved past that part of my life, it still haunted me from time to time. I couldn't imagine if something like that ever happened to someone I loved and I wasn't given the chance to make it right. I grabbed his hand in mine and rubbed my thumb against the back of his hand, willing him to continue.

"When I finally found you, I flew to Florida as fast as I could. I just wanted to see you again. To find out what I did to make you leave. Damon was an old friend of mine from the academy before we went our separate ways, so I asked if I could stay with him while I looked for an old flame. This was before he was dating Jill so he happily let me crash in his spare room. I went with him to some bar, The Sand Dollar, or something like that. He ended up ditching me to make out with Jill in some dark corner that night."

He smirked at the memory but as he mentioned the name of Heath's bar, my heart tripled its beats. That was the night Kate had finished her first manuscript and we had gone out to celebrate. Fate was a cruel mistress it seemed.

"But then I saw you dancing. It was like fortune smacked me in the face that night and said, 'Here, you idiot, go get your girl.' There you were and there I was at the same time in the same place. I started to walk toward you but then when I truly looked at you I saw how different you looked. You looked so young and flush with joy and ... you were happy." I felt my tears flow down my cheeks as I watched him relive that night.

"Of all the times we had been together, I had never seen you so carefree. I hadn't realized how miserable you truly were back then. I hated myself for not being able to see it then. I walked away that night. I just knew you were better off without me. But then destiny proved to be an even bigger bitch than both of us could ever know and brought us back together anyway."

I closed my eyes and let every revelation spoken here tonight wash over me. My head swam with all the information it was taking in. Everything Leo said sounded true. As tangled as it all was, it made complete sense.

I had been a complete fool to believe the three people in this world who had always treated me like shit. Why had I ever taken the word of an abuser and two neglectful parents over the one person that proved their love for me time and time again?

I dropped the flight tickets from my fingers and grabbed both sides of Leo's face. I stretched up on my tiptoes and brought his head down to me. Placing my forehead against his, I looked into those honey eyes that showed me the truth I had always been looking for.

"I'm sorry," I spoke around the emotion still clogging my throat.

His eyes closed as he gripped my hips, pulling himself closer to me. I shook my head.

"I am so sorry I just left like that, Leo," I cried.

His eyes sprung open and he lifted me against him.

"You are so fucking strong, do you know that? You found a way out of an abusive relationship and lunged for it. Don't you dare apologize for that," he murmured to me as he carried me to bed. He cradled me to him as he laid us both down on the soft duvet. He brought those lips down to my cheeks and kissed away my tears as I held the sides of his face.

"I should have given you the benefit of the doubt. I should've asked you outright if you had truly wronged me. I never should have run from the only man to ever show me the type of love I needed," I admitted. "I loved you and I believed an abuser over you." I sobbed. I wanted to tell him I still loved him but I couldn't get the words out. I didn't deserve his love after what I'd done.

"No, Emy, don't cry. It shreds me up," Leo begged me as he kissed my lips. His lips were soft but firm as he gently dominated me.

The tears continued to leak from me as I kissed him back but it was a cleansing thing. The overwhelming regret that lurked in my heart was quickly overshadowed by the joy I felt spreading in my belly. I was finally where I was meant to be. In the arms of the man I hadn't been able to stop thinking about for years now. I was in the arms of the man I hadn't been able to stop loving.

I let my hands flow down his sides as he ate at my lips with lazy kisses. My fingers deviled between the towel and his waist. Leo growled against me as he pushed his hips into me. His cock perked up to attention.

I moaned into his mouth as he thrust his tongue in, begging mine to move with his. I licked into him as I pulled the towel down, revealing his taunt ass to my waiting palms.

"You'll be sore," he murmured against my lips.

"I don't care," I whispered back as I tried to shove my hand between us. I wanted to feel his thick length in my hand.

He chuckled as he pulled out of my reach. I frowned up at him with a pout on my lips.

"I do, Princess. As much as I love you and I would love nothing more than to take you right now, you need a break from that part of me."

I continued to frown at him as he pushed up away from my mouth. I almost begged him until he started to kiss his way down my body. He held my eyes with him as he pushed my robe open, revealing my breasts to his hungry gaze.

"I thought you said I would be too sore," I teased

before he leaned down to lick my puckered bud. I arched into him as I watched that wicked tongue lap at me.

"I said you were too sore for my cock, I never said anything about my tongue." His deep voice vibrated straight to my pussy as he continued his descent.

He played, licked, and sucked my breasts until I was all but begging for more. The vision he made as he spread my robe wide was enough to fuel any wet dreams I would have for years to come.

When he reached my navel he stared up at me before he dipped his tongue inside. I squirmed under him at the unique form of torture. I was so hot for him, I nearly begged for it.

He kissed the rest of the way down until I felt his moist breath fan over my most delicate area. He used his hands to spread my thighs further apart. He stared at my pussy with such lust in his eyes I shivered under his scrutiny.

"This is the prettiest, pinkest, sweetest little cunt I've ever tasted. Even if I died tomorrow, I would still be able to taste your sweet cream on my lips," he breathed before he ran his middle finger down my cleft. I jerked as he grazed my clit before going lower. He dipped his finger into my weeping hole, groaning at the wetness he found.

I winced a little as he gently fingered me. I wouldn't ever admit it to him, but he was right, I was sore.

"All I want to do is sink into this heat right here and feel you squeeze my cock until I can't breathe. And this," he said before he withdrew his finger and traveled even lower. His wet finger rimmed my asshole and I sucked in a surprised breath. "Oh, I'm not even going to talk about what it will feel like to sink into this. You will snatch my very soul when I fuck this little asshole."

As if to drive his point home, he pushed that big finger until the tip slipped in. I moaned at the taboo feeling. I could feel myself getting wetter the longer he teased me. My hips undulated themselves as he pushed into me in slow tantalizing passes.

"That's it, Princess. Use me to fuck yourself." His words urged me on. I rolled my hips faster as he thrust harder.

I watched him as he became entranced in what he was doing to me. The love and heated lust in his face lit me up. Something was building inside of me I had never felt before. It was foreign but delightful all the same.

I dug my heels into the mattress and moved with him unashamed. When he sank all the way in, his groan of satisfaction sent a surge of feminine pride through me.

"That's my good little Princess. God, you're throbbing around my finger. You love this, don't you?" he growled as he spoke, like what we were doing was speaking to that primal part of his soul.

I nodded my head as I panted.

"I love everything you do to me. Please, lick me," I begged as I felt sweat break out along my brow. I was so close already, I just needed a little push. My clit was throbbing so hard it was almost painful.

"Just because you asked so prettily, Princess. Come for me," he rasped before pulling his finger out, lighting up every nerve I didn't know existed, before pushing back into me. I gasped at the sensation and shook uncontrollably as I felt the orgasm crest over my head.

Leo leaned down and used his other hand to pull up on the hood that covered my bundle of nerves. Just exposing it to the cool air was enough to hurtle me over the edge. I screamed as I came. Feeling every muscle I owned clench and seize as the orgasm gripped me.

"That's my good girl," Leo groaned right before he brought that scorching mouth onto me.

I bucked into his mouth as he sucked at me. Screaming so hard my throat felt like it was on fire. I had never felt an orgasm as intense as this in my entire life.

Leo never let up. He fucked his finger into my ass fast now as he continued to pull on my clit. When my release started to subside, he would bring me back to the top again just to crash me back down. I was shaking my head back and forth by the end. No longer able to take any more.

"I can't!" I panted. "No more!"

Leo released me from his lips but didn't stop pumping into me. He smoothly added another finger and that building sensation started all over again.

"You will," he replied harshly. "One more, Princess. Come for me," he ordered right before he pinched my clit and I went flying again.

I squeezed my eyes closed as euphoria cascaded over me. The blood rushing to my ears blocked out all sounds, even the ones I was making. I saw stars behind my eyelids before I felt strong arms wrap around my spent body.

Leo pulled me to him and rolled us so we were spooning. He closed my robe as he wrapped his big body around me. Smoothing down my hair before hugging me close.

I felt his hard length against my ass and pushed back against it. I moved my arm around to grip him but he stopped me with a grunt.

"What about you?" I asked.

He kissed the side of my temple as he whispered to me, "We can take care of that needy bastard later. I just want to hold you," he admitted as he kept his lips in my hair. The deep breaths he inhaled pulled at my heart.

"I love you so fucking much, Emily. If you let me, I will prove it to you every damn day of my life until I die."

I twisted my face toward him and nodded. I let my kiss against his lips be my answer.

Chapter Fifteen

"This was the last time we saw your brother," Leo explained as he slid the black and white photo across the small bistro table. I took a sip of my coffee before placing the cup back on its saucer. I brushed my fingers over the photo of my brother walking on a side street, tents from street vendors littering the background. Another man was slightly out of focus in the background, as if he were my brother's traveling companion, but stood further away. Crowded streets, teeming with shoppers both local and tourists, flowed around the two.

I slid the photo closer to me before picking it up from its place. My brother looked slightly different than he had three years ago. Still just as athletic looking to a point where he toed the line of intimidating. In his hands, he held what looked like two cloth bags stuffed with food. He wore a simple button-down, short-sleeved shirt and cargo shorts. His arms looked slightly bigger and his exposed skin tanner. His hair looked longer but he had it pulled back away from his face in a stylish bun. The dark sunglasses he wore covered his expressive eyes from my view.

The man walking several paces behind him was a wiry little guy I didn't recognize. He was shorter than Tanner by quite a few inches, skinnier too. His skin was pasty white, as though he never went outside. His eyes were not covered like my brother's. If I were to write him in a book, he would be described as a jittery, manic, unpredictable man. His bulging eyes and sharp nose almost looked rat-like. Dark short cropped hair only made his features seem far sharper. His hands were both shoved into his front pockets as if he was hiding something. If that something was substances or intentions, I didn't know. He looked strung out and almost desperate for his next fix. I didn't like the way he stared at my brother's back.

I rubbed my thumb along the still of my brother's profile before closing my eyes at the emotion I felt building there. *What have you gotten yourself into, Tanner?*

"When?" I croaked out before placing the picture back between us.

Leo's head was cocked to the side as he observed me. It was at times like this when I remembered he was a private investigator and not the bodyguard I'd known him to be. He had been trained to observe people, to discover what made them tick.

He straightened before he gripped his coffee mug and brought it to those same lips that had spent hours worshiping me when I woke this morning. Flashes of sleepy eyes, ruffled hair, and a warm tongue replayed behind my eyes like my own personal home movie. Leo in the morning was … well, he was something to behold.

I cleared my throat and tried to trample the coil of knots in my stomach. I needed to focus.

Leo smirked like he knew exactly what I was thinking. I flushed as I glanced around the crowded observation deck we sat on. It had been an internal struggle this morning to leave our little private love chamber, but the view of the sea as we ate breakfast almost made it worth it. The only thing that made it less than perfect was all the prying eyes around us.

If we had opted to eat breakfast in our room, I was almost certain the only thing I would be eating would be him. I had yet to get my mouth on him and I was almost to the point of begging him to let me taste him.

Last night he said he didn't want me to take care

of him, he just wanted to hold me. I allowed it thinking I would be able to return the favor this morning. That plan had proved futile.

When I tried to crawl down his body this morning, he had quickly flipped me under him and pleasured me with *his* mouth instead. It was as though he couldn't get his fill of the taste of me on his tongue, not that I was complaining. He had then taken me in the shower. He had me so worked up and slick that it had been no trouble at all for him to slide into me with ease.

He took his time and brought me to multiple orgasms before allowing himself to find his own release deep inside of me. Then he washed every square inch of my body with only his hands and soap. By the time the shower was done, I was ready for him all over again.

When I told him we should stay in for breakfast, he declined. He told me if we didn't get out of that room soon there was no way he would be able to take his hands off me. I had pouted mightily. I didn't see a problem with that. We were just making up for lost time after all.

He had shown me those dimples beneath all that scruff before delivering another panty-melting kiss. I only sobered when he pulled away and told me we needed to talk about Tanner.

Guilt panged through me at the mention of my brother. Shamefully, I'd been so wrapped up in everything Leo, I had put Tanner on the back burner.

I nodded my head and quickly got dressed. I let Leo lead me by the hand to this very spot and now here I was. Sitting in this beautiful place, surrounded by worry-free people, eating our very privileged meal, and daydreaming about losing myself within my lover's body once again. All while my brother was God knows where with Satan knew who. I was the worst kind of sister.

"That was taken from a CCTV camera the night we arrived here." Leo's voice pulled me from my thoughts. "I left the morning after we checked in and went to that shopping center. I scoped the place out for a few hours in hopes of seeing him again but had no luck." He frowned at the photo as he sucked his teeth in obvious disdain.

I nodded before I picked my coffee cup back up. Bringing it to my lips, I searched for the right words to say. I could tell Leo was frustrated by the situation at hand. I knew him well enough to know he hated loose strings.

I mulled over my response as I sipped at the bittersweet beverage in my hands. If this were a book I was writing, how would I find the stolen damsel in distress? I snorted quietly to myself at the flash of Tanner in a dress, flailing about like some type of heroine in need of saving.

"What was that?" Leo was smirking at me when I looked back up.

I flushed. "Nothing." He arched his brow, silently imploring me to share with him. I shook my head. "I was just picturing Tanner as a lady in need of saving. Sometimes I have a hard time shutting that creative switch in my brain off." I smiled bashfully. Leo smiled back at me before a look of inspiration crossed his features.

"So, you see Tanner as the victim in this way," he stated as he searched my eyes. I could see the cogs moving in his mind. "Who's the villain?" he asked as he leaned forward.

His mannerisms gave me the idea that he smelled something and he latched onto it like a lifeline. I flicked my attention back to the photo between us before pointing.

"Him, that's your villain in this story," I offered with a frown on my brows.

Leo observed the photo as he pulled it toward him again. His brows creased in obvious confusion before glancing back at me.

"You think he's with your brother?" he asked as he pointed to the wiry man behind Tanner.

I nodded my head. "I thought it obvious they were together. Normal strangers don't follow other people that closely unless they know them, or they want something from them." A shiver clawed up my spine as I thought of worse.

I pointed to the man in the photo again. "Look at the way he's watching Tanner. I know he's a little out of focus, but he knows him. From the look in his eyes, I would say he's angry with him." I stared at the small man.

Words formed behind my lips and I didn't stop them as they made their way out. It was like the same process I had when I was writing, the idea hit me and I had to get it out before I lost it.

"If this were my book, if these were my characters, the two in the photo would be friends at first. Their mutual need to escape using drugs and alcohol fueled their relationship. They met stateside at some local druggy house party and became fast friends. Tanner always did like to hang out in the seediest environment he could possibly find. His friend, let's call him Cole, has only ever known that type of life." I paused as I disassociated from everything going on around me. The full creative imagery flowed through my mind.

"Cole came from nothing, probably grew up in foster care, and ended up at the same party as Tanner by a stroke of fate. Tanner didn't tell Cole he came from money right away. Cole entered the friendship thinking the two were in the same boat all along. That they were equals. They probably had a few drunken nights where Cole opened up, saying he couldn't wait to 'get out.' To leave his shithole of a life and never look back." I spoke to Leo but it was almost like I was talking to myself at this point. My eyes were unseeing as I continued.

"After telling him about his hopes and dreams, Tanner went and bought two tickets to Columbia to 'get them out.' The two left the States with nothing but the clothes on their backs and a pile of cash Tanner withdrew from the family bank account. Cole was so happy to just be a part of this plan, he didn't ask questions. He got on the plane with my brother and they didn't look back." It always amazed me when I could see the vision in my mind like I was watching a movie. This is why I wrote, it was like I got to live thousands of different lives at once.

"Months went by with the two just bouncing around. A long line of shitty bars, fleabag motels, and drug houses to keep them happy. For a while." I swallowed to bring moisture back to my dry mouth.

"Until Cole starts putting pieces together. He realized he and Tanner hadn't struggled once since being in Columbia. Never once have they had to steal or find another source of income. Tanner just kept paying for things." My heart rate ticked up with each passing word that escaped my lips.

"Cole did some research one day. If you had a decent internet connection and knew how to use Google, it wasn't hard to find out Tanner came from money. You could easily find the family's net worth if you knew the right place to look. Time moved on and Cole became more and more distant. He was angry Tanner never told him who he was. He's livid Tanner had gotten to grow up with such privilege and pissed all over it." My fingers started trembling as I trailed on.

"Cole made a plan. He distanced himself enough from Tanner so that if any of his family came looking for him, they wouldn't see the desperate man lurking in the background. He's going to make his move soon to hold Tanner for ransom. He hasn't quite planned out how to get ahold of Patricia and Frank yet, but that's what he plans to do. He will not go back home without some sort of consolation prize. He's unhinged and believes he deserves the life that Tanner never wanted." I looked up at Leo as reality crept back in around the edges of my subconscious.

"He's either going to get paid or … he's going to kill Tanner." I swallowed thickly as I felt a single tear roll down my cheek. "Find Cole and you find Tanner," I said darkly.

Leo gaped at me like he just watched a physics teacher describe time dilation. I brushed the tear away from my face with a sniffle. I glanced around the table to see if anyone was staring at me. I may have spoken quietly, but I felt like I screamed the information at the top of my lungs.

I heard the screeching of a chair being shoved away from the table before I snapped my head back in Leo's direction. He rushed to my side of the table and got on his knees in front of me. Without saying a single word, he gripped my chair and turned me to face him roughly. When he grabbed both sides of my face and forced me to look at him, I blinked and sighed heavily at the contact. When I looked into his eyes I could almost see the emotion swirling around there.

"You got all that from a single picture?" His voice was raw as he spoke.

"I'm probably wrong." I huffed a self-deprecating laugh.

Leo shook his head before pulling my lips to his

for a fast kiss.

"I think you're exactly right. I've been trying for almost seven months to figure out why Tanner would just take off the way he did. It didn't make any sense to me why he would withdraw that large amount of money and then buy two tickets here. Nothing about this case has made sense until now." He shook his head as he continued to study me. He smiled before he laughed at the blatant transparency of it all.

"I consider myself a damn good profiler, but what you did just now..." He continued to grin at me as he shook his head. "I've never seen anything like that."

I couldn't help the smile on my lips at his praise. I was truly just going off the feelings I was getting from that photo. The look Cole gave my brother was one of desperation and jealousy. Or at least that's how I would write it.

Leo grabbed my hands and stood, taking me with him. He hugged me to him in a fierce embrace before pulling back. He kissed me again as he held me. I couldn't stop the grin that split my lips.

"I need to call Isabelle and have her check into the man in the photo. We've been looking at recent rental transactions with local landlords. We haven't ever seen Tanner's name and that makes sense if his friend is the one with the lease. We need to figure out what his real name is." Leo rambled on so quickly, I could feel his thrill at finally getting a break in the case. "The day is still young, so hopefully she will know something by this evening. Do you want to stay here or can I walk you back to our room?" he asked as he searched my eyes. I felt a flutter of butterflies in my belly at the mention of *our room*. He didn't say mine or his, it was ours.

I shook my head before answering. "I think I will stay here for a bit, enjoy the view for a little longer." I didn't mean for my voice to sound so small. I was happy to help Leo find answers but I couldn't ignore the building dread in my stomach. If I was right, Tanner was in some serious trouble.

Leo kissed my forehead before telling me he would meet up with me later. He had a little extra pep to his step as he walked away. I slumped back into my chair and leaned against my palm, covering my mouth with my fingers. I stared out at the sea and thought about my brother. When we found him—because we *would* find him—I was going to kick his ass for doing this to me.

I glanced back over toward the direction Leo receded. His figure became smaller and smaller as he practically jogged back to our room. He was excited at finally, maybe, getting a break in this case. I just hoped for our sake, if I was right, we weren't too late.

Chapter Sixteen

We spent the next three days at the resort waiting and researching. The longer we looked into the man who was with Tanner, the more I fretted over his safety. I was so terrified for my brother but I swore when we found him I was going to kick his ass.

Ever since my hypothesis about Tanner and "Cole," I couldn't quite get the image out of my mind. We had learned a couple of things in the last few days, though. "Cole" was actually Peter Broderick. Leo had proven he had some really good connections stateside. It took less than twenty-four hours to find out everything there was to know about Mr. Broderick.

I'd been wrong about him being in foster care all his life, but it turned out he probably should've been. I was still very saddened by the fact that his life had been so unforgivingly hard.

Peter and his two younger siblings had grown up with a neglectful heroin addict of a mother. His father, if he even knew him, was nowhere in the picture. He never had much of a home to speak of as every place they had tried to settle ended in an eviction notice. By the time Pete was thirteen he was already doing whatever he could to raise his two siblings, ages one and five. Department of Family Services had been called multiple times but the courts kept placing the kids back with the mother. By the time Pete reached eighteen, his siblings had been taken from the home permanently and placed in foster care. He was left to fend for himself as he was no longer a minor.

Peter tried to fight for custody of the two children but was denied by the judge. He'd been told he had nothing to offer and that the foster home would be better for them. That part broke my heart the most I think. Imagine having someone tell you, you had nothing to offer your own siblings who you had practically raised yourself.

I don't know what was sadder, the fact that he had to grow up in that situation or that he grew up just to repeat the same cycle his mother started.

In the years since then, Peter made quite the name for himself with local law enforcement. His rap sheet was a mile long with offenses ranging from possession of illegal substances to petty theft. He spent most of his twenties in and out of lockup with an endless list of public defenders to keep him company.

When looking into the crowd he normally ran with, we found that most of those people were known for various nefarious criminal activities as well. It didn't take much digging to find that some the same names on Pete's list were on Tanner's. My assumption of them meeting at a mutual party was proving to be spot on.

The more Leo and I dug into Peter's past, the more my imagination seemed to run rampant. I even started having bad dreams about it every night. It was always the same. We would find Tanner walking the streets at some local market. Peter was walking behind him with his hands in his pockets looking the same as he had in the photo. Hateful, jealous, and maniacal. I watched helplessly from the vehicle Leo kept me locked in as Peter started to pull something from his pocket. I could still feel the utter helplessness as I watched the gun appear in his hand. My screams went unheard as he pointed the gun at my brother's back and pulled the trigger.

I woke up with a jolt every time, drenched in sweat and my lungs heaving. It always took me a few beats to realize where I was. When Leo's hand would gently graze my damp back, I would jump as if I just remembered he was with me.

When another one of the same dreams awoke me early this morning, I was shocked when I immediately searched for Leo's comfort only to find cold sheets instead. My brows furrowed in confusion as I glanced all around the suite, only to find it completely empty apart from myself. That's when I noticed the open sliding glass door. Early dawn light trickled in across the cream-colored tile.

I wrapped the crisp white sheet around myself and slipped from the bed. The cool tile against my feet felt almost refreshing as I padded toward the door that allowed a slight breeze to waft over me. The sheet gathered on the ground behind me as I walked across the room. The stillness of the room made the sound of the starched fabric dragging across the floor almost too loud in my ears. I could hear a hushed mumble from where I stood just inside the door.

When I poked my head outside the slightest bit, I finally laid eyes on the main star of my fantasies. The sun was starting to rise just enough that I could see his striking features in the dim lighting. He paced back and forth slowly in front of the pool. He held his phone to his ear as he listened intently to the voice on the other end.

I lost all focus on what he was saying to whoever he was speaking to when he turned away from me. Maybe I was just a sucker for a strong back, but *damn*. He forwent the shirt altogether, leaving all that golden skin covered in dark ink exposed. His shoulders were defined to perfection. My gaze blazed a trail down his lats, and further still. The top swells of his toned ass poked out of the fabric that hid the rest. I squeezed my thighs together as I thought about all the delights those shorts were hiding.

When he turned again to face me I almost lost all concentration as I looked at his rugged beauty. His brows were furrowed in frustration as he raked his hand through his wild locks.

The way his muscles seemed to glide so smoothly underneath all that soft flesh was almost hypnotizing to watch. God, would I ever get used to this man's immaculate beauty? He was the epitome of perfection. I feared I would always want him as much as I did at that moment. The unrelenting urge to constantly be around him and touch him was almost maddening.

I let my gaze trail down from his broad chest to his washboard abdomen and further still. He had slipped on his shorts but didn't bother to button or zip them. Those shorts of his were barely hanging on as it was and I wanted nothing more than to give them that final push. I had to catch my drool when I noticed the top of his thick cock poking out. I sucked in an almost startled breath as I watched that cock twitch under the fabric.

"See something you like, Princess?"

I jumped from my spot by the door as my gaze jerked back up to his eyes. He was obviously done with his conversation and had caught me ogling him. He had a mischievous look sparkling in his eyes as he set his phone down on the side table before straightening to his full height again.

"Did you have another bad dream?" he asked softly as his gaze raked me from head to toe.

I nodded and said nothing else. He held his arms out for me to come to him and I didn't think twice. I clung to the sheet at my chest as I practically ran into his open embrace. When I hit his chest, I expected him to hug me but instead, I squealed in delight as he picked me up into his arms and cradled me to him. He always made me feel so feminine and delicate even if we both knew I was anything but.

He grinned down at me as he walked us both on those strong legs over to the hammock. More gracefully than I would have, he laid me down before crawling in next to me. Once he was situated he pulled me to him and draped me over his warm chest. I snuggled down into him as a sigh of contentment left my parted lips.

We lay like that and watched the sunrise for long silent moments before I gained the courage to ask the question that had begged for an answer this whole time.

"Where's Tanner?"

Leo pulled in a deep breath before he ran his hand down my back firmly. "Isabelle has been working with the local police department all week. She's been given access to the CCTV cameras. Unfortunately, she hasn't seen anything else since the last picture was taken with Peter and so far we've come up empty-handed with the local landlords." He sighed heavily against my hair as I closed my eyes.

Come on, Tanner, work with me.

I squeezed my arm around his stomach before I lifted my head. I placed my chin on his chest and looked up at him. "I can't believe neither of them has come out at all. Even for food? By the looks of the last picture, Tanner only had a couple of shopping bags with him. They must be running low by now. They may even be completely out," I said then immediately winced. Would it even matter if they didn't have any food? I knew some drugs made you not want to eat at all.

I lifted my head and looked down at my lover. The worry and empathy I found staring back at me were almost enough to break me. Leo was thinking the same thing. Tanner may be too strung out to know he needed to eat.

I laid my head back down on his chest and took

soothing breaths as I listened to the steady rhythm of his heart. His fingers played in my long strawberry-blonde locks while I gained the courage to speak again.

"I think we should go to the shopping complex, where the picture was taken. It's been almost a full week since the last time they were there. Maybe they'll venture out again today and we'll get lucky," I muttered as I played my finger along the black lines on his chest and abdomen.

Leo kissed the top of my head before he spoke. "I think that's a good idea, Emy. I'll call Isabelle back and let her know when I'll meet her."

I lifted my head again and went up on my elbows to look into his eyes. "I'm going with you," I said firmly.

Leo frowned up at me and shook his head. "No. It'll be safer for you to stay here," was all he said.

"He's my brother, Leo. I'm going with you and you're not going to tell me no. *I* was sent here to get him so *I* will be the one to retrieve him." I glared at him. "He doesn't even know you, so please tell me how you plan to get him to come with you?" I raised my eyebrow at him in challenge.

Leo glared right back at me before raising onto his elbows and coming closer to my face. I could feel his breath puffing across my cheeks as he spoke. "*I* was *hired* to find your brother, Princess. Not only that, I have to keep you safe as well. I can't do that if you're running willy-nilly down the streets of fucking Columbia," he seethed.

"I'm coming with you and you're not going to stop me," I growled right back.

We stared at each other then. Neither of us was willing to back down. When it came to who was more stubborn in this relationship, it was a toss-up. If it was anything else we were talking about, then I wouldn't have a problem backing down. But this wasn't just any argument we were having. This was my brother we were talking about. I would be damned if I wasn't allowed to help look for him.

In the end, it was Leo that caved. I held my frown in place as his softened into a grin. He huffed a small laugh as he leaned in the rest of the distance and kissed away the crease between my brows. "You win," he mumbled against my lips. "But, you will stay in the car. If we see him then you can come with me to retrieve him. Even then, you will listen to everything I say and will not put yourself in unnecessary danger. Am I understood?" he said firmly.

When I started to bristle at his tone he pulled me to him so there was no space between us. He gripped the back of my neck as he grazed his lips against mine. "I can't have anything happen to you, Emy," he whispered.

Unhashed emotion clogged my throat as he admitted his fear. I sighed against him as I nodded. "Okay," I whispered back before he kissed me fully and held onto me like a lifeline.

****

"Have I told you how incredibly sexy you look in that getup?" Leo's sultry voice sounded in the otherwise quiet car.

I grinned at him before looking down at myself and shrugged. My outfit was less than eccentric for our outing today. I'd opted for denim shorts, a tight hot-pink tank top, and my Nike running shoes. I wanted to be comfortable enough to sit in a car all day but also functional enough to get out of the car and walk around if I needed to. I had wanted to wear the bright top for safety reasons more than anything. It was harder to find someone in a dark color rather than a bright one. Not that I was planning to get lost away from Leo, but a girl could never be too careful.

So far we'd been sitting in Leo's rental car for about two hours and had yet to see anything out of the ordinary. Locals and tourists of all shapes and sizes littered the streets today, some buying things and others just browsing. Looking around at all the colorful people of different backgrounds, I had a hard time seeing why Leo was so worried in the first place.

Sure, the crime rate in certain areas was higher than others, but everything around here seemed safe. The only thing different than some places in the states was the constant stream of police walking in and out of the crowd with their weapons on full display.

It was almost unsettling to think that this was everyday life for most of these people.

I shook off the thought as I glanced back over to my traveling companion. I made a show of puffing my chest out a little more for him to get a good eyeful of my cleavage. I giggled at him when his eyes flared and he readjusted himself through his dark jeans.

"You have literally seen me naked and bent every which way to Sunday, and this outfit turns you on?" I laughed as I spoke.

He leaned toward me in a way that made me think of a lion stalking its prey. "Just because I know what's underneath those tight clothes, doesn't make me any less intrigued to see every part as I search for new ways to make you crumble in my arms." His husky voice sent heat straight to my core.

I smiled brightly as I leaned over the center console to get face-to-face with him. I let my hand grip him just above his knee before making the slow ascent toward his manhood. When he was a breath away I dodged his lips quickly before moving on to his ear. "Maybe we can see what it would take to make you fall apart for *me*," I whispered before nipping his earlobe as I rubbed him through the thick denim of his jeans.

The only warning I received was a low growl before he pounced. He gripped my throat in his big hand before he brought me back to his mouth. His kiss was all-encompassing as he thrust his tongue past my lips. I gripped him as best I could through his jeans and he sucked in a sharp breath.

"Be careful what you ask for, Princess," he growled. "I'll have your arms tied behind your back and this cock shoved past those perfect lips before you can even think to beg for mercy."

His wicked threat made me shiver before I smiled against his lips. *Did it make me a masochist if I wanted everything he threatened?*

"Promises, promises," I cooed before flicking my tongue out for another taste.

The look of feral gratification passed through his eyes before he smiled. Just as he started to lunge back for my mouth, there was a knock on the window that jolted me back into the present. I tried to pull away from his grasp but he held me firmly before he gave me one last kiss. As he released me, the grin on his lips told me he thoroughly enjoyed our banter.

He readjusted himself before pulling his searing gaze from me to roll his window down. As he did, a tall female came into view as she knelt. She had a knowing grin on her lips as she propped her elbows on the opening and squatted to eye level with us. She was attractive enough with her cropped short black hair. Her eyes were so dark they were almost black. Her lips were nice and plump. She had no makeup on and she was dressed for business in her blazer jacket and matching slacks. The chain hanging around her neck told me she was law enforcement. Possibly a detective.

She looked me up and down with an appreciative gaze that made me think she was either very curious or very gay. My guess was the latter. She extended her hand through the window and over Leo as an offering to me. I gripped her outstretched hand and gave it a firm shake.

"Isabelle Paseo," she said by way of greeting. Her thick accent only added to the persona that was her. I opened my mouth to return the greeting when she cut me off. "And you're the famous Emily." She grinned. "I've heard a lot about you. And I see that Cruz here wasn't exaggerating about your beauty." She winked as I blushed.

Definitely gay.

She released my hand and looked at Leo. "Can I speak to you for a moment?" she asked him before glancing back at me briefly. "Outside," she finished.

Leo nodded and rolled the window up as Isabelle stood back to her full height. He looked at me before opening his door. "I'll be right back," he said before slipping out of the vehicle.

I'm not one to eavesdrop normally but I'm not even ashamed to say that I tried to listen to their conversation. Although, they were talking way too calmly and quietly for me to make out anything at all. If they were discussing Tanner, shouldn't I be in on the conversation?

Just as I made to grab the door handle, the driver's door jerked back open to reveal Leo. He didn't climb back into the car as he squatted to look at me.

"I've got good news and bad news," he said with a half-smile. I said nothing as I willed him to continue. "Isabelle is pretty sure she's located where Tanner and Peter are staying. She says multiple eyewitnesses say they've seen two white men that match their descriptions coming and going out of the apartment building. We think they're a few blocks south of here. We need to go talk with the landlord."

"What are we waiting for then? Let's go," I said as I straightened in my seat, grabbing my seatbelt.

Leo's hand stilled mine before I could click the belt into place. "That's the good news," he mused. "The bad news is that the building they seem to be staying in is not known for its … friendliness." He searched my eyes for a reaction he wouldn't find. I snorted around an audacious laugh. I knew the type of people Tanner was known to hang out with. They weren't known for their friendliness, but it had never been intimidating for me to be around them.

When Leo said nothing else I had to assume he didn't want to tell me he wasn't going to let me go. "Like I said, let's go." I tried to sound calmer than I felt.

"Emily…" He frowned.

"You promised." I didn't try to hide my annoyance. "You said I could go with you when you found him," I gritted behind clenched teeth.

"That was before I knew how dangerous it was going to be," Leo defended himself.

"You know you can't save me from everything, right?" I challenged.

"But I can save you from this," he said firmly.

I rolled my eyes and straightened my spine. "He's my brother," I said. "He needs me and I'm not going to let him down," I growled. "Not again."

"You don't think I know that?" A look of frustration crossed Leo's eyes. He ran his hand through his messy hair before releasing a sigh of exasperation. When he looked back up at me, his eyes seemed to beg. "I'm trying my best here, Emily. I can't do what I need to do in order to get Tanner back if I'm worried about you getting hurt in the crossfire. If this Peter is as dangerous as we think he is, then there's a big chance someone could get hurt. I can't have that be you," he pleaded with me. "I just got you back. I can't stand the thought of losing you again."

I didn't want to feel the tugs on my heart his words caused. I wanted to scream and thrash at him. To be able to tell him to go fuck himself, that I was coming along one way or another. Even though Tanner was older than me, I felt as though he was my responsibility. I left him three years ago and look what happened. All of this was *my* fault.

I studied Leo for long moments before speaking. In the end, the logical side of me won out.

"Go," was all I said.

"I need to take yo—"

"If you take me back to the resort now you are wasting valuable time. I don't want you to miss him because of me." I swallowed thickly as I closed my eyes. I hated this feeling of defeat and helplessness. "I won't leave the car. I'm going to stay here and watch for him a little while longer and then I can find my way back to the resort on my own. I have my phone and the directions." My voice sounded numb even to my own ears as I spoke. I turned around to face the windshield and Leo was left staring at my profile.

I felt him climb into the car before he grabbed my chin and forced me to look at him. Honey-colored eyes searched my own before he kissed me softly. "Call me if you see anything at all and I will be here. I'm going to bring him back in one piece, Emy. I promise," he whispered.

"You better," I murmured before I kissed him one last time.

He exited the vehicle with the parting order to lock the doors. I did as I was told before I watched him walk away from the vehicle. I sighed heavily as I climbed over the center console into the driver's seat. I leaned my head against the steering wheel and swallowed thickly before releasing a shaky breath.

I knew logically Leo was right. The place he had to go to find Tanner wasn't safe for me to be in. Ultimately it was dangerous and it was no place for a woman who didn't know the slightest bit of self-defense. I was just too stubborn to admit he was right.

I swore as I thumped my head against the wheel. Tanner was going to get the thrashing of a lifetime when we found him. I think the sheer stress from this whole experience had shaved off at least a year of my life.

I straightened in my seat and looked out the windshield. I would sit here for a few more minutes searching the crowd before I headed back to the resort. Even in a locked car, it wasn't safe to be a single woman around this many strangers.

As I scanned face after face, I felt my heart rate increase. My grip on the steering wheel relaxed as I moved. I blindly searched the door with my hand as I kept my gaze trained forward. I gripped the door handle and opened it. I stepped out of the car and kept a steady eye on what I was seeing hundreds of feet in front of me. The humid midday heat smacked me in the face so hard I had to squint when my eyes immediately dried. I still kept focused on my target.

I realized Leo was going to come back to me empty-handed. Even though he was probably one of the most competent people I had ever met in my life, I knew he was going to fail on this mission. The reason I knew this was because I was looking directly at the one thing we had come here in search of.

I felt my feet moving of their own accord toward the one person I had shared so much of my life with. He looked just like he did in the photo right down to those sunglasses that covered the eyes that mirrored my own. I waved my hands above my head as I shouted above the massive crowd.

"Tanner!"

Chapter Seventeen

By the time I started to walk I had almost lost Tanner in the sea of people. Faces blended together and adrenaline clogged my vision. I raised my hands above my head and waved wildly at his profile to grab his attention. "Tanner!"

No use. There was no way he could hear me over the number of people at the market today. Strangers looked at me wearily as I weaved through the crowd as fast as I could. The mob of people was way too thick to try and run through.

The whole time I steered through the crowd I kept my eyes trained on the man not two hundred feet in front of me. He had an easy smile on his face as he seemed to be haggling with the short dark man at one of the many fruit stands.

I tried to pick up my speed but the sheer clutter of the busy street just wouldn't allow it. Slowly, oh so slowly, I pushed closer. "Tanner!" I tried again but to no avail.

I watched as he passed his money to the vendor and filled his plain burlap satchel with the fruit he purchased. I started to panic then. What if I couldn't make it to him on time? Would this be my only shot at getting him?

I scrunched my brows together as I felt a thick sheen of sweat coat my back. I couldn't lose him again. I walked further and further into the mass of people, offering quick apologies when I knocked into some a little too harshly. I had to get to my brother.

One hundred feet now. I almost felt relief until I watched as Tanner turned his back to me and started to walk the opposite way. Panic laced my blood as I watched in horror as someone I vaguely recognized started to follow him.

Just like in the dream, Peter looked as desperate and strung out as we were led to believe. His eyes darted around him almost nervously before he followed the trail my brother was leading. It was like a flashing picture show as I watched his hands that were shoved in his pockets. I wanted to scream for Tanner to watch out but he wouldn't hear me if I did. My chest tightened as visions of a gun being pulled filled my mind's eye. In reality, no such thing was happening but that didn't stop my mind from conjuring the thought. I watched as their forms weaved in and out of the people in their path as if they'd done this for years.

I hadn't realized I'd come to stand completely still until I felt my feet start moving again. If I wasn't panicking before, I was now. I shoved my way around multiple people as some halted to stare at the crazy white woman who interrupted their shopping day.

My breath came out of my lungs in labored pulls and releases as my heart raced wildly in my chest. I watched in horror as Tanner stepped further and further away from me with each passing second. It may have been my mind playing tricks on me, but it felt like he was even further away from me than before.

I lost track of him as he continued to walk. I cursed the crowd as it just seemed to get thicker the more I pushed. The panic in my system only made it harder to focus as I stood on my tiptoes to try and find Tanner again. I was tall for a woman but still not tall enough to see much more than what I could flat-footed.

I glanced all around me to see if I could find something—anything—that would put me at a height advantage. I needed to find him. I spotted a ledge of a store window I would possibly be able to stand on to get a better view. I quickened my pace as I approached the store.

Two men were standing in my way as if they didn't have a care in the world. I searched the recesses of my mind to conjure the words I knew lay there. I needed them to help me up onto the ledge.

"*Por favor, ayúdame,*" I begged.

The men looked at me and then at one another as if silently communicating. When they looked back toward me, confusion marred their brows.

I pointed to the ledge. "*Arriba,*" I spoke the one word, *up,* and then beseeched them once again. "Please, *por favor.*"

Recognition registered on their faces at my plea and they both moved out of my way. I released a breath I hadn't known I was holding as they held their hands out to me. I gripped their rough palms and they helped me up onto the ledge. As they released me I quickly thanked them before they walked away, disappearing into the crowd.

The midday sun beat down on me, making me feel as though my skin would melt right off my bones. A deep fear that I was missing my only shot to bring my brother home settled in my gut like a ball of lead. Radiating tremors coursed from my chest into my extremities as I continued to seek my brother in the ocean of strange faces.

I sucked in a deep breath as I caught the slightest glimpse of him once again. I raised my hands to my mouth and shouted his name as loudly as I could. I didn't care if I looked like a crazy person, I needed to get his attention.

It seemed to work as I watched him and Peter stop walking. Tanner's head swiveled around, searching for the source of the call. I smiled as he started to turn more and more toward me. I reached up to cup my mouth once again. One more shout of his name and he would surely be looking in my direction.

"Ta—"

I was cut off from my shout as something knocked my feet from under me. I screamed as my body went careening to the side. My arms flailed wildly as I searched for anything to grab onto. The ground seemed to come up quickly to meet me as I fell. At the last second, I tried to catch my footing only to land on my ankle the wrong way. I yelped again as I felt the tendons twist in a way that wasn't natural. The rest of my body caught up with the ground as I landed with a hard thud on the concrete below me. I moaned in pain as I felt the skin on my legs rip open from the harsh fall. I caught the rest of my body with my palms, scraping them as well.

I felt as though my body was vibrating still as I came to a full halt. I hissed as I assessed the damage on my hands. My fall seemed to have stopped some people in their tracks as they surrounded me. I was slightly confused as I searched for the reason I'd fallen.

Before I could fully see who had pushed me out of the window, a rough sticky hand gripped my wrist and began to drag me away from the front of the store. I thrashed against my attacker as my ass scraped against the hot concrete below.

"What the fuck are you doing? Stop!" I shouted as I felt road rash on my exposed legs. As they pulled me to the alley next to the shop I reached up to hit the hand that held me.

I got one good hit in before they violently threw my wrist down away from them. I slumped to the ground before I swiveled to face my attacker. I scowled at them as I took in their details.

Dirty, torn, ratty tennis shoes came into my view

suddenly. My gaze traveled up from those used-to-be white shoes to weathered-looking bare legs. Up I looked, taking in the seen-better-days dress with barely there floral print. To the dirty bloodstained apron that covered much of her form. All the way to a very livid middle-aged woman's face. She held a deep scowl on her face that was framed by unruly tendrils of hair escaping her haphazard bun.

It wasn't the scowl that had me trying to scoot away from the woman, but the butcher knife she held firmly in her right hand that was sticky with old blood. I held my scraped palm up to ward off her advance but she swatted it away like a pesky fly.

"*¡Estúpida Americana!*" she shouted down at me.

I didn't need any help translating that. When you went to a country that didn't speak your native language, it was always best to brush up on insults. I tried to stand so I didn't feel like a child being scolded. I put the slightest pressure on my ankle I twisted only to have white-hot pain lace straight up my leg. I whimpered as I plopped back down to the hard ground.

"*Por favor, lo siento,*" I tried as I held my palm out once more to stop her advance.

Once again, she swatted my hand away and continued to tower over me. She bent at the waist to come further down to my level before she brought the knife closer to my face. I cringed away from her, leaning back onto my sore hands. She didn't let me get far as she gripped the back of my head and pulled my hair into her tightened fist. I bit back a whimper as pain scattered across my scalp. I attempted to thrash away from her until she held me tight and began to drag her blade lightly across my cheek.

"*Te atreves a faltarle el respeto a mi negocio, maldita perra,*" she seethed.

I had no idea what she was saying that time as I kept my mouth closed. I was afraid to move or speak with that sharp knife so close to my eye. My chest labored fiercely as I stared into her dark menacing eyes. The raw meat smells permeating off her hands and blade were enough to make me gag. Out of all the stores I had to find a ledge on, my stupid ass picked a fucking butcher shop.

Once again I tried to jerk away from her only for her to hold me tighter. I glanced around at the other market patrons hoping someone would help me. It was as though they were all blind to what was happening just feet away from them. Some stared at me while others continued with their day.

The woman's raspy laugh puffed across my cheeks as she leaned closer still. The smell of stale cigarettes assaulted my nose. *"Ellas no te ayudaran,"* she murmured as she pushed the knife against me. I hissed as she pricked the skin below my eye.

I squinched my eyes closed as she continued to push the knife further into my cheek. A scream stalled on my lips as I heard the familiar sound of a gun being primed.

"I would rethink that if I were you."

Leo's voice sounded like a beacon of hope as my eyes sprang open. I could just barely see him as he held the gun pointed at the woman. His face looked harsh as he kept his eyes trained on her.

If she was threatened by Leo's presence she didn't show it as she continued to hold the knife just below my eye. I watched her as she rolled her eyes before glaring at Leo.

"Another stupid American," she spat in broken English.

"Déjalo, Luciana. ¿Recuerdas lo que pasó la

última vez?" Isabelle's voice chimed as she came into view, gun aimed at the woman.

I watched as disgust crossed her face before she lowered the knife. I released a heavy breath as I scurried away from her. She spat at my feet before dropping the blade completely and facing Isabelle.

Isabelle put her gun back in its holster at the same time Leo did before rapid-fire Spanish ensued between the two women. I tried to stand once more and had to smother my shout as pain radiated through my foot. Somehow, I managed to stand but didn't dare put any pressure on my left ankle.

I glanced up at Leo just in time to see him take two big strides in my direction. He said nothing as he scooped me up and cradled me to his chest as if I weighed nothing. I wound my arms around his neck quickly as he started back toward the busy market street.

I didn't even need to look at him to know he was pissed at me but I risked a glance up at him anyway. His jaw was clenched so tightly I feared he would break his teeth before long. He didn't look down at me as he continued to walk through the crowd as if he didn't have a problem with the clutter. It was as though he had done this before and knew exactly how to navigate the busy street where I failed so spectacularly.

It took me a few beats to realize we were headed back toward the car. I craned my body to look over his shoulder back to the direction I'd last seen Tanner. He was nowhere in sight.

I deflated in his arms with a sag as I turned to face Leo once again. "I saw Tanner," I offered as he continued to walk. The crowd got thinner and thinner the closer we came to the car.

Leo's jaw clenching was the only indication that he'd heard me at all. He offered me nothing more as the car came into full view.

"I had to get to him before we lost him again," I said as I stared up at him. Still nothing, no reaction. "I couldn't see over the crowd so I thought standing on that ledge was a good idea. It worked until that psycho ripped my ass down. I shouted Tanner's name and he turned around right as I went down. I don't know if he saw me. Peter was with him," I blurted rapidly as if making excuses for running off on my own.

"Stop. Talking," Leo said between clenched teeth as he came to a stop. He managed to open the passenger door and smoothly deposit me into the seat. He shut the door much calmer than I thought he would and walked around the front of the car to the driver's side.

I studied him as he stood outside his door for a beat longer than normal. His muscles looked primed for a fight as he raked his hand through his soft waves. I couldn't see his face from my angle but I could tell by the way his arm was positioned he was pinching the bridge of his nose in frustration.

When I meant to lean over the console to see him more clearly he moved suddenly. I jumped and jerked back into my seat as he slapped the roof of the car so hard I was sure his palm was stinging. The loud thump that rippled through the car made my heart leap in my chest as sweat broke out along my forehead. My heart beat rapidly as I kept my gaze trained on my lap while he composed himself. He calmly opened the door and ambled into the vehicle.

He held onto the steering wheel with white-knuckle force and stared out the windshield. He said nothing for a long moment before he suddenly twisted in his seat to face me.

I didn't mean to do it but I flinched away from him. Logically, I knew Leo would never treat me the way

Chris did. He would never lay a finger on me if I didn't want him to. But sometimes old habits die hard.

When I realized what I'd done, I quickly looked at him. His eyes widened before they took on a sad glaze. He started to reach for me as if to console me and then thought better as he pulled away again. I tried not to let the movement hurt my already fragile feelings. "I'm sorry," he murmured. "I didn't mean to scare you." He swallowed thickly.

I laughed nervously as I buckled my seatbelt. "I've seen worse," I said before staring forward.

Leo reached over and gripped my chin, forcing me to look at him. "Don't joke. I should've done better to control my temper. I don't ever want to give you a reason to fear me," he said as he searched my eyes.

I nodded before he released me and started the car. I settled in as I watched the buildings and vendors of the market disappear. When it finally dawned on me that we were headed back to the resort, I gripped his arm.

"What are you doing? I said I saw Tanner. We need to go back to that apartment you said he was staying at. They may have gone back there."

Leo huffed a humorless laugh before he completely navigated away from the area. "I'm taking you back to the resort. I'll go with Isabelle later this evening and check the apartment again," he said, not bothering to look in my direction.

I felt heat rise from my chest to my face as I tried to control my temper. "You promised you would let me go with you to get him," I ground out behind clenched teeth.

We came to a "stop" sign and Leo turned in his seat to face me fully. "And you said you would stay in the fucking car when I wasn't around. We both made promises we couldn't keep." he snapped.

I scowled at him before responding. "What the fuck was I supposed to do, Leo? He was right there." I pushed my arms out as I spoke as if Tanner were right there in front of me. "That could have been my only chance at getting him."

"You were supposed to call me!" Leo's deep shout filled the car and I snapped my mouth closed. "You had your phone on you and you didn't even stop to think and call me. I would have made it back in time to get to Tanner. I needed you to *trust* that I would be here to help you and you didn't." His chest worked double time as his breathing accelerated. I'd never seen Leo this worked up before.

"You put yourself in a dangerous situation for no goddamn reason, Emily. I was right around the corner. Do you even realize how sideways today could have gone for you? I mean, just look at what that woman did to you," he growled toward me before flipping down my vanity harshly.

I pulled my searing scowl away from him to look into the mirror. The gasp left my mouth before I could think to smother it.

My usual freckled face was streaked with dirt and blood on one side. I had an inch-long gash across my cheekbone where she had held the knife to me. The cut was deep but not deep enough for stitches, though I was sure it would leave a scar. I hadn't even felt the now-dried blood as it trickled from the cut down my neck and cleavage, disappearing under the fabric of my shirt.

My gaze continued down as I took a moment to look at myself. My bright-pink top was stained with dirt and blood. My palms were scuffed up so badly I would need to pull the dead skin from them later. My knees were equally as scuffed but they also had dried blood all over them. I could tell my ankle was already swelling and bruised even around my Nike. I wiggled it slightly, testing for a break. I gritted my teeth together as dull pain radiated through the extremity. Though it hurt something fierce, I thought it was just a sprain. I would need to elevate and ice it later if I wanted any shot of walking on it the next day.

When I was done inspecting myself I snapped my gaze back up to the mirror and stared at myself. Leo was right. I put myself into unnecessary danger because I didn't think to call him. If I would have taken two seconds to do that, we could have easily navigated through the crowd together and gotten to Tanner in time.

Now, because of me, Tanner was gone again and I was a wreck. It would be just my luck if Peter saw me as well and convinced Tanner they needed to move locations again.

I squeezed my eyes shut before slamming the vanity back into place. Tears burned the back of my eyes as I fought for them to stay where they were. This was all my fault.

"Emy," Leo started, his voice much calmer now.

"Drive," I whispered.

When I felt his hand grab mine I jerked away from him. I opened my eyes and the tears I held back escaped down my filthy cheeks.

"I said, *drive*," I said more firmly.

His gaze held mine for a beat longer than necessary. I saw the flash of concern in his eyes before he returned them to the road. The car lurched forward and I let my head fall back onto the headrest.

The ride back to the resort was just long enough for me to ruminate on just how much I'd fucked up today.

Chapter Eighteen

"Is this really necessary?" I grumbled as Leo pushed through the bathroom door to our suite with me in his arms. Why he still felt the need to carry me everywhere was beyond me. How he always managed to open doors so gracefully while holding me baffled me.

When we had finally gotten back to the resort, I stood from the car before he had a chance to cut the engine. I had limped halfway to the main lobby by the time he caught up with me just to scoop me into his arms. The only protest I offered was an exasperated sigh as we passed a very pleased-looking Gloria.

Leo said nothing as he sat me down on the toilet before he turned away from me. He walked to the bathtub and flipped the water on the hottest setting. After plugging the tub, he stood to his full height and stalked back toward me. I watched him as he gracefully sank to his knees in front of me.

He gripped the bottom of my shirt before gently taking the ruined garment above my head. His eyes gobbled up the sight of my lace bra before bringing the strap from my shoulder down my arm. He leaned into me before planting a soft kiss against the indent the tight strap had made against the skin there. He repeated his process to the other side before reaching around my back to unstrap it completely. My breasts bounced free as the thin fabric slid down to reveal my tightened nipples.

I was so sore and tired from the events of the day but that didn't stop my body from reacting to Leo's ministrations.

His mellowed gaze never left me as he tossed the bra to the side. I half-expected him to pull me to him and put his mouth on other parts of me. I tried not to think too much about it as he moved on to my shorts. His deft fingers quickly unbuttoned them. I lifted my hips for him as he slipped the thin denim along with my panties down my legs.

His nostrils flared as lust registered in his gaze as he looked me up and down. His rough hands grazed down my legs. Starting at my upper thighs, I nearly moaned as his big hands kneaded the tight muscles he found there. He worked his way down my exposed flesh until stopping briefly at my knees. He inspected the scrapes quickly before moving on.

When he reached my swollen ankle, I gasped and then held my breath as he gently prodded the area. As softly as he could, he unlaced my shoes before slipping them off my sore feet. Next, he pulled my shorts completely from my legs before removing my socks.

He moved my sprained ankle in slow circles as I winced down at him. He deemed it not broken before gently placing it back onto the cold tile. His hands traveled back up my legs and his eyes followed. His gaze continued its uphill climb as his hands stilled along my hips. When he squeezed the flesh there I felt hot arousal flood my core.

He then met my gaze and I saw more than lust in those honey eyes. Worry, fear, and deep love are what I found lurking there.

I surrendered myself as he leaned forward to take my lips with his. He didn't demand entrance like I had become used to. He gently ate at my lips with soft presses and licks. I moaned against him as I immersed myself in the feeling.

When he finally pulled away, I found myself leaning in toward him seeking more. I nearly whimpered as he stood again and stepped away from me. I watched as he picked up the sweet-smelling lavender soap beside the tub before dumping the contents into the steaming water. He opened the jar of Epsom salts and poured a healthy amount into the water as well. After the water was frothy, he turned the faucet off.

He then walked over to the first aid kit and pulled out a disinfectant wipe. After ripping the package open, he gently cleaned the open wound on my cheek. I winced at the sting but didn't move away from him. It hurt to the touch but not as much as the turmoil that rolled in my gut.

When he was done, I stood from my spot and opened my arms for him as he stepped up to me. It was useless to try and fight him about it. If he wanted to carry me, who was I to stop him? He obviously felt the need to take care of me after the scare I'd given him.

He picked me up with ease before striding back to the bathtub and slipping me into the water. I hissed at the sudden heat against my chilled skin before moaning in pleasure. I closed my eyes as I relaxed back and felt my muscles release all at once as the heat seeped into every one of my pores.

When I opened my eyes again, Leo was gazing down at me with hooded eyes. I grinned up at him as I played with the bubbles around me. "Aren't you going to join me?" I asked before letting my hands dip below the waterline suggestively. I needed to feel the bliss of being with him now more than ever if only to quiet my racing thoughts.

When Leo made no move to ditch his clothing, my smile left my lips. He shook his head before glancing at the door that led back to the suite. "I need to call Isabelle. She said she was going to stake out the apartment complex to see if Tanner and Peter return," he said before bending down above me.

My face fell as I looked down at the water. I

knew he wasn't rejecting me but that still didn't stop the sting I felt.

Leo gripped my chin and forced me to look up at him before he kissed me sweetly again. I was left wanting more as he pulled away slightly to speak. "Wash up and relax for a bit. I'm going to get you some ice for your ankle and order us some food. Call for me when you're ready to get out of the tub and I'll help you." He paused to search my eyes. "I—" he stuttered. "You scared me today, Emy. I just need a minute to collect myself." He swallowed thickly.

I nodded my acceptance as he released my chin and turned to leave the room. I watched his receding form as emotion swamped me. When he closed the door I released a shaky breath and leaned my head back against the cool porcelain of the tub.

I sat there like that for long drawn-out moments as I listened to Leo in the suite. I heard as he ordered our room service as well as a bucket of ice and clean towels. He hung up the phone only to dial another number I knew to be Isabelle's.

I stopped listening to him and sat up in the now-cooling water. I grabbed the clean washrag and applied a healthy amount of soap to the damp cloth. Once the soap lathered into a foam I took to cleaning all the blood and grime from my face.

Today couldn't have gone any worse as I replayed this afternoon in my head over and over again. Why didn't I stop to think about my actions before I bolted straight into danger? I could have my brother with me right now instead of nursing a cut-up cheek, sprained ankle, and broken pride. I could be on my way back home instead of wondering if I'd ruined everything with Leo.

I knew deep down it would take more than one

fuck up from me to chase him off but I still felt as though he was pulling away from me. Normally, there wouldn't be a chance in hell that Leo would leave me high and dry after getting me naked. I knew he still loved me but I couldn't help feeling as though he wanted to be apart from me now.

I splashed the dirty washrag into the water and thumped my head against the back of the tub a couple of times. What could I do to show him that I was sorry about how shit went down today? I knew I'd hurt his feelings earlier when I flinched away from him. That, and even if I hadn't done it intentionally, not reaching out to him when I needed him hurt him the most.

I needed to show him I trusted him completely. Because I did trust him both physically and mentally. But I had done a shit job of showing my confidence in him by completely ignoring his warnings to keep myself safe.

The truth was, I had never known what it was like to trust a man until Leo came into my life. The men in my life hadn't exactly been good examples.

My father was obviously one of the most untrustworthy people I'd ever known. He would probably still be lying and cheating until the day he took his last breath. If your father is supposed to set the bar at which you expected men to treat you, I'd been doomed from the start.

Then there was Tanner. Don't get me wrong, I loved him to pieces, but I wasn't stupid enough to think I could completely confide in him.

Chris was next on this list. Clearly, he proved to be just as honorable as my father had been, if not worse. So, that left only Leo.

At the beginning of our affair, I confided in him with most aspects of my life. I shared my deepest secrets and regrets with him. The only thing I hadn't shared was what Chris was doing to me. I couldn't ever bring myself to show him that shame. It wasn't like I couldn't have entrusted him with those details. I knew without a doubt he would've taken care of me if I'd told him any of it. I trusted him that much.

When I thought he betrayed me, I'd lost that confidence in him immediately. It wasn't fair to him that he had to build that trust back if he never really did anything to lose it in the first place.

I raised my head and hardened my resolve as I quickly washed the rest of my body. I was going to show Leo just how much I trusted him even if he did want some space right now. He wouldn't find such a thing with me. I thought I had needed space from him all these years and I had been dead wrong. I never had distance from him as he had always ruled my thoughts.

After I rinsed my body, I rose from the tub carefully. I slowly limped to where my robe was hanging and wrapped the soft cotton around my wet body. I hobbled toward the door and opened it slightly to glance out. What I saw nearly broke my heart.

Leo was sitting in one of the chairs in the little carved-out seating area in the suite. His phone lay on the table next to him as he slouched in the plush seat. His eyes were closed and his head had fallen back to rest on the cushion behind him. His arms slumped almost uselessly beside him. He looked so tired, so worn down.

I silently opened the door the rest of the way and slipped into the suite. I padded carefully in his direction, ignoring the pain in my foot. To know what was going on in his head was something I wished for at that moment. I knew he had to be deep in thought if he didn't hear me approach.

Once I was within reaching distance, I less than gracefully sank to my knees in front of him. He still didn't move or open his eyes as I watched him. The only indication he was even alive was the steady rise and fall of his chest as he breathed.

I tentatively reached up and ran my palms up his thighs. His eyes sprang open and he sat forward with a start as he stared down at me. When he realized I'd snuck up on him he sat back in his seat with a huff.

"You were supposed to call me when you were ready to get out," he murmured before laughing to himself. "Of course, why would you call me?" He shook his head, clearly exasperated by me.

I closed my eyes and took a deep breath before opening them again. "I'm sorry," I offered.

His eyes softened before he raked his fingers against my sore cheek. "No, I'm sorry. You didn't deserve that," he said as he smoothed his thumb across my lower lip.

I smiled at him as my hands continued their uphill climb. "Yes, I did. You were right, I didn't trust you when I should have. The moment I saw Tanner I should've called you. I should've had more faith in you."

He stared at me before he stilled my hands with his. His warm fingers rubbed against mine as he studied me. "It's fine, Em—"

"No, it's not," I said cutting him off. I swallowed thickly before moving my hands further up. He released me and moved his hands to the armrests of his seat, gripping the plush fabric tightly. When I came to the bulge in his jeans I rubbed him firmly through the thick denim. I felt a surge of satisfaction course through me as he pushed up against my hand involuntarily.

"You have done nothing to lose the confidence you gained all those years ago and yet I still doubted you. I need to do a better job of showing you how much I believe in you," I said as I reached for the button of his jeans, releasing it. "How much I trust you to take care of me."

I watched his expression shift to something hotter as I pulled his zipper down. One of the best things about being with Leo was the easy access he always offered. He didn't bother with trivial things such as underwear most days. A fact that proved very useful as his thick cock sprang from the restraining garment.

His jaw clenched tight as I palmed him and he thrust into my hand. I stroked him from root to tip as I watched him. His mouth parted with a gasp as I used my other hand to cradle his heavy balls. He groaned as my fist tightened just as he liked. My mouth watered as I watched pearly liquid gather at his tip.

When I couldn't take it anymore, I leaned forward and sucked his bulbous head past my lips. I swiped at him with my tongue, gathering that liquid and moaning against him. His hands remained where they were as he tightened his grip on the chair.

I continued to stroke him as I pulled away enough to speak. "I trust you, Leo. Utterly and completely, with my mind, body—" I swallowed thickly. Now was a pivotal moment for us. Either I could keep acting as though this man still had no effect over me, or I could tell him how I felt. What he ultimately meant to me. "With my heart." His gaze softened as heady emotion glimmered in his eyes. "I'm truly sorry it's taken me this long to tell you that," I whispered. "I need to prove how much faith I have in you."

I watched his eyes flare as he sat forward, forcing me back on my heels. I bit back a whimper at the pressure it put on my ankle. He gripped the back of my neck and kissed me with such intensity it nearly left me dizzy. He shoved his tongue inside my mouth as I stroked him harder now. He devoured my mouth as his hand traveled further into my hair. I hummed a moan against his lips as he tugged just hard enough to light me on fire.

When he pulled away from me he stared down at what I was doing to his cock. With a long groan, he pulled my hands away from him before he stood. I half thought he was pulling away from me because he was still angry. The relief I felt when he shoved down his pants was almost enough to bring a tear to my eye.

He reached down and gripped the sash of my robe quickly. He yanked the knot free before pulling it completely away from the rest of the robe. The fast movement pulled the garment apart, revealing my naked form.

I watched him as he walked around the back of me and quickly grabbed a pillow from the bed. He urged me to move so he could place the pillow under my knees, taking the pressure off my ankle. He just kept proving to me how stupid I had been by continuously being thoughtful of my needs. Once satisfied with my position, he knelt behind me. He pushed the robe and my hair off my neck as he trailed kisses from my shoulder up to my jaw. I leaned into him as he gripped my wrists, bringing them behind me. I smiled to myself as he started to tie the soft sash around them.

"You want to show me how much you trust me?" he asked as his lips grazed my ear. At my nod, he continued. "Are you going to sit like a good girl while I fuck your mouth? Trust me to take you to your limits and no further?" His voice seemed to go deeper with each erotic word spoken.

He tugged on my binding before standing, taking his heat with him. My mouth watered as he came back into my view. I watched as he pulled his shirt over his head. I nodded again, answering his questions.

His smile was feral as he gathered my hair into his hands. He worked the long strands until his fist held them like a ponytail holder. I was completely at his mercy as he held me still and gripped his big cock with his other hand. I watched helplessly as he stroked himself in front of me. Liquid fire built between my legs at the image he was making.

"Open," was all he said as he stepped forward. I obeyed immediately as I opened my mouth and stuck my tongue out as if it were a one-way road for him to follow. He guided his thick cock past my lips and I sucked him down greedily.

His fist tightened on my hair as he tunneled into my mouth only to pull out again. His groans of pleasure sent surges of arousal straight to my pussy.

"Fuck yes, Emy. You're going to take all of me, aren't you?" he growled as his cock reached further into my mouth.

I hummed my agreement as he moved my head back and forth in tandem with his thrusts. I had no choice but to let him fuck my mouth the way he wanted and I loved every second of it. With each pass he made, he tunneled deeper and deeper into me. Soon he was knocking the back of my throat. Once there he held himself still as my throat convulsed around him. He then pulled completely out and I gasped for air each time before he would slap his cock against my tongue once more before doing it all over again.

I focused on my breathing as he fucked my throat. I could feel tears streaming down my cheeks as I choked on him but I kept silently begging for more as I watched his face contort with pleasure. Soon he stopped pulling all the way out and thrust into me faster and faster. I sucked and swallowed as if my life depended on it.

"That's it, Princess. I'm going to come. You swallow every fucking drop. Don't you lose any of it." He groaned as he held me still and his thrusts became erratic.

I moaned against him as he shoved in. I swallowed around him one last time and he exploded down my throat.

"Fuck!" he shouted above me as he emptied himself inside of me. I gagged as his release spilled thickly into my mouth but I swallowed it down greedily all the same.

When he had no more to give, he popped out of my mouth and I gasped for breath before he knelt in front of me. He hastily reached behind me and ripped the sash from my wrists. When I was free, I rushed to grip his face and kissed him like a starved woman.

He pulled me up and wrapped my legs around his lean hips before he forced me to my back as he laid on top of me. My robe fell completely open as his hands roamed my body. I arched into him as he palmed my breasts, tweaking my nipples as he went.

"You sucked me like a good little slut, Princess. Now it's my turn to make you come," he murmured against me before he slid easily inside my pussy. How he could come the way he did and still be ready for more was beyond me.

He pulled away from me as he sat up, taking my hips with him. I squealed as his thumb pressed down on my clit and I clenched around him. He fucked into me hard as he rubbed me in tight circles.

"Now, be a good Princess and fucking come for me," he commanded as he slapped the outside of my thigh with his free hand. "Now!" he roared and I went flying.

I crumbled in his arms with his name on my lips.

He fucked into me with harsh thrusts as I convulsed around him. I gripped his back and dug my nails in as he rode me. When I came floating back down from my orgasm, he slowed his thrusts before stopping altogether.

"Do you trust me, Emy?" His voice was hoarse as he pulled his glistening cock out of me.

"You know I do," I panted.

He reached over into his nearby bag and grabbed what looked like a bottle of oil. I quickly realized it was lube as he used it to lather up his already slick cock. Right when I thought he would thrust back into me, he quickly crawled down my body and latched his lips around my engorged clit.

I shouted as I gripped his hair and pulled him to me. He groaned against me before I felt his slick finger find my asshole. I sucked in a startled breath as he easily slid his lubed digit inside of me.

He was the only one I had ever done any sort of backdoor play with, so the feeling was still a little foreign to me. Not to say it was bad, in fact, it was quite the opposite as he slowly pumped into me as he tongued my clit. He built me higher and higher as I felt him stretch my little hole with his big fingers, first one, then two. He worked me over thoroughly as my orgasm began to raise. I started to move with his fingers as my body took control. I churned my hips as he finger-fucked my ass and sucked at my clitoris. He groaned long and deep against me and that was all it took to make me come crashing back down to earth. I screamed his name as he fingered me hard.

I don't know when it happened but one minute my vision was going dark around the edges and the next Leo was posed above me gently breeching my ass with his hard cock. I moved with him as he slowly gained inch after inch. His breathing was just as harsh as mine as we moved together. He was stretching me impossibly tight with each passing moment.

"Leo," I whined as I thought he would never make it all the way in.

"Shh, I have you, Emy. You can take me. You were made for me," he grunted before he reached down to rub my pussy again.

I shuddered as he slowly rubbed me from my entrance to my clit and back again. I pushed against him as another orgasm built inside of me.

His thrusts became smooth and languid right before he fully seated himself. He sat still, letting me adjust to him. His fingers never stopped moving along my pussy as he stared down at where we were connected. I could feel myself clenching around him as he continued to play with me.

When I couldn't take it any longer, I churned my hips against him. Imploring him to move inside of me. He groaned before meeting my gaze and he started to fuck me.

Nerves I never knew about flared and flashed as he pulled out of me just to tunnel back in. I was ready to come by the time he really started in on me.

"This isn't going to last long, Princess. You're so fucking perfect and this tiny little asshole is strangling my cock," he choked. "Come for me, baby."

I shook my head as I held my orgasm at bay. "I need you to go with me," I cried.

My words must have broken his tightly held restraint as he slammed into me hard. His balls slapped against my ass as he pulled me down to his every thrust.

"Oh yes. Fucking come with me, Emily," he groaned heavily as his cock spasmed. I felt him spill his hot cum inside of me, sending me over the edge with him. He pinched my still throbbing clit, demanding I come again as his hips churned against me. I came with a scream as he leaned back down to take my lips.

We both held each other as we panted loudly. He stayed inside of me as he explored my lips with his own. "You have my heart too, Emy. You've always been its keeper," he whispered against me. "Even if I had to work every single day of my life to make you trust me, I would for you."

To some, it may look like I had just given him trust with my body and nothing more. But to an abuse survivor, giving my body to someone without any holds meant so much more than that. He didn't need my words when I had just given him undeniable proof that I trusted him unequivocally in every way that mattered.

Chapter Nineteen

Hours later, Leo and I sat outside in our private patio area eating the most delicious cheeseburger I'd ever had. I was starved. Maybe it was because it was late in the afternoon and I hadn't eaten anything since breakfast, or maybe it was because I had exerted so much energy today. Either way, when that burger and fries had been set in front of me, I wolfed it down almost immediately.

Leo sat across from me the whole time with my ankle propped up on his thigh with a rag filled with ice sitting atop it. To some, our earlier activity may have seemed rough, but to me, it was nothing but loving. Especially after we were done and all he had done since was dote on me.

He refused to let me walk at all on my injured ankle as he carried me back to the bathroom to clean us both up. He was gentle as he knelt in front of me to wipe away the evidence of what we had done.

When he was satisfied with his work, he had shed me of my robe and gathered me back into his arms. He then walked us both into the pool where we'd floated together, never taking our hands off each other. The cold water immediately took most of the pressure off my ankle as well as helped with the swelling. We stayed there well past the point of being pruned. It was only inevitable that we both found multiple releases once again. After a day like today, I think we both needed to find extra comfort with one another.

We only separated once the knock came at the door signaling room service had arrived. I propped my head on my hands against the edge of the pool as I watched him gracefully exit the pool. I loved seeing the water slide off his naked body, leaving his smooth skin slick and shiny. His cock hung heavily between his legs as he grabbed for the towel hanging nearby. I didn't think I would ever get tired of watching his naked ass as he walked away from me. The sight alone was enough to make me want to take a bite out of it.

He wrapped the towel around his waist, taking away my view as he strode through the open door of our suite to retrieve room service. I giggled behind my hand as I watched from my place in the pool as he answered the door. The little Colombian woman's eyes doubled in size as she gave Leo a once-over. I didn't know a hell of a lot of Spanish but I could recognize when someone stumbled over their words. I couldn't even blame her at this point, Leo was one fine piece of man.

I smiled broadly as I watched Leo rub the back of his neck almost bashfully at the woman's reaction to him. I felt like sometimes he was completely oblivious to the fact that he was hot. He'd quickly moved out of the way for her to enter the room and I swear I saw her cheeks brighten with blush as she walked past his still-dripping form. Everything important was covered on him but those stunning tattoos were still on full display. His chest and abs gleamed with wetness.

I giggled again as I watched him try to help her take things off the cart. The woman was having a hard time keeping her focus on her task and he was far too oblivious to the fact that he was the cause of her frustration.

I decided to take pity on the girl and called for Leo to come help me from the water. My ankle was feeling a lot better at this point and I didn't feel like I needed the help, but it was obvious she needed him to leave the room.

He immediately dropped the tray cover he was holding and rushed back to me. I snorted as I watched the woman take a steadying breath before calmly resuming her task. Leo pulled me from the pool and wrapped me into my robe before helping me walk back into the suite. By the time I entered through the door, the woman was done unloading her tray.

She waited to be dismissed but not before I handed her a hefty tip as I searched my brain for the right words to say.

"*El es guapo, no*?" I asked and the woman blushed before nodding. *He's handsome, isn't he?* I smiled broadly at her as I tapped my temple. "*No te estás perdiendo mucho, la belleza y el cerebro no existen.*" I lied through my teeth, beauty and brains did in fact exist. Leo was probably the smartest person I knew.

The woman giggled before she nodded her thanks. I hid my smile behind my hand as she exited the room. Once the door was closed, I heard Leo chuckle as he approached me from behind. "*Ah, de verdad*?" His deep voice sounded against my neck as he kissed me there, sending shivers down my spine. "Oh, really," he repeated in English that time as his strong arms wrapped around my waist and pulled me back to him.

I smiled again. "The poor girl needed to have something wrong with you. You're too perfect otherwise," I said as I turned in his arms to face him.

"Hmm," he hummed before his smile broadened. He kissed me swiftly before scooping me up into his arms. I giggled unabashedly as he carried me to the patio and sat me down at the little table.

And that's where we were as I licked the remaining sauce off my fingers after shoveling the last bite of burger into my mouth. I was less than ladylike as I chewed the overly large bite.

I closed my eyes and moaned as the flavors exploded on my tongue multiple times as we ate in silence. I'd caught Leo more than once as he glanced at me while I ate, a small grin playing along his lips. Once again, I had caught him staring as I sucked the last of the juices from my thumb. I swallowed my last bite before I snorted a laugh. "What are you staring at?"

He sat the rest of his burger down before answering me with a playful grin. "I just didn't know I would ever be so jealous of a burger." He chuckled before he picked his food back up.

I squinted at him as I smothered the urge to laugh. I was probably doing a terrible job of hiding my smile as he grinned around his bite of food before he winked at me. I lunged at him.

I crawled onto his lap as he held the burger to his lips. Before he could move, I bit down on the other side of his burger, taking a huge bite from it. His eyes widened before he pulled it away from me. His shocked expression had me fighting a laugh of my own as I tried not to choke on his food.

I chewed and swallowed as he threw his burger back onto his plate before gripping me around the ribs. "You little shit," he growled playfully as he tickled me. I screeched as I pushed away from him. Giggling, I shoved at his chest as he brought me closer to him. He stopped tickling me long enough to wrap his arms around my ass and pulled me to him. My robe separated at the movement, exposing me to him.

I watched as his eyes went from playful to full of lust within seconds. I felt myself getting wet and ready for him. *Would I ever tire of this man?*

His hands moved up my back before gripping the back of my head. He pulled me down for a brief kiss before letting his hands travel down the front of me. My breath caught in my throat as he lowered the robe off my shoulders, exposing my breasts inch by inch.

His eyes stayed locked on mine as his hands moved lower. He grinned up at me as his thumbs brushed over my tightening nipples. "I love you, Emy. And this may be a fucked-up situation that brought us back together, but I thank the universe every day for bringing you into my life," he murmured.

I leaned forward to kiss him again, letting that be my response. I felt him harden under me as his tongue swept inside my mouth. I shuddered as his hands kept their downhill advance. He gripped my naked hips and ground me onto him.

I moved my hands down his chest and further still before I reached the plush towel around his waist. He hissed against my lips as I raked my fingernails against the skin below the towel.

Just as he started to move me so I could release him from his constraint, a shrill tone broke through our bubble. I jerked away from him as I realized it was his phone. He sighed heavily as he tore his gaze away from me before grabbing the device.

"Cruz." His chipped tone sounded annoyed as he answered the call. I was feeling playful as I leaned forward to kiss his neck.

His free hand squeezed my bare thigh as I ran my tongue up his pulse point. My grin was apparent as I nipped his earlobe. I snorted as he cleared his throat in obvious frustration.

"I'll be there in thirty." His harsh words registered in my lust-addled brain and I sat up. He sighed as he put the phone back on the table beside us. "I gotta go," he said as he stood from the chair, taking me with him.

He walked us into the suite and deposited me on the large bed before turning his back to me. I tightened my robe around myself. "Where are you going?" I asked, already knowing the answer.

I watched his shoulders bunch as stress crept into them. He didn't want to tell me. "That was Isabelle, she's been staking out that apartment building since we left the market. She said Tanner and Peter just walked in. Now's the chance to get him," he explained without turning around.

My gut rolled as the food I just ate turned leaden. We were finally going to get Tanner. And if I was right, it was going to be dangerous. I stared down at my hands in my lap as I worried. Leo told me I would be able to go with him when they found Tanner but I could tell from his body language that he didn't want me to.

The internal struggle I felt at that moment was enough to make me nauseous. I wanted nothing more than to go get Tanner with Leo so we could all go home. But I also wanted to prove to Leo I did trust him completely to handle this.

We both knew it could be a dangerous situation he would walk into. I had to learn to shove down my wants and let logic take over. I knew without a doubt that Leo would do everything in his power to bring Tanner back to me safely. I just needed to let him do it.

I studied Leo as he released his towel before gripping a pair of light denim jeans. I said nothing as he shoved his legs through them and pulled them up into place. He then pocketed his phone. His shoulders were still tight as he grabbed a clean white shirt and tugged it on over his head.

I shook my head and took a deep breath before pushing myself further up the bed. There was no way I was going to make this situation harder than it had to be. For Leo or myself.

I tore my gaze away from his back as he checked his pistol and shoved it into its holster under his shirt. I glanced at the side table and grabbed the distraction I was searching for. I pointed the remote to the TV and switched it on. Out of the corner of my vision, I saw Leo's head snap in the same direction. If he was trying to hide his obvious relief, he was doing a terrible job at it. His heavy sigh released all the tension that had built around us.

He turned toward me and I met his gaze with my own. He said nothing as a slight grin formed on his sensual lips.

"Before you go, can you grab the ice for my ankle? I would like to be able to walk normally tomorrow." My voice sounded much calmer than I felt.

Leo nodded as he approached me. "I won't be gone more than a couple of hours," he said as he knelt over me. I nodded as I watched his eyes search mine. His still-damp waves dangled over his forehead before I pushed them back. He leaned down and pressed his lips to mine as I sighed. "I know this is hard for you, Emy. Thank you for trusting me enough to bring your brother back to you in one piece."

I snorted despite myself as I rolled my eyes. "It would be easier if I knew exactly where you were going," I said as I grazed my fingers through his short beard at his cheek.

"Ah," he said before pulling his phone out of his pocket. He unlocked the screen and tapped until he found what he was looking for. Before I could ask what he was doing, my phone dinged from its spot on the bedside table.

I reached for the device and my eyes burned slightly as I read the screen. It was a silly thing to get emotional about but that didn't stop it from being so.

"Now you'll be able to see where I am," Leo murmured from above me before I glanced back up at him. He had shared his location with me.

I put my phone down and shoved my hands into his hair. I tugged him down to me so I could taste his lips. His hands slid between my back and the mattress to hold me to him as I explored. I was breathless when I pulled away.

"A couple of hours?" I whispered.

"A couple of hours," he repeated.

I nodded and swallowed thickly before speaking again. "Go get my brother."

Chapter Twenty

I winced slightly with each step I took. I knew I needed to stop my brisk pace if I wanted any shot at walking normally tomorrow but I couldn't seem to stop myself. I'd wrapped my robe around myself so tightly, I wasn't even sure how I was breathing normally. I took six steps forward before reaching the chair at one end of the suite, only to turn and take six more. Pulling my fingers up to my mouth, I nibbled at the nails nervously as I glanced at the clock once again.

It had been three hours since Leo left to get Tanner, and nothing. Not a single call or text. I had no idea what was happening or if either of them were even alive at this point. I once again glanced expectantly at my phone which lay silent on the bed.

I'd sent Leo a message asking him if he had any news. When I received nothing in return I sent another one ten minutes later. That one I'd teased him with sexual promises, masking my concern with humor. Another silent ten minutes had passed and still nothing so I'd sent another, asking if everything was okay, voicing that he was making me nervous.

This had gone on for the last hour. I even went so far as to threaten that I'd show up there if he didn't answer me. Absolutely nothing. The worst part about it was that he wasn't even reading the messages. The notification had been delivered but nobody was seeing them. I wanted to be able to trust Leo in this. For both of us, I needed to give him this. But how long was I willing to wait?

I huffed angrily before marching over to my phone yet again. I pulled his name up and hit the call button. Fear prickled down my spine as the call immediately went to his voicemail. Leo never shut his phone off. Something was wrong.

I raked my fingers through my hair hastily as I considered screaming my frustration. I tapped my phone against my palm as I continued to pace. What was I supposed to do? I didn't have Isabelle's number so it's not like I could just call her. I didn't even think calling the police would do me any good either.

I looked down at my phone again before opening the location tab. I tapped Leo's name and it pinged him in the same damn spot it had an hour ago. He hadn't moved at all. I clicked on the location and took a screenshot of the address.

"Fuck it," I murmured to myself before walking to the bedside table. I gripped the en suite phone and dialed the front desk. After I ordered a taxi, I rushed to the dresser where my clothes were and grabbed the first thing I could find. I didn't care anymore if I pissed Leo off. If he didn't want me to show up and save the fucking day, then he should have answered my call.

I tried to tramp down the feeling of dread as I stood and grabbed my bag. Tried to tell myself nothing was wrong as I exited the suite as fast as my ankle would allow. I didn't want anything bad to happen to anyone, but the feeling that something had gone terribly wrong clung to me as I slid into the taxi and gave the driver the address.

****

"*Gracias*," I said to the taxi driver as I handed him cash from my bag. I didn't bother to count it all out. I was too nervous to worry about trivial things such as money at the moment.

I surveyed my surroundings as I stepped away from my ride and into the dark, humid evening air. The sounds of Columbia at night filled my ears. Dogs barking, people talking, and traffic flowing down a nearby street. It was late in the evening and most people were inside their homes, aside from the few that hung around outside.

If it weren't for the nearby streetlight, it would be almost impossible to see the area around me. I looked up at the run-down building in front of me that I knew held my brother at one point. Whether he was still here or not wasn't the real question. The real question was, was Leo still here?

It didn't strike me at that moment about the odd situation I found myself in. I had come to Columbia in search of my brother, the one person I cherished most in this world, and now I searched for the man I chose for myself. The man I didn't think I'd be able to survive without. Not again.

I had wasted so much precious time that we could have had together. I wasn't going to allow myself to waste any more. I wanted Leo in every single way that one person could have another. I wanted him as my protector, my reason for waking up each day, my husband, and fate willing, the father of my future children. I would not allow anything else to come between us. I loved Tanner but if it came down to it, I would choose Leo. It was well past time I started choosing my own happiness above others.

A loud rattle and bang sounded to my left and I nearly jumped out of my skin. I gripped my chest as I faced the noise only to find a cat lightly pawing the inside of a garbage can it knocked over. I released a shaky breath as I glanced away from the mangy feline and down the street.

A pebble of dread sank in my gut as I spotted Leo's rental car parked a few spots away from me. I walked as briskly as I could toward it. My heart sank slightly as I noticed the vehicle was empty. Saying a silent prayer, I gripped the handle and tried to open the door.

I nearly cried happy tears as it opened. I grinned to myself before glancing around to make sure nobody was looking in my direction. When I was certain no one was, I knelt and opened the glove compartment.

The pistol Leo put there the first day we arrived in Columbia gleamed in the low light of the vehicle. I had shot a gun only a handful of times in my life so I couldn't say I was an expert. I knew where the safety was and how to hold the firearm, but that's about it. If this experience in another country had shown me anything, it was that I was sorely prepared. I promised myself I would ask Jill about her self-defense class as well as ask Leo to help me train with firearms. A woman, no matter where she grew up, needed to know how to protect herself.

I checked the safety and made sure there was a bullet in the chamber before carefully shoving it into my waistband at the small of my back. I pulled a few Columbian bills from my wallet, shoving them in my back pocket before grabbing my phone. I palmed it as I threw my bag onto the floorboard. When I shut the door and turned to face the building again, I could feel my adrenaline spike.

I fortified myself as I walked toward the building. As I neared the front door, I felt eyes following my movements. I forced myself to keep my eyes ahead of me but I could see a few people leaning on the railings of their balconies as they watched me. They seemed just as leery of me as I was of them.

I released a steadying breath as I reached for the handle before pushing through the threshold. The building was less than nice as I let my eyes adjust to the crappy fluorescent lighting. The bright lights flickered as I walked to the set of stairs directly in front of me. The smell of mold and mildew had me scrunching my nose up in disgust. The air was hazy with what I could only hope was cigarette smoke.

The graffiti on the walls was enough to show me that whoever allowed these people to live like this truly didn't care. I avoided the scuzzy railing as I ascended the stairs. The sounds of a baby crying through the thin walls was not nearly enough to drown out the thoughts running wildly through my mind.

I had no idea which one of these apartments Leo could have gone to. I only hoped I would get some kind of clue as to where he was. If I had to resort to knocking on doors, no matter how dangerous that might be, I would do it.

As I stepped up to the second-floor landing, the sound of a door slamming made me jump once again. I cursed at myself, I needed to calm down. I glanced around the next set of stairs as I watched a woman leaning against the wall outside of her apartment.

She looked to be around her early twenties, though the bags under her eyes said otherwise. She was dirty, but not in an unbathed way. She looked like she'd just had a long day and it seemed like her evening was proving to be even longer. I watched her as she pulled a cigarette from the pack in her pocket. She dangled it from her lips as she lit a match. She pulled a long drag from it before leaning her head against the wall at her back.

Under different circumstances, I would call her beautiful. Under her haphazard bun and her too-tired eyes, was a lovely young woman.

As though they had a mind of their own, my feet started moving toward her. I really should have known better than to approach anyone in this place. Although, it seemed that if I had a shot at all at finding Tanner and Leo, she might just be it.

Among other things, Tanner was always known to be a charmer. Although he never really had a preference between men or women, if he spotted a pretty girl within a fifty-mile radius, you could bet he would go out of his way to talk to her. This woman was the type he would do that for. If I had to guess, I bet Tanner had tried his luck with this one. She would know where he was.

As I stepped closer, the woman's head snapped in my direction. I held my hands out to show her I meant no harm. "Hello," I said softly as she pushed away from the wall. I panicked as she made a dash for her door. "*No, por favor,*" I begged.

She paused and I advanced. When she looked back in my direction I held my phone up. "*Mi hermano.*" I stepped closer to her as I pulled up a picture of Tanner. When I was within reaching distance I held the screen toward her. "Have you seen him?" I asked.

I allowed the worries I felt to shine through on my expression as her eyes flickered from my phone to my face and back again. I saw the recognition in her gaze as she stared at the picture of Tanner. Dread curled in my stomach again as she shook her head before turning away from me. "*No,*" she said as she gripped her doorknob.

I panicked and shoved my hand into my pocket. I gripped the wad of bills and thrust them in her direction. "Please!" I nearly shouted.

The woman eyed the stack of bills and then me again. She brought her cigarette back up to her lips and took one last pull from it before throwing it onto the ground. She stomped it out before grabbing for the money in my hand.

When she gripped the bills, I didn't let them go as

I stared at her. *"Donde esta el?"* I asked with a firmness in my voice I didn't know I possessed. *Where is he?*

She frowned at me before pulling on the money in my hand. I released the bills but not her gaze. She glanced down at the money before looking me up and down. I nearly panicked again when she grabbed for her door.

"Fourth floor, unit seventeen," she spoke in a thick accent before slipping past the door and back into her apartment.

I nodded to myself as I turned back toward the stairs. I had to force myself to slow down as pain flared in my ankle again. I was glad it was just the fourth floor. I didn't think I'd be able to make it much further than that.

As I ascended the stairs, my heart beat more heavily in my chest. With each step, I could feel my breathing accelerate. I was so close now to finally finding Tanner and in turn Leo.

When I stepped onto the fourth-floor landing, the first thing I noticed was how quiet it had gotten. I didn't know if that was good or bad, I was leaning toward bad. I quietly strode further down the hall and surveyed each door as I went. My heart nearly leapt from my chest as I spotted unit seventeen.

The door was slightly open as I stepped forward. I could vaguely hear mumbling on the other side. I breathed as quietly as I could as I tried to see past the small opening. At first, I saw nothing in the dim light of the unit, then what I finally saw made my blood run cold.

Isabelle lay still on the hard tile with her hands tied behind her back. I could just barely see a thin trickle of blood that marred her forehead. It looked as though she had been hit from behind and knocked out cold. Glass was littered on the floor surrounding her as if she had been thrown against a mirror in the struggle.

I leaned against the doorway and tried to see more than just the detective. Movement caught my eyes further into the room and I angled myself to see better. I nearly whimpered when I saw Leo sitting on the floor with his arms also tied behind his back. His eyebrow had a deep slit in it that I guessed he got after Isabelle had been knocked out. He had stopped bleeding a long time ago, if the dried blood on his face was any indication.

His once clean white shirt was ripped at the collar. He had a dirty rag shoved into his mouth and tied around the back of his head. He was conscious.

I slipped slightly as I leaned forward a little more to get a better view. The move pushed the door open a fraction more than it had been. I cringed at my own stupidity as Leo's head snapped in my direction and he spotted me. His eyes widened and his nostrils flared as he stared at me. A mixture of fear and anger filled his scowl.

I didn't stop to think about the repercussions as I pushed the door even more. Leo shook his head at me but I ignored him as I slipped into the apartment. I stayed low as I got a look at my surroundings.

It was filthy, the floors, the walls, all of it was grimy. It wreaked of stale smoke and mold as I crawled along the stained floors to get to Leo. To my right, there was a single ripped, dark-green couch pointed at a TV that looked like it came straight out of the 80s. I tried my hardest to ignore the coffee table in front of the couch. I just knew it would be littered with evidence of my brother's drug problem. To my left was an equally grimy kitchen. The tiles were white but stained brown from lack of basic cleaning. The number of dishes stacked in the sink surmounted the number of flies swarming them. I could hear quiet talking coming from another room in the unit but it didn't sound like they were headed this way yet.

I slid up to Leo and pulled the rag from his mouth before replacing it with my hand. His eyes flared with anger as he released a harsh breath through his nose.

"I know you're angry, but from the looks of it, you need my help. Let's get you untied," I said before releasing his mouth. I grabbed for his tied hands.

"You need to get the fuck out of here," he hissed at me as I fumbled with the knot at his wrists.

"And do what? Leave you here? Ha," I whispered. The knot was proving more difficult to untie than I expected.

"Emily—" His eyes jerked toward the other room. Voices became clearer now as if they were coming closer.

"Just think about this for a second, man," a familiar voice begged.

"No, they were following us, Tanner." My heart leapt in my chest at the mention of my brother's name. He was alive. "I'm gonna find out what the fuck they want one way or another," the shaky voice finished as it became louder.

"Hide, now!" Leo demanded, his eyes wide with worry. I nodded hastily as I shoved the rag back into his mouth.

My eyes darted around the room for a place to hide and landed on a closet next to the front door. I crawled as fast as I could and quietly opened the shuttered door. I slid inside and silently shut the door. The shutters were open just enough I could see out but no one would be able to see in unless you knew where to look.

Leo straightened back up and turned his head as two figures entered the room. I watched in horror as Peter stepped in front of Leo, blocking him from my view completely. I had expected him to be here so that wasn't the part that terrified me

The part that had me horrified wasn't the fact that he was Leo's captor, it was that he had a gun. And he had it pointed directly at Leo's head.

Chapter Twenty-One

I moved forward to burst back through the door as another tall figure entered my view. The only thing that stopped me was when the man put his hand on Peter's arm to lower the gun. No, not a man—Tanner. Tanner stopped Peter from shooting Leo.

"Whoa, stop, man. I didn't sign up for this. What the fuck are you doing?" Tanner's deep voice sounded clear as a bell and I felt relief flood me for a moment. He was whole. For the time being, he was okay.

Peter glared at the hand holding his arm before shoving Tanner away from him forcefully. For a smaller guy, he had some strength to be able to push a guy built like Tanner.

"Nah, fuck that! I'm going to find out what this prick wants with us. Then we're going to move again." His eyes were crazy as they stared at my brother. "Then I'll know what to do," he mumbled as if to himself.

My breath left me in a woosh as I moved my gaze back to Leo. He was staring at me again and I could read the unspoken words in his eyes. *Don't you fucking move*, he was silently imploring me. I started to throw him a look that said, *The fuck if I will sit by and watch him shoot you*, when Peter stepped back into his space. Leo's eyes immediately diverted to his captor as he glared up at him.

Pete roughly pulled the dirty rag out of Leo's mouth before speaking. "Who the fuck are you? And who is she?" His voice seemed to get louder with each word as he pointed toward Isabelle.

"I'm not here to hurt you, Peter. Just untie my hands and then we can talk like civilized pe—" Leo's last word was cut off as Peter brought the gun down to his face in a harsh hit. I covered my mouth to smother the screech that climbed up my throat. My eyes burned as I watched Leo's head whip to the opposite side.

"Pete, stop!" Tanner begged as he rushed Peter. "You can't do this," he continued as he made to pull Peter away from a now freshly bloodied Leo.

My chest ached as I watched the blood trickle from the new gash that split his lip. The only sign that he was hurting was the wince as he straightened once again.

Peter was about to turn on Tanner when Leo spoke again. "Tanner's parents hired me to find him and bring him back to the States. That's it. I'm not here to arrest you or hurt you in any way. I just need Tanner," he explained.

"See, he's here for me. Okay? Not you. So you can let him go and I'll just go straighten this out," Tanner rambled quickly as he grabbed Peter's arm once more.

Peter looked down at the hand on his arm as if stunned into silence. I could hardly see anything from my vantage point, but even I could tell he was nervous as his hands began to shake. I just hoped his finger didn't pull that trigger that was pointed in Leo's direction.

"Everything's fine, man. I'll just call my parents and tell them I'm staying here. They can fuck off. I don't need them," Tanner said calmly as he pushed Peter's arm further down, lowering the gun.

My breath left me with a sigh of relief as the gun no longer pointed at the man I loved. But that sigh was quickly replaced with a sharp inhale as Pete shook his head before screaming at Tanner. I watched in horror as he jerked away from my brother only to pull the gun back up. Only this time he pointed it at Tanner.

Tanner put both of his hands up in front of him as he stepped back. I saw his throat work as he swallowed thickly. Sweat beaded on his upper lip as he stared at the gun. "Pete…" he tried calmly.

"Don't!" Peter screamed as he stepped closer to my brother. "Don't lie to me and tell me everything is fine. Nothing's fine!" He sucked in sharp breaths as he mumbled to himself, "Not gonna take you from me, no one can take you."

I looked between Leo and Tanner in a panic now. I couldn't just sit here and do nothing. I searched all around me for something to cut Leo free. I had a gun to defend myself but since I didn't really know how to use it, my best bet was to get it to Leo. The closet I sat in was completely empty and useless to me. I looked back down at Isabelle to see if she had some sort of pocket knife. That's when I remembered the glass surrounding her body.

A loud crash jerked my attention back to Peter as he pushed Tanner back further into the kitchen. Tanner hit a chair at the small dining table and stumbled back as he tried to keep his balance.

"You had everything given to you on a fucking silver platter. And what did you do with it? You shit all over it!" Peter's voice cracked with emotion as he continued to stalk my brother. "Do you know what I would give to have even a sliver of your life?" He pinched his fingers together as he spoke.

My eyes darted all around until they landed on a huge shard of glass. It may not be a knife but it would be sharp enough to free Leo. The only problem was that it was in the middle of the room. I would have to leave the closet to reach it.

I glanced up from the glass to Leo who was staring at me with panic in his eyes. He shook his head at me, knowing exactly what I was going to do. *No*, he mouthed toward me. He wanted me to leave so I wouldn't get hurt. Well, I had news for him. Watching both him and Tanner get hurt would ruin me more than anything that could physically be done to me.

I raised my eyebrows in an apologetic expression before tearing my gaze away from him. I risked a glance back toward Peter and Tanner. Peter was so busy tearing into my brother he wouldn't notice if I snuck into the room. I took a deep breath and pushed the closet door open.

"Pete, man, please. I thought we were friends." Tanner's voice was shaky as he stared at the gun.

Peter let out a horrifying laugh as I crawled silently behind him. "We were. That was until I found out that you're a fucking millionaire. What? Poor little rich boy couldn't buy himself some real friends so you decided to slum it with the first sad sack you could find?" Peter mocked him.

"It's not like that! You have no idea what my childhood was like," Tanner scowled as he lowered his arms. He was done cowering. "You are my real friend, Peter. Please stop this."

I reached out as far as I could and grabbed the shard of glass. Peter and Tanner were both so distracted neither of them could see me sneaking just a few feet away from them. As silently as I could, I slid the shard of glass toward Leo. I tramped down my happiness when it reached his foot.

He put his heel onto it and slid it up closer to his body. When he was satisfied, he twisted until he got it in his hands. I smiled briefly at him as his eyes screamed at me to hide. I tried not to snort at his silent command as I retreated once again but not before I grabbed the gun out of my waistband and slid it over to him as well. His sigh of relief was obvious as he eyed the firearm.

"You have no idea what hardship really looks like." Peter's booming voice caused me to jump from my place on the floor. "To have your life ripped away from you. You have your own fucking *rescue* team and I get told I'm not good enough!" he screamed.

I seemed to be rooted in my spot, stricken by horror as I watch the complete mental breakdown that was occurring before my very eyes. Peter pulled the gun up to himself and held it against his head as he screamed again. The type of bloodcurdling scream that rips your heart out.

"You have everything!" he repeated. "And now, you're going to give me everything." He pulled the gun away from himself and straightened.

I felt my body moving before I could fully comprehend what I was doing. I stood to my full height as I heard Leo harshly whisper his protest.

It was as though everything slowed down as Peter primed the gun to fire and raised it to my brother's head. I knew without a doubt that this was the moment he would shoot my brother in cold blood. It didn't matter what his plans were before this night. If he had meant to hold Tanner for ransom or not, it no longer played as a thought in his head. Right now he was out for one thing and one thing only—he was going to teach Tanner a lesson.

"Stop!" I yelled in a voice that seemed foreign to me.

Tanner's gaze locked with mine and surprise registered in those hazel eyes that were a twin to my own. Pete turned around on a dime with his gun still held up. I sucked in a sharp breath and prepared for the worst as he aimed it at me now.

Before I could think of my next move or even tell myself how stupid I was for pulling this one, Leo jumped up from his spot on the ground. He stepped in front of me and aimed the gun I slid to him at Peter.

"Put it down, now!" his booming voice echoed throughout the apartment.

Peter's eyes darted from me to Leo and then the gun nervously. His hands shook as he tried to decide who to point the gun at first. His eyes were watery as he desperately thought of his next move.

At that moment, I knew I wasn't looking at a killer. I wasn't seeing a criminal looking for his next big payday. I was seeing a very broken man who just wanted one thing in his life to work out the way it should. He was desperate for the love he never received a day in his life and that he rightfully deserved in some shape or form. He needed what everyone needed, someone in his life he could trust and love. Someone he would be able to call a friend no matter the circumstances. It was the lack of a basic human need that led him to this road, and giving him that was going to save us all.

"Let us help you," I said softly from behind Leo's broad back.

Peter's eyes glazed over at my words and I feared the next few moments.

"Help me?" he whispered as he stared at the gun in his hands. "There is no help for me."

Peter moved so fast it was hard to track his movements as chaos erupted. One moment he was pointing the gun at Leo and the next he was shoving it under his chin. Tanner shouted as he lunged for his friend and Leo pushed me away as he grabbed for the gun. I staggered back and regained my footing just as Leo ripped the gun from his hand and threw it to the ground. Tanner pulled Peter back to him and held him steady as he thrashed wildly.

"Let me go!" his hoarse voice cried, tears streaming down his grimy cheeks. My heart clenched in my chest as I watched Tanner hug his friend tightly to stop him from hurting himself.

"We're going to help you, Pete." Tanner's voice broke as he glanced from me to Leo and back to me again before mouthing a silent thank you.

Leo nodded as he holstered his gun and pulled me to his chest. I wrapped my arms around his waist as I buried my face into his neck. "I want to kiss you and thrash you at the same time, Princess," he said as he kissed the top of my head. "That was incredibly brave and so fucking stupid, Emy."

I snorted as I breathed him in. "You said a couple of hours. Someone had to save your sorry ass," I teased.

We pulled away from each other then and I watched as Tanner slowly rocked a now sobbing Peter. It was incredible how my brother had the capacity to love a person who just tried to kill him.

Leo kissed the side of my head before getting on the phone with local dispatch. He called in the "officer down" code as he knelt to check Isabelle. All of which was background noise as I knelt on the floor in front of Tanner.

He glanced up at me with wetness glistening in his eyes as I gripped his outstretched hand. "He's my friend," Tanner's voice was wobbly as he spoke.

I nodded. "We will get him some help," I promised.

He nodded at me and continued to comfort his friend. I sat with him the whole time as the sirens sounded in the distance. Even after the local authorities arrived to take Peter and Isabelle to the hospital, we comforted each other until it was time for us to clear the area.

Leo and I had done what we came here to do and now it was time to go back home.

Chapter Twenty-Two

"Can you believe they just give you this shit for free?" Tanner smiled broadly down at me as he returned from the bar in the first-class lounge. His arms were filled with all the complementary snacks they offered with this airline. Leo sat next to me with his head leaned back against his seat as he squeezed my thigh. He was tired, we all were. I flashed him a small smile as I resumed looking down at my phone.

I wasn't really looking at anything important. I just didn't feel like speaking. The last twelve hours had left me exhausted, to say the least.

After the authorities showed up to take Peter and Isabelle to the hospital, we had a lot of phone calls to make. Tanner and I stayed with Leo as he coordinated with the police to get Peter transferred to the States to one of the best psychiatric hospitals in the country. Just because the man had a mental breakdown and tried to kill all of us, that didn't mean he didn't deserve the help he desperately needed.

Tanner said he would be taking full financial responsibility for Peter while he was receiving his treatment. I didn't bother asking how he planned to pay for it.

We had stopped by Isabelle's room in the hospital after she woke up. Apparently, Peter had gotten the jump on her as she was trying to search the apartment she thought had been empty. She said she'd seen them both enter the complex and immediately called Leo. While she waited for him she'd knocked on their apartment door. When no one answered, she'd quietly snuck in to investigate—a poor decision she wouldn't make again in the future. Peter proved to be quite sneaky as he crept up behind her and hit her over the head with a dirty pan. She'd fallen into the mirror by the entrance and shattered it on the way down.

She was sore and had to stay for observation because of a possible concussion, but other than that she was fine. How Peter got the jump on Leo was another story altogether.

When he'd gotten to the apartment complex, he had gone looking for Isabelle. When he found her on the floor in the unit, he rushed in without really thinking it through. Peter was waiting with Isabelle's firearm and held him at gunpoint before knocking him out with the butt of the gun. The rest was history.

Even though the thought of the whole experience terrified me, I still couldn't stop teasing Leo about it. How a scrawny little boy like Peter got the jump on a big guy like Leo was truly astonishing. I didn't bother hiding my giggle every time Leo grumbled about being in the moment.

After we left the hospital, Leo had driven us in an all-too-silent car back to the resort. Once there, we packed up our things and headed to the airport. We were on the first flight out of Columbia within the next hour.

Hours later, here we sat, in the first-class lounge in Miami, waiting on our connecting flight to JFK. I was happy to be back in the States, but I was still not looking forward to seeing my family again in the next four hours. I wouldn't wish that mob upon anyone.

Tanner plopped down in the seat next to me and I did my best to ignore him. The truth was I was still angry with him and rather than thrash him like I wanted to, I bit my tongue.

He was doing a pretty good job at hiding the fact that he was coming down from some sort of drug, but I could tell. He seemed jumpy like his nerves were firing off of their own accord and he couldn't stop them. That, and he was sweating like a whore in church. When we got him back home I would personally be taking his happy ass to rehab. My only hope was that this time he would take it seriously.

"Da-ym," he stretched the word as he riffled through his treasures. "They even give you the name-brand shit on this airline." I could hear the grin in his words.

I resisted the urge to roll my eyes as I scrolled my social media. Not really seeing anything I was looking at.

"You definitely don't get this kind of shit in economy seating," he said as he nudged me with his elbow. I squeezed my lips tight together to keep my mouth shut.

"All they gave me and Pete on the way to Columbia was one bag of stale fucking peanuts." Tanner's voice seemed to be getting louder and louder the longer he spoke. All the other people in the lounge were starting to look at us wearily.

"We had to share that bag of nuts too. Can you believe that? Fucking billion-dollar airline and all I got was one bag of nuts." He laughed at himself causing more people to look in our direction.

"The only thing that made the whole flight worth it was the sexy-ass flight attendant. Oh yeah, I liked her. I even offered to give her my bag of nuts if she met me in the little bathroom so she could suck my c—"

"Would you shut the fuck up!" I broke my silence and glared at my big brother. Anger built in my gut like liquid lava as he grinned at me.

"Finally. There you are." He laughed at me as my eyes flared. "I was just joking, they didn't really give us anything to eat."

"Well, I believe I need to use the restroom," Leo

grunted as he stood suddenly from his seat beside me. He kissed the top of my head before making his quick exit. I kept my heated scowl on Tanner.

"Is all of this a big fucking joke to you?" I asked behind clenched teeth.

Tanner shrugged. "I mean, it's kind of funny. I take a vacation and Patricia suddenly acts like she cares about me. That alone is hilarious." He resumed looking through his snacks as though what he said made all the sense in the world.

"Tanner, you were gone for months. You said nothing to anyone at all and you just disappeared." All my blood rushed to my ears. How could he treat this with such little care?

"What the fuck does that matter, Em?" He looked up at me before he used his teeth to open a bag of chips. He shoved a few in his mouth and chomped down before leaning back in his seat. He looked so unbothered.

"What does it matter?" I repeated with a screech. "Nobody even knew if you were dead or alive."

He snorted at me. "Right, even so, who cares? Everyone has moved on with their lives. Frank and Patricia are still just as terrible as ever and you moved across the country and seem to be doing just fine. So who does that leave?" He looked at me with sad eyes. "No one needs me, so why does it matter what happens to me?"

"I need you, you fucking idiot!" I screamed. If there was anyone in the lounge that wasn't looking in our direction before, they sure were now. Not that I cared.

Tanner stopped chewing and swallowed hard as he looked at me. He sat up in his seat before clearing his throat. "You're just s—"

"No, I'm not." I practically vibrated with rage as I stared at my big brother. The one person who was always there for me growing up. My first protector, my first best friend. How had either of us let our relationship stray so far apart?

"Em … you have your own life. You don't need me in it to fuck it up for you."

"Listen," I cut him off as I sensed Leo approaching us. "I know this is mostly my fault. I should have been there for you. I shouldn't have left you like I did."

"No," Tanner said firmly. "You're not going to apologize for getting away from that cocksucker of a husband you had. You needed to leave."

"I should have taken you with me." I choked on the emotion clogging my throat. "I should've and I didn't and for that I'm sorry."

Tanner sat silently as I searched for my next words.

"You say nobody needs you, but that's the furthest thing from the truth. I've always needed you, Tanner. I still do. I need you to help me with this part of my life because it's all really fucking scary. I don't know how to be this person. How to jump first and ask questions later. But you do. You've always been able to let your heart take you wherever you need to be and trust that you will come out whole on the other end."

I took a fortifying breath before continuing. "This man behind me is going to be my husband one day and I *need* you to walk me down that aisle. To hold my hand while I make the biggest leap in my life." Leo gripped my shoulder as I said the words. I could feel his deep love practically flowing from his body for me at that moment.

I'd never leapt into love the way I did with Leo. I had married Chris but that had been a thing to do just to survive, to escape my shitty life. It had never been a decision made with my heart.

I glanced up at the man that reminded me what it was like to truly love. "And I want babies." I smiled as his grin widened. "At least two, to raise the right way. We will show them what it's like to grow up with parents that would do anything for them and each other." I glanced back to Tanner who was looking at both of us with indiscernible emotion in his eyes. "And they are going to need their crazy uncle Tanner to get into trouble with. They are going to need you to love them just as much as I do." Tears dripped from my eyes down my cheeks as I gripped Tanner's hand in mine.

"Now boarding flight 203 to JFK. First-class ticket holders, please have your tickets ready to scan. I repeat, now boarding flight 203 to JFK," the man over the intercom recited as I stared at my brother

"So can you please get your shit together? If not for me, for your future niece and nephew?" I said with a watery smile.

Tanner snorted before he wiped his eyes with the back of his hand. He grinned at me. "Yes, Em. I will try to get my shit together."

We both laughed and leaned into one another. Our foreheads touched before I spoke. "I love you, you asshole."

"I love you too, you crazy bitch." He laughed.

The final boarding call for first-class came over the intercom and we separated. Tanner grabbed his bag and walked toward the plane while wiping his eyes. Leo helped me stand and pulled me in for a brief kiss.

"Was that your way of proposing?" he teased.

I snorted before grabbing my carry-on. "Only if you're saying yes," I said as I looked up into those honey eyes.

He wrapped his arm around my lower back and

pulled me toward him. I gasped softly as he ground his thick excitement against me. "That's definitely a yes," he murmured right before he sealed his lips to mine again.

Chapter Twenty-Three

I swallowed down my raising dread as the town car pulled up to the sprawling estate I used to call my home. I scoffed at the thought. *Who was I kidding?* This place had never been my home. This was just the place I had been forced to grow up in.

Our driver was a man that hadn't been in my parents' employment when I lived here, as I had never seen him before. He had been waiting on us as we landed at JFK with a sign that read *Donaleigh/Cruz*. I'd rolled my eyes as we walked up to him. My mother knew my last name was not Donaleigh, but she just liked to keep digging in that knife any chance she got.

Thank goodness for Leo. If he hadn't grabbed my hand and distracted me, I feared I may have tried to maim our driver. He'd pulled me to him and whispered in my ear that I shouldn't worry about the name. Soon enough it would no longer be a question as to what name I had because he would be changing it to Cruz the first chance he got.

Our driver had driven us through the busy streets of New York as we made our way to the richer part of the city. When we rode further upstate, the changes in scenery always left me slightly breathless. Even if some of my worst memories occurred in this place, it never ceased to amaze me with its beauty.

When we reached the private drive that would lead to my parents' mansion, our driver stopped at the decorative iron gate and typed in the code. As the doors swung open for us to venture further, my heart leapt forward as the car did.

I watched from my place between Leo and Tanner as the trees that lined the perfectly manicured driveway flitted past my vision. I could feel my stomach rolling the closer we came to the house as we drove across the pristine pavement. I knew deep down I was being ridiculous. I shouldn't be having this visceral reaction to a place. But even common sense held no ground in a place like this. My body and mind knew this was a place it never wanted to be again and yet here I was.

Just when I thought about jumping from the vehicle, the big house finally came into view. I breathed in a sharp breath as I closed my eyes and fortified myself. It was almost time to meet with these monsters again. Only this time I wouldn't be the scared little girl I once was. I had some hard questions for Daddy Dearest and I would be getting some answers.

I frowned when I noticed cars lining the half-circle drive. *Were they having a party?* It seemed odd they would be having a party given that it was still early afternoon. Even odder that they knew we were coming and still decided to have the party.

I risked a glance over at my brother. He looked paler now than he had at the airport and I was almost certain he had sweat through his t-shirt. His eyes darted from the front door to the driver in hurried movements as if he too contemplated jumping.

I reached over and gripped his hand in mine. It was cold and clammy as though there was no blood flow going to his fingers. He glanced at me and that's when I saw a brief glimpse of fear in those hazel eyes. The car came to a stop but we didn't stop staring at each other. Call it an unspoken bond siblings share or whatever, but we knew we would need each other if we were going to get through the next few minutes.

"Are you ready?" I asked, forcing a smile to my lips.

Tanner snorted and squeezed my hand. "That's a hard no, you?"

I mimicked his snort. "Absolutely not." I glanced at Leo who was looking at me with concern in his gaze. "Let's get this over with," I said as I squeezed Tanner's hand one last time before releasing him.

We all exited the vehicle and made our way up the huge brick staircase that led to the front doors. To an outsider looking in, this place was like a dream come true. The beautiful white house was pristine and the manicured lawn and surrounding shrubbery were straight out of a magazine. Only Tanner and I knew the truth that lurked behind all this beauty. Lies, neglect, and mental abuse lay behind those doors.

As we crested the top of the staircase, an elderly woman with hard eyes greeted us. Like the driver, I'd never seen this woman before. I eyed her warily as we came face-to-face. At first, she said nothing as she looked at us with disdain plain in her gaze. Her eyes roamed over Leo first then me and finally landed on Tanner. The scoff under her breath didn't go unnoticed by me.

"Gretta, so nice to see your sour puss again," Tanner tossed her way as a mischievous light gleamed in his smile.

Gretta said nothing as she scowled at my brother. I didn't think her face could hold any more disgust.

"Still as delightful as ever I see. You still haven't taken my advice and gotten laid? I think a good cock would help turn that frown upside down, my dear," Tanner poked.

I hid my smile behind my hand as I watched Gretta's eyes squint at Tanner before speaking. "If you are quite done, Mr. Donaleigh, your father requests your presence in his study. He left explicit instructions to stay away from the garden, as your mother is entertaining guests this afternoon." With that, Gretta turned on her heel and disappeared into the house.

Tanner smirked after her before he turned to me and Leo. Even though he looked like he was enjoying himself, I knew he was hating every second of this.

"Let's get this over with," he said as he extended a shaky hand toward the door. His tremor seemed to get worse as the hours ticked by. His body was trying to process not getting what it had gotten so used to—drugs.

Leo gripped my hand before we walked into the house. Nothing had changed with the interior since I'd left. The shiny wooden floors and staircase seemed just as disinviting as ever as we walked through the foyer. Our footsteps echoed behind us as we walked past the stairs toward my father's study. The clean marble walls screamed luxury as I scanned my reflection in them.

I always thought looking into someone's home was like getting a peek at that person's soul. My thought proved true as I looked at this house. It was just like my parents—cold, hard, inhospitable.

As we stepped up to the door that would lead into my father's study, I felt Leo grip my hand reassuringly. I looked up into that honey gaze before he leaned down and brushed his lips against mine. I released a breath I hadn't known I was holding until now as I relaxed against him.

"That's better. I thought you might pass out soon," he murmured against me.

I chuckled as I put my hand against his chest. He pulled away to kiss my forehead as I fortified myself once more. After one last deep breath, I pushed the door open and stepped into the room.

This room was different from the rest of the

house. It was dark with its wooden walls and dark plush carpet. It also smelled of the sweet cigars my father was always smoking. This was the only room in the house my mother never ventured to, so it stood to reason my father was always in there. It was almost comical that my dad held as much disdain for my mother as we kids did.

I let my fingers glide along the felt of the billiards table as we walked deeper into the study. The huge piece of furniture was beautifully hand-carved mahogany. The felt had been imported from some foreign country and added to the custom piece. During all the years I'd seen this table, I had never once seen anyone use it. It was like most other things in this house, just another show of the family's staggering wealth.

"Emily," an all-too-familiar voice sounded from across the room.

I moved my eyes away from the billiards table to the imposing figure that sat behind the matching desk. He looked as though he hadn't aged a day. His thick strawberry-blond hair still had the same amount of gray speckling throughout. His mustache was trimmed to perfection, seeming to only draw attention to his sharp chin. His almost too-white teeth gleamed in the low light of the study as his dark blue eyes traveled the length of my body as if looking for any damage. As if he would care at all.

"God, you've changed, haven't you?" he said as he stood from his seat behind his desk. He smoothed down the front of his black suit jacket before straightening his cherry-red tie. He was dressed for a party that was obviously happening today.

"I can't say the same." My voice sounded dull even to my own ears as he approached me. I gripped Leo and jerked him to me before Frank could come any further. Leo wrapped his arm around my waist and hugged me to his side.

Frank stopped his advance, his eyes moved to where Leo was gripping me tightly. His smirk almost pissed me off as he gazed back up into my eyes.

"I figured you would end up spreading your legs for him again. I tried to tell Patricia it was a bad idea to hire him. You always were a little slut when it came to Mr. Cruz," he scoffed as he relaxed against the front of his desk.

Before I could retort anything back, Leo pulled away from me and started toward my father. A look of rage clouded his eyes as he clenched his fists together. I quickly pulled him back to me and forced him to look down at me. He clenched his jaw before yielding to me.

"Don't listen to him," I whispered as I smoothed my fingers along the scruff of his cheek. I needed to de-escalate the situation before Leo killed him. "You like it when I'm a little slut for you," I teased, hoping to defuse the bomb that was Leo with sexual humor.

His eyes flared and his jaw twitched as he fought a grin. I knew how hard it was for him to let the disrespect go, but it would do him no good to beat the shit out of Frank.

"Way to welcome her back with open arms, Frank," Tanner's voice rang out. I moved my gaze to him as he fingered my father's crystal decanters full of scotch. He pulled the lid off and brought it up to his nose for a smell. He gripped a glass and looked it over like he was going to pour the amber liquid into it and decided otherwise. He threw the glass over his shoulder and didn't even flinch when it shattered against the wall. He smiled deviously at Frank as he plopped down in the plush armchair and took a long pull from the bottle.

It was just like Tanner to distract our parents' negative attention away from me. He always found a way to do something so off-key to drag their engagement toward him instead of me. Even when we'd been kids he had protected me from their harsh scrutiny.

"You look like shit, son," Frank's voice held all the disgust his expression showed.

"Awe, I missed you too, Dad," Tanner said as he pulled another drink from the decanter. "Ah," Tanner sighed after he swallowed. "You did always have the good shit, I will give you that."

Frank practically vibrated as he stalked up to my brother and ripped the bottle out of his hand, sloshing the liquor all over him and the chair. Tanner simply dragged his fingers across his shirt and slurped the wet digits into his mouth before smiling back up at our father. I snorted at the show of annoyance directed at the one person in this room we both hated.

"You little prick. You're a good-for-nothing druggy and I'm not wasting this good scotch on someone like you." Frank's face turned beet-red as he slammed the crystal back onto the little table by the chair.

"Whatever, Frank. Let's just get this over with so I can get the fuck out of here. Which rehab are we going to try this time?" Tanner picked at his nails, not bothering to look up.

Frank balled his fists up before he grabbed my brother's collar and ripped him out of his chair.

"Hey!" I yelled and started toward the two when Leo pulled me back.

"You think I'm going to waste any more money on a piece of shit like you?" Frank seethed. "You're going to pay me back every cent you stole, you worthless little fucker. The only reason I had your sister go and get you is so I could do this in person," he said right before he pulled back and punched Tanner in the face.

The sound that left me was pure rage as I tried to

push away from Leo. He held me to him too tightly as he pushed me toward the wall.

"Let me go!" I said as I watched Tanner shake off the hit.

"Stay here and I will take care of this," Leo growled.

He released me and I stayed where I was. I watched as my big brute of a man took two big strides toward my father and gripped the back of his suit. Frank's eyes grew to the size of saucers as he released Tanner and went flying.

Leo threw him back until he hit his desk with a thud. He then gripped his collar, lifted him, and slammed him down onto the desk. Pens and papers when flying as Leo bore down on him.

I felt a smile of pure delight as Leo pulled back just to give Frank the same treatment he had given Tanner. Frank yowled in pain as blood gushed from his nose. He kicked and flailed his arms just to come up short. Leo looked savage as he bared his teeth and held him still on the desk.

I rushed over to Tanner and helped him off the chair. His cheek would be sporting a bruise tomorrow but other than that he'd be fine.

"Get the fuck off me! You work for me," Frank screamed at Leo as Tanner and I approached the desk.

"Actually, no, I don't. Consider this my formal resignation." Leo smiled down at him before winking up at me.

"I will fucking ruin you, Cruz. You'll never find work again," Frank seethed.

"Not before we ruin you first," I said with a grin.

Frank stilled on the desk as he looked up at me, disgust written all over his face. I made sure to get down to his level before speaking again.

"The jig is up, *Dad*. We know all about your employment with Chris. I know you were on the verge of bankruptcy before you took a deal with the Devil. We know all about his embezzling and we have proof you were his right-hand man," I said. Up until now, everything I was saying was a pure educated guess. After today, I would know the whole truth.

"How?" he gritted behind clenched teeth as he squeezed Leo's wrists.

"You hired the best PI money could buy, that's how." Leo smiled down at him. "I do my homework on everyone that hires me."

"We know you've been working with Chris this whole time. We know you're the one that told him about Leo being hired to dig up dirt on him." I tapped his nose with my finger to solidify my point. "Clearly, you twisted it to make it seem like I was the one who hired him when he confronted you. Why did you do that to me? Was it just a desperate attempt for you to weasel your way into Chris's circle and happily take the money that came along with it?"

Frank glared at me, then at Leo and back to me again. "I told that fucking bitch this would never work," he spoke as if to himself. "You don't know as much as you think you do." He smirked at me. "Chris never confronted me because he never knew I was the one that hired Leo. *I* never told him you betrayed him."

I furrowed my brows in confusion. If Chris had never confronted Frank about hiring Leo, then who told him I was the one that hired him?

"Your mother was the one that told him you hired Leo. She knew we were broke and she didn't think the way I was doing it was going to work. The cunt never did trust me. She said that if I had absorbed Chris's company like I intended to, I would run it into the ground as I had mine. She also said if Chris found out I was the one to hire a PI he would've shown no mercy. You knew the man, did he seem like a merciful guy? We would have been completely ruined," he admitted with a sneer, as if talk of the past put a bad taste in his mouth.

"He never even spoke to me until after you left and it was all over. I was as much in the dark as you were, Emily. She's the one that made the deal with him and didn't tell me. It was a mutual take, he got info about his treacherous wife and we gained his trust. She told him you were looking for any way you could to get out of the marriage so you were going to blackmail him. He bought it. That's when he let me in on his scheme and started making me millions."

All the pieces fit so nicely together now. Leo had guessed wrong but the outcome was the same. I'd been betrayed by my mother this whole time. She knew the way Frank was handling things would end badly for them so she threw her own daughter into the flames. She was the mastermind behind it all.

I thought after all these years that she couldn't hurt me anymore. I thought everything I had experienced in my childhood had hardened me against her. I was wrong, as I felt a deep sadness form in my gut. I knew I would never have a mother/daughter relationship most had gotten but that didn't stop the heartbreak that was happening as I pushed away from my father's desk.

I covered my mouth to smother my sob before Tanner wrapped his arms around me. He held me from behind as I squinched my eyes closed. He gripped me tightly as if to hold my pieces together before I completely fell apart. How could the person that brought me into this world be so truly vile?

I heard a scuffle and a thunk before I felt another set of strong arms around me. I sighed and leaned into

Leo as his familiar scent surrounded me. Tanner released his hold on me but kept his hand against my back nonetheless.

"The past is the past, Emily. It's time to get over the things you can't change," Frank's voice pulled me back into the now and I pushed away from Leo. "Honestly, you should be thanking your mother. You still get to cash in on the family's wealth because of her," he spat.

"You want me to thank that monster? Because of her lies, I was kicked like a dog and beaten. I lost the last three years of my life because of her." It was true. If she hadn't set all this into motion, I would have never left Leo because I never would've thought he lied to me.

Frank did what he did best and blatantly ignored me. "Tanner, I expect my money back in full in a month. Otherwise, I will be speaking with the authorities. Stealing is not something I take lightly. And as for you, Mr. Cruz…" Frank sat down in his desk chair and straightened his rumpled jacket as he stared at Leo. "You'll be hearing from my lawyer before the day is up. Assault is a real thing, young man." He sniffed.

Leo gripped my chin and smiled before capturing my lips for a light kiss. "Totally worth it," he murmured.

I turned toward my father and scowled at him. "None of those things will be happening, Frank," I said sternly.

"The fuck if they won't," Frank scoffed.

I held my finger up as I reached into my purse and dug around for the thing I was looking for. Once I found it I pulled it out with a broad smile.

"You see, you aren't going to do shit. Because if you do, I'm going to release this." I pressed "play" on my phone, and Frank's voice filled the room. *"That's when he let me in on his scheme and started making me millions."* I smiled as I paused the recording. I reveled in watching the blood drain from his face.

"You will go to jail for a very, *very* long time," I said and smirked.

"Why, you little bi—"

His next words were cut off as Tanner rushed him and decked him across the jaw. Frank immediately slumped over, knocked out cold. Tanner shook his hand in pain as he grinned like a loon.

"Totally fucking worth it!" he preened.

I snorted at him as I turned to Leo. "Let's go home," I said before looking back at Tanner. "All of us."

Tanner grinned at me before grabbing the scotch decanter and heading toward the door. I rolled my eyes as Leo gripped my hand, leading me after Tanner.

"He's going to be a handful," I muttered

Leo kissed the back of my hand as we walked back into the foyer. "We can deal with him together." He grinned.

I smiled as I glanced back toward the entrance that would lead to my escape from this terrible place. I almost made it to the door when I noticed something I'd missed before. I stuttered to a stop as I read the words on the big sign propped on the easel. *Could they really be* this *cruel?*

Emy, what is—" Leo's words were cut off as he too saw the sign.

Christopher Hasting's
&
Brittany Siphon's
Engagement Party

Chapter Twenty-Four

It was almost as if I was in a dream as I felt my feet moving. I could vaguely hear Tanner and Leo in the background calling my name. I hadn't realized I was running until I was pushing out the glass doors into the garden.

I squinted as the brightness of the day assaulted my vision. I stumbled forward in search of one person and one person only. I was going to strangle my mother and enjoy every last second of it.

How could she do this to her only daughter? She knew how Chris had treated me while we were married and she continually took his side. But to throw him a fucking engagement party? Was the woman truly daft?

I walked forward as I scanned the immediate area for the bitch that birthed me. The garden was as gorgeous as ever. The thick bushes full of perfect flowers made the area smell sweet like spring. Little cauldrons of fire scattered across the area, making it seem cozier than I knew it to be. Everywhere you looked were servers in white coats and black pants holding silver trays filled with alcoholic drinks.

I walked down the flourished steps until my feet hit the plush grass covering the expanse of the ground around me. A server walked right past me and without thinking I reached out as quickly as I could. I grabbed the first thing I could on the tray before gulping it down. I tried not to cringe as the warm liquor slid down my throat and warmed my belly.

The server looked at me in horror before signaling someone behind me. One glance over my shoulder had me cursing. The fucking security guard rushed down the steps after me.

I held my hands up as he gripped my upper arm. "I'm just looking for Patricia," I said as I handed the glass back to a very disgruntled server. I nearly laughed as they scoffed back toward the bar.

The guard looked me up and down as if deciding if I belonged there. That's when I looked around at the other partygoers. Some stared at me as they whispered behind their hands while others openly frowned my way as if I were beneath them. All of them in summer dresses, slacks, and blazers. I knew these types of people. They all thought they were better than me in my jeans and t-shirt.

I frowned back as I started to raise my middle finger at them all. The guard grabbed my wrist and started to drag me back to the house. "You don't belong here," he whispered harshly.

"No shit, Sherlock. I just need to talk to my fucking mother and then I will leave. Trust me, I don't want to be here anymore than you want me here," I said as I tried to pull from his grasp.

He held me fast as he continued to drag me back the way I came. I glanced up as we continued and spotted another two guards holding Leo and Tanner back as they tried to come for me. Tanner was grinning like a madman as he seemed to play with his guard while Leo kept trying to push past his. I could practically feel his impatience to get to me from where I stood.

"It's okay, she's a guest," a soft-spoken voice came from behind me.

I whipped my head in the direction the voice came from and immediately frowned. *Who the hell is she?*

The short woman with long bottle-blonde hair stood behind me. Her light-brown eyes reminded me of a doe. Prey-like. Her small frame was almost swallowed whole in the thick long-sleeved gown she was wearing. I raised my eyebrows at the weirdness of her attire choice. It was at least eighty degrees outside and yet she wore a gown more fitted for winter.

She smiled brightly up at the guard before extending her hand to me. "Emily, right?" she inquired with a small wink.

I looked between her and the guard before nodding.

She returned my nod. "Your mother asked me to fetch you." She grinned before looking toward the guard expectantly.

The guard stammered as he released my arm as quickly as he had grabbed it. "I'm so sorry, miss," he said to the woman before he took a step back.

"It's quite all right, Henry. You were just doing your job." The woman glanced over my head toward Leo and Tanner before nodding. "Can you please assure Emily's traveling companions that she will be right out? They may wait where they are or go back inside but I'm afraid,"—she looked back toward me before raking a judgmental gaze down my wardrobe—"they are not fit to enter as they don't adhere to the dress code."

I scowled at the little doe and thought to myself that maybe she wasn't prey after all. She had claws underneath that soft exterior she presented to the world.

"Yes, miss." Henry gave a head nod before turning on a heel and heading back up the stairs. I looked after him until the woman gripped my wrist.

She was so much shorter than me, I almost felt enormous as I looked down at her. "Come this way." She smiled up at me and I could have sworn there was a little darkness lurking behind those perfect teeth.

I nodded as I followed her away from the prying

eyes of the party. She led me down the winding path that led into the closed-off area of the garden. Tall bushes and scattered fountains would assure nobody saw or heard what we spoke about.

This was just typical of Patricia. Rather than face her own problems head-on like an adult, she would rather send someone else to do her bidding.

Once we were in the closed-off area in the garden, my chauffeur stopped to admire the huge fountain at its center. I walked around her warily as I searched each seating area for my mother. When I came up empty-handed, I glanced back at Miss Perfect for answers.

"So, you're the famous Emily. I have to admit, I didn't think I would ever get the chance to meet you. You're much prettier than I expected." The woman's voice held no small amount of awe as she pulled her gaze from the water back to me. I ignored her backhanded compliment and studied her closely. The look she gave me had me regretting my earlier thought. This woman was no prey. She was all predator and she had done such a good job hiding it.

"Who exactly are you?" I asked as I sidestepped away from her.

She laughed as if what I asked was the funniest thing in the world. "It figures you crash *my* party and you don't even know who I am." She grinned ferally toward me.

Her words dawned on me then. "Brittany," I whispered.

"The one and only." She held her hands out as though presenting herself. "What? No congratulations for the blushing bride?" Her eyes darkened as she studied me.

"You're marrying Chris so I think the word

you're looking for is condolences," I murmured as I really looked at the woman in front of me. I now noticed the slight darkening under her eyes that she tried to hide with makeup. If he was already hitting her, the long-sleeved dress was making sense now.

"What did you just say to me?" she gritted behind clenched teeth.

"I said my condolences. I've been in your shoes and I wouldn't wish it on anyone," I said as I straightened my spine.

She crossed her arms over her chest and scoffed at me. "You don't know shit."

"I know that it starts small … I bet it's already started, hasn't it?" I asked. If I hadn't been studying her so intently, I would have missed the way her shoulders bunched at my words. "First, he's quick to get angry with you over small things, like that one time you may have forgotten to pick up the dry cleaning," I continued as she glared at me. I could tell she hated me. Whether she was told to hate me or she just truly made her own judgments about me didn't matter. What mattered was her safety.

"Then it turns to explosive anger, screaming at you for not doing as you're told. All that is mild compared to what happens when he gets really comfortable. When his cruel words turn into rough hands." I didn't miss the way Brittany rubbed her wrist as though it pained her. My bet was there was a dark bruise that marred the skin there. "Might be an arm yank here and there, maybe he will shake you a little too hard."

I stepped toward her now. Coming closer and closer to the woman that was now residing in my old place. Even if she was nasty to me, that didn't mean she deserved what was going to happen to her. "Even that is easy compared to the first time the back of his hand flies across your cheek the one time you stick up for yourself," I whispered as I tried to grab her hand.

She jerked away from me and stared up at me like I was her enemy. "I would never do anything to upset him the way you did," she hissed at me. "I have heard stories about you, *Emily*," she said my name as though the words soured on her tongue. "You weren't a good wife. You never treated Christopher the way a wife should treat her husband." She raised her perfect nose to me as if I was the crazy one here. As if she were better than me.

I gritted my teeth before stepping into her space. Even though this woman pissed me off to no end, I wouldn't be able to leave unless I knew she had a way out.

I used my size to my advantage as I gripped her elbow and brought her closer to me. "You don't have to believe me now, but when it starts, if it hasn't already," I whispered before handing her a business card from my purse, "call me and I'll help you."

Nobody deserves to be abused by the person they're supposed to be able to trust most in this world.

I watched her eyes widen as she studied me. She swallowed thickly before looking at the card in my hand. She didn't look me in the eye as she took it from me. I sighed as a little relief coursed through my body. *At least she had a way out.*

"What in the hell are you doing?" a shrill voice caused Brittany to jump and I released her. The woman behind the voice may have scared her, but it held no such power over me. Not anymore.

The sound of high heels clicking against the stone path filled my ears as I turned to face the true monster of my past—my mother.

"You come into this party, uninvited, and accost

Christopher's fiancée. What was your plan, Emily? To scare her into not marrying him?" Patricia's shrill voice made me cringe as she approached us.

"I mean, that isn't a terrible idea. But no, I'm just making sure she has a scapegoat for when she needs it," I said calmly as my mother grabbed my wrist.

"Oh, really, Emily, you're still on this. You and I both know Christopher treated you like a queen. He didn't abuse you. If anything, you did the abusing when you decided to cheat on him with that *man*." She referred to Leo as if he was the gum beneath her shoe. Her hazel eyes that looked too much like my own were full of so much hatred.

I yanked my hand away and stalked closer to her. I took satisfaction from the brief glimpse of fear I saw in her eyes.

"That *man* is the only person to ever treat me with the love I deserved. He is the reason I didn't kill myself when Chris refused to give me a divorce. He was never the villain in this story, *you* were," I seethed.

Patricia had the common sense to back away from me. She shook her head as she turned around and headed back toward the party. I followed closely.

"Oh, what? Now you have nothing to say to me?" I bated her as she walked faster down the path. "You're the one that told Chris I hired Leo, and do you know what he did to me?" I asked.

She didn't stop walking as I continued, "He beat me, *Mother*. He left me bruised and broken on the floor as he taunted me with pictures of Leo and me together." We rounded the corner and the rest of the party came into view. I gripped Patricia's wrist and jerked her around to face me. She winced as a pop sounded in the joint and I had to smother my grin of delight.

"Are you happy with what you've caused,

Mother? Do you have anything to say for yourself?" I yelled so that everyone would hear me. These people were bloodthirsty vultures for any tidbit of gossip they could find, and I would be the one feeding them tonight.

Patricia wrenched her arm away from me before facing me. "You spoiled little bitch!" she screamed and I smiled. "Do you have any idea what Chris is worth to this family? You were going to fuck it all up because he was a little too rough with you. Boo fucking hoo." She sneered at me. "I had to do what I did to make sure we could still cash in on that wealth. Telling him you were the one to hire the PI *and* that you were fucking him was the only way I could make Chris trust us again," she admitted.

"So, you're the one that told him I was sleeping with Leo too. Why am I not surprised?" I said.

I saw red as Patricia started to laugh. "Who do you think gave Chris the pictures?"

Before I could stop to think about my actions, I raised my hand and slapped her across the face as hard as I could. The crowd behind us gasped as her whole body snapped to the side. My palm screamed at me, but that didn't stop the surplus of satisfaction coursing through my body as I saw the red mark appear along her cheek before she covered it with her hand.

"You're a wretched, heartless bitch and I hope you rot in hell," I gritted out as I stepped around her. I was done with this life. I had gotten the admission I came here for and I could finally put it all behind me.

"Don't you walk away from me, Emily! You stop right now or I will cut you off permanently. Do you hear me? You are no longer a part of this family!" she screamed behind my back.

I rolled my eyes and smiled to myself as I stopped at one of the fire cauldrons. I found my wallet and removed that little black card I'd enjoyed abusing all these years. Without a second thought, I tossed it into the fire.

"I have my own family, I don't need yours," I announced as I walked toward the front drive and smiled proudly at the gawking faces.

Chapter Twenty-Five

One Month Later

Beu smiled down at Harper while wiping away her tears. "I know I ain't got much, but what I have is yours. It's always been yours. You have my heart and I don't ever want it back. I want ... no, I need you to keep it," he finished with a shimmer of tears in those light-green eyes.

Harper looked up at the love of her life and opened her mouth to say the words she had been dying to say since the first time she'd seen him.

A soft hand wrapped around her wrist and tugged her away before she could speak.

"I will be damned if you're going to ruin our good name because of some dirty, no-good, ranch hand. You are getting in that motorwagen," Harper's mother hissed as she pulled her away from Beu.

"Momma, stop. I can't leave him." Harper clawed at the hand coiled around her wrist as she looked back toward Beu. He was hot on their heels as he pleaded with her mother.

"Please, ma'am. I love your daughter and I would give anything to be wi—"

She never dropped Harper's wrist as she whirled around to face Beu. She pointed a delicate finger in his face as she snarled at him. "You will never come near my daughter again, do you hear me, boy!"

Beu held his hands up as if to show he was of no harm. Harper tried to pull away but came up short as her mother held onto her like a vice.

"Momma, stop. I love him. I'm not going anywhere with you!"

"You shut your mouth, little girl," her mother

gritted out before facing Beu again. "It's bad enough Harper has made a fool of herself, sleeping with the likes of you. But she's also made a fool of me. This ends now," she seethed as she attempted to tug Harper along. "That boy is lucky I don't write a letter to his employer and have him punished for assaulting you."

Harper saw red as she watched the light in Beu's eyes vanish. Enough was enough. "I said stop!" she screamed as she jerked away from her with all her strength. Her wrist screamed as she pulled away, but she was free.

She rushed back to Beu and he enveloped her in his arms. "I'm so sorry," she cried as he breathed her in. Beu shook his head before capturing her lips with his once again.

"Harper Louise, that is quite enough. That boy isn't good enough for you." Her mother stalked toward them, her face red with frustration.

Beu turned Harper so his back was facing her mother, protecting her from the wrath that was headed their way. "I'm not letting her take you away from me," he whispered before turning to face the monster that was her mother.

"No," Harper whispered to herself. She would not allow Beu to take the brunt of this punishment. She refused to let the man she loved become a martyr to the person that raised her.

She pushed past Beu and faced her mother. The smirk that formed on her lips was enough to make Harper start seeing red again. She thought she'd won this fight. She was wrong.

"I knew you'd come to your senses. That boy is trash, Harper. You were about to give up your life being full of riches and prestige for some disgusting ranch hand." Disgust was plain in her voice as she continued her rant. *"You'll thank me later for saving you from a lifetime of dis—"*

Her words stalled on her lips as Harper smiled at her mother, pulled back, and slapped her open hand across her face. The look of shock and then pain registered in her mother's eyes. Harper's hand stung but it was a small thing as the triumph she felt overwhelmed everything else.

Her mother was overly dramatic, as usual, as she cupped her cheek and sank to her knees. Good. This was a better position to get her point across anyway.

The hot breeze ruffled her nightgown around her ankles as she stooped to her mother's eye level. She looked her in the eyes and almost smiled at the slight fear she saw waiting there for her.

"That's for never being the mother I deserved, as well as speaking ill of the man I love," she spoke calmly and softly to get her full point across. "I'm done letting you control my life. So here is how this is going to go from now on. I am *leaving with Beu." Harper held her hand up to silence her mother when she started to protest. She was delightfully surprised when she closed her mouth. "He makes me feel things I've never experienced in my entire life. It doesn't matter that he's a poor ranch hand. He has shown me what it means to be truly loved by someone else. Something I should have learned from you as a child, I'm just now discovering from him."*

Harper paused to look back at Beu who was smiling down at her with such love in his eyes it made emotion swirl inside Harper's chest. She didn't take her eyes off him as she spoke again. "It doesn't matter if I never see riches ever again in my life, as long as I always have him."

Her mother scoffed and Harper glanced back

down at her. The red mark along her cheek looked angry and puffy as she scowled at her daughter.

"At the end of the day, it doesn't matter what you think or what you want, Mother. This is my decision and you will respect that or you will no longer be included in my life. I will leave you here to think about that."

Harper stood to her full height and walked back toward Beu. This time when he hugged her to him, she released a long calming breath. Neither of them said anything further as they walked to Beu's steed.

"You're going to regret this!" her mother sobbed as Beu helped Harper up onto the saddle.

Once she was situated, Beu climbed up behind her and pulled her flush against his front. Harper's breath caught as he clutched her around her middle. She looked up into those green eyes as he gazed down into her blue ones.

"Never," she whispered. Beu smiled down at her before catching his lips to hers. She moaned and melted into him as his hands roamed her torso. Before she was ready, he pulled his lips away and grabbed the reins. He gave the command and the steed turned and trotted down that old dirt road. Away from her mother and toward her freedom.

****

I smiled as I stared at the blinking cursor. The ending to the book may have seemed a little cliche but to me, it was justifiably perfect. I looked away from the screen and glanced at the clock. It was almost time to leave and I'd finished right on time.

The month since we had all returned home, had seemed to go by quickly. Once we arrived in town, Tanner checked himself into a great rehab facility close by. Leo and I had taken him there and left him with everything he needed. He was told that if he needed anything at all he was to call me.

Honestly, that had been the first time I had ever taken him to a program that I felt would actually work. Tanner had been excited at the prospect of starting a new life for himself away from New York, and he would have all the support he could handle from Leo and me.

Speaking of Leo, he'd wasted no time at all when we got back to Pensacola. He had moved what little he had with him into my home almost immediately. I giggled to myself and blushed slightly as I remembered that conversation. He had driven us straight to my house and promptly unloaded his suitcase.

"Yeah, make yourself at home," I teased as I watched from the doorway of my bedroom. His ass looked scrumptious as he bent at the waist to remove his clothing from the bag. When he stood to his full height, the smile that played along those sensual lips caused my heart to skip a beat or two.

"Is there a problem with that?" he asked as he slowly stalked my way.

I grinned up at him as he placed his hands on my hips. I coiled my arms around his shoulders as I answered, "Normally, a girl needs to be asked if she wants a roommate before one just moves in."

"Is that so?" Leo grinned as his gaze bounced between my eyes and my lips. I nibbled my bottom lip as I nodded and loved the way his eyes flared with lust.

"Well, my apologies," he murmured before he kissed the side of my mouth. His fingers found their way under the hem of my shirt and rubbed the skin there. My breath caught in my chest as they traveled further up toward my breasts.

"Emily?" he said as he found the border of my bra. His fingers tickled me as they delicately moved to the clasp.

"Hmm?" I hummed as arousal flooded my core. He was teasing me with slow movements as he unclasped the restraint. My breasts bounced free under the fabric of my shirt and I had to bite back a moan. I was so turned on by what little touch he was giving me. My tightened peaks rubbed lightly against the fabric of my loosened bra, only adding to my arousal.

"Is it all right with you…" His breath brushed across my cheek as he breathed against me, traveling to my neck with soft kisses.

I shivered as his hands cupped me. His fingers tweaked my tightened nipples and I had to lean into the doorframe for support. I squeezed my thighs together to ward off the ache that built there.

"W-what?" I stuttered before he pulled my shirt and bra up and over my head. His gaze gobbled up the sight of my bright pink nipples as his fingers plucked at me.

He then kissed his way down my neck and sank to his knees in front of me. He gripped the bottom of my breasts and lifted them. He held eye contact with me as he swirled his hot tongue over one before nipping it with his teeth, pinching the other with his fingers. I jerked and fought the urge to sink my hands into his hair. I wanted nothing more than to pull him to me and never let him go.

"If I move in with you?" he finally asked before he sucked hard on the nipple he was torturing. I arched into him then and couldn't stop myself as I gripped him to me. He groaned against me as he licked and sucked at me.

"Yes," I breathed.

He groaned again before he moved. Before I could blink he was standing and pulling me toward him.

"Thank fuck," he growled before his lips crashed

down onto mine. He pushed his tongue past my lips as he gripped my ass. He ground his erection onto me and I cursed the barrier that was our jeans.

I tried to push my hands between us to tug at his jeans when he picked me up. I had no choice but to hold on for dear life as he walked us toward my bed. I giggled when he dropped me and I bounced onto the soft comforter.

He grinned down at me before hastily unbuttoning my pants. He seemed just as desperate as I was as he jerked the denim and my panties down my legs. Before he could do anything further, I sat up and gripped his waistband.

I watched his hooded gaze as I released the button and pulled the clothing down. His cock sprang free and grazed the front of my breast. I moved my hands then and gripped him around his thick shaft. His mouth opened with a sigh as I stroked him softly. When I moved my gaze to what I was doing to him, my mouth watered to taste him. The pearly liquid at the tip of his cock begged for me to swipe it up.

I leaned forward and pulled him past my lips without thinking about it. As soon as his taste bloomed along my tongue, I moaned my pleasure and closed my eyes. He groaned from above me and threaded his fingers through my hair. He tugged hard enough to light me on fire as I sucked at him. I nearly whimpered as he pulled at my hair, tugging me off him. He forced me to look up at him as he knelt to take my lips with his.

"Not now," he said against my lips as he laid me back. "Need to be inside of you."

He gripped my wrists and held them above my head as he descended on top of me. I could feel the wetness coating my inner thighs as he spread them with his knees. He never let go of my wrists as he lined himself up with my entrance and pushed into me.

His groan blended with mine as he fully seated himself. No matter how many times he took me, it was always as if I was filled to the brink each time. He stretched me as he slowly fucked me, and it wasn't long before I was craving more.

Without the use of my hands, I had to find other ways to urge him on. I wrapped my legs around his ass and tried to pull him into me. I wanted him to fuck me hard and he was going so slow.

His lips moved from mine and danced along the skin of my neck, making his way to my upthrust breasts with soft kisses and sharp nips. I moaned and arched into him as he took my achy nipple into his mouth once again. He still fucked me slowly even though I was urging him on with my legs and churning my hips. If he didn't pick up the pace soon, I would explode with frustration.

"Please," I whimpered breathlessly.

I could feel his grin against my breast as he continued his slow thrusts. He was making sure I could feel every one of his inches as he slid into me over and over again. The bastard was going to make me beg for it.

"Please, what?" he said as he popped my nipple from his mouth and looked down at me with mischief in his eyes.

I scowled at him as I squeezed him between my legs. "Fuck me," I groaned.

He smiled at me then and I felt the overwhelming urge to headbutt him. "I am fucking you," he said.

As if to accentuate his point, he pulled back ever so slowly just to sink back in at the same rate. It was maddening.

He moved both of my wrists so he could hold me with one of his big hands. He then slid his other hand down my body before settling in between us. I sucked in a sharp breath as he pushed down on my pelvis with that hand and rubbed his thumb against my clitoris.

I churned my hips with movements as he watched me with a dark gaze. I throbbed for him as he continued to work me over but it still wasn't quite enough.

"Faster," I gritted between clenched teeth.

Leo stopped his thrusts and brought his face inches from mine then. He kissed the tip of my nose and then my lips ever so sweetly. His eyes sparkled with laughter before he finally spoke.

"Anything for you, Princess." He grinned.

The relief I felt was short-lived as he pulled out of me. He released my wrists and I opened my mouth to protest as he pulled away from me. Whatever I was going to say died on my lips as he gripped my hips and flipped me so fast I became dizzy.

Before I could comprehend what was happening, Leo pulled my ass into the air and a second later slammed into me. I screamed as he pounded into me from behind.

The orgasm that had seemed so far out of reach barreled down on me with the speed of a bullet now. I gripped the sheets under my palms as Leo threaded his fingers into my hair once again. He tugged at me until I was on only my knees. I reached back and gripped his hips for balance as he held me tight.

"Is this what you wanted?" he panted against my cheek as he kept up his grueling thrusts. I felt a coiling deep in my core as his hand at my hip dipped down toward my pussy. His fingers grazed over my clit and I nearly screamed.

"I can feel you squeezing me, Emy. Don't hold back. Come on my cock." His breath puffed across my cheek as he spoke.

I moaned deep in my chest as he pinched my clit and I went flying. I squealed as he pounded into me. Colors flashed before my eyes as I exploded around him. If it was possible, Leo sped up even more as he fucked me.

"Fuck yes," he groaned before pushing me back to the bed. His hands moved to my lower back. He pushed until my ass was in the position he wanted. The sounds of fleshy smacks filled the room as his thrusts became erratic.

I felt another orgasm rise within me. As if my body knew he was almost at his end and I needed to meet him there.

"Leo!" I screamed as he pulled me back for each thrust.

"Too good, gonna come." His broken words spurred me on. I reached underneath me and back until I felt where we were connected. Leo groaned deep in his throat as I gripped his sack in my hand and squeezed him.

He smacked my ass in one swift swipe and I went flying again. His balls tightened as he cursed and spilled himself inside of me. The twitching of his cock prolonged my own orgasm.

We both collapsed into a pile of heavy limbs and shaky breaths. I allowed him to pull me the way he wanted until I was draped over his chest and my leg curled over his lower abdomen.

"That," Leo panted as his hand rubbed down my back. "Was one hell of a homecoming," he finished as he kissed the top of my head. I laughed against him as I leaned up and offered him my lips.

It was good to be home.

****

I was snapped back to the present as the front

door shut and Leo appeared in front of me. I smiled up at him from behind my computer and he returned my grin.

"The wedding starts in a few hours, we better get ready if you don't want to have Jill freaking out. And we still have to pick up Tanner on the way," he said as he leaned down to peck me on the lips. "How's the book coming along?"

I nodded as I saved my work and glanced back at my writing one last time. Leo straightened and held his hand out for me. I shut my laptop and set it beside me before I gripped his hand.

"I'm done now," I said as I stood to meet him face-to-face. I went up on my tiptoes and grazed my lips against his. "I finally found the perfect ending."

The End

Please enjoy this sneak peek into the next book in The Wicked Series:

Lindsey

"You look absolutely stunning, Aunt Jill. And the wedding was perfect," I said as I hugged Jill around her neck. It wasn't an exaggeration when I thought she was the most stunning bride I think I'd ever seen. A lot of women with her petite frame would be gobbled up in all the tulle that came along with a wedding dress. But not her.

The tightly fitted bodice of the dress clung to her every curve and accentuated them even more. Her hair and makeup were immaculate in a way that most would never be able to imitate. I was firmly jealous of her slender body and perfect posterior. Where she was slim and fit, I was soft and what I would consider pudgy.

Even though everyone always told me I held my weight well for my build, it didn't stop that little voice in the back of my brain that screamed I wasn't as pretty as the other girls around me. The one that always spoke too loudly every time I pushed any food past my lips. It yelled I'd never be able to find a good man to love me the way others seemed to be finding without even trying. That voice sounded vaguely like my father's.

That's on Daddy issues, I internally scolded myself as I squeezed Jill. This was no place to think of that monster and what he had done to my family.

"Thank you, Lyns." Her smile beamed my way as she released me and stepped back only to hold my hands. "I'm glad you and your mom were able to talk me down earlier," she mumbled as she gave Damon the side eye. I could almost see her sigh of relief when she realized he hadn't heard her. He was too busy talking with his brothers.

I giggled as I squeezed her hands in mine. "Are you kidding me? Like we would ever let you talk yourself out of keeping a guy like Damon," I said in a hushed tone so as not to raise suspicion. Even though Jill had overcome a lot of her past, her insecurities still shined through under times of stress. And anyone who has ever been involved in one knows how stressful weddings can be.

It's not like she tried to talk herself out of marrying Damon, it's just that she had to be reassured she was indeed good enough for a guy like him. As one of her maids of honor, it was my mom's and my job to kick her ass when she started having doubts.

Jill beamed at me one last time before releasing my hands as Damon approached. The way they looked at each other sparked feelings of yearning I didn't think were possible for me to have.

I'd never had a boyfriend unless you count that one date I went on with Georgie Bluff in junior high. We were barely sixteen at the time and all we did was hold hands at the local movie theater while watching some gory zombie movie. I grinned now when I thought back on the craptastic date.

He had asked me out and I had been so quiet and shy back then that I hadn't had the gall to say I really wasn't interested. He'd picked me up in his mom's old Dodge Neon and we'd split the cost of tickets. I even bought my own popcorn. Why he ever thought I would make out with him in the backseat after the movie was beyond me.

That was my first and last date. Sure, there had been other times in college when I had gone a little further with some guys after a few too many drinks, but it had never been more than some kissing.

That's right, I was going to be a twenty-one-year-old woman in just a couple of days and I didn't have any experience with the opposite sex. How pathetic was that?

It's not like I was saving myself for marriage or anything like that. It's just that I had never met any man that sparked that part of me. Well, all except for one man.

I shook my head to clear my thoughts. Now was not the time to think about Dr. Young. It was a childish fantasy, for one thing. We had only had one encounter but for some reason, I couldn't stop thinking about him. To think a man like that would want anything to do with someone like me was a cruel joke.

I mean, sure, I wasn't completely unfortunate-looking. I had a pretty enough face. I liked my eyes and my long dark hair, but come on. The thought of an older guy like him even having a single fleeting thought about me was ridiculous. But I couldn't fool myself into thinking that when we bumped into one another at the hospital, it hadn't made me feel … something. Just the thought of him sparked feelings inside me I honestly didn't think were possible.

I pushed those inappropriate thoughts aside as I watched Damon envelop Jill into his arms and kiss her like his life depended on it. I couldn't stop the blush from staining my cheeks as his hands wandered lower toward her behind. His smile when he released her lips was enough to make any single woman beg to have a love like that. I couldn't hear what he whispered so close to her ear but whatever it was made Jill throw her head back and laugh.

I looked away from the intimate scene in front of me and watched my mother who looked on toward the newlyweds with such love in her eyes. Heath and Reid flanked both of her sides and were touching her lovingly.

It was like they were inseparable. Heath was the first to trail his hand up my mom's neck and nudge her chin in his direction. She grinned before meeting him halfway for a tantalizing kiss. Mom hadn't even fully opened her eyes before Reid was pulling her toward him for their own sensual kiss.

I couldn't keep the smile from my lips as I looked away. I was so happy she finally had found the ending she always deserved.

Emily and Leo were the next in this wedding party. I always thought Emily was a happy-go-lucky person, but I think that may have been a mask all this time. Because as I looked at her situated in Leo's arms, she truly looked happy.

I was surrounded by happy couples and I felt an overwhelming feeling of loneliness. I mean, sure, I was only twenty. I had my whole life ahead of me. Plenty of time to date and meet new people. I could have any life I wanted.

So, why did I want exactly what was in front of me?

I didn't want to party as my peers did. I didn't want to sleep around with a bunch of different people and figure out what I liked. I wanted to meet the person I was supposed to be with for the rest of my life. I wanted to feel like I belonged.

"Hard not to be a little jealous surrounded by all this mushy shit, isn't it?" a deep voice murmured next to my cheek. I flinched and gripped my chest as I faced the person speaking. Damon's brother, Liam. I'd been so busy in the depths of my self-pity I hadn't even seen him come to stand next to me.

"Sorry, I didn't mean to startle you." He grinned down at me and I couldn't help the nervous giggle that rose from my throat.

"It's okay. And yes, even though I'm extremely happy for everyone in this room, I kinda wish they would all get a different one." I winced at my awkwardness. "Room, that is, get a different room." I shook my head to myself. *Good God, Lindsey, get it together.* The first handsome man to speak to me today and I was tripping over my words.

Liam tilted his head back and a deep laugh boomed out of him. I couldn't stop the smile that spread across my face. "I knew what you meant, Lindsey." He smiled.

"Oh." I blushed and then fell silent. This was my problem. I couldn't handle being around the opposite sex, especially if they were vaguely attractive, and not make a fool of myself. And Liam was more than vaguely attractive. He was downright hot. From his perfectly coiffed hair and deep-brown eyes to all those alluring black tattoos, Liam could have any woman he desired. I was sure of it.

Well, except for Emily, I suppose.

I didn't know the whole story of Liam and Emily but I wondered if it hurt Liam to watch her and Leo together. I risked a peek up at him and found him still grinning at all the happy couples, so maybe not.

"Well, what do you say we get this party going?" he said as he turned his attention back to me. I nodded hastily and moved to take my place by the big doors that led to the reception hall.

Liam clapped his hands together loudly to get everyone's attention. "All right, all you perverts, it's time to get in there and get our drink on." His raised voice quieted all the murmuring around us. "I for one need a stiff drink after witnessing this son of a bitch tie himself to one woman for the rest of his life. Poor fucker," he said as he slapped Damon on the shoulder playfully. I covered my laugh as Damon and Jill both raised their happy middle fingers at him. Liam snickered as he sauntered back toward me.

The intro music for the wedding party started to play over the loudspeakers as everyone lined up behind Liam and me. He intertwined my arm with his as the doors sprang open.

The wedding had been beautiful but the reception was where all the real planning had been. The room was artfully decorated with tables on either side of the makeshift aisle we were to walk down. Black tablecloths with beautifully crafted centerpieces dotted the entire area. People that had just come from the wedding sat at said tables with bright smiles. The dance floor had been assembled and waxed to perfection. The DJ had his huge setup at the far end of the building with all the lights and speakers you'd be able to find at a rave. The open bar held all of Damon and Jill's favorites along with top-shelf liquor. This was topped off with tuxedoed waiters and waitresses to make the evening go off without a hitch.

"Nobody knows how to throw a party quite like a Santos does," Liam whispered into my ear before leading us into the room.

I giggled as he threw his free hand up into the air and started swaying his hips to the beat of the song, "Crazy in Love." He tugged me along with him and I tried to keep the blush from my cheeks as he made a fool of himself.

"Come on, Linsey. Dance with me," he shouted over Beyonce's famous lyrics. I shook my head but he didn't take that as an answer as he gripped my hand and twirled me in a circle. The giggle that bubbled up was involuntary as he settled his hand at my waist.

Fuck it. How often did I allow myself to act

carefree? Never.

I gripped his hand in mine and put my other one holding the bouquet in the air. I swayed my hips and flipped my hair around as we made our way further into the room.

"Yeah!" Liam shouted as we both danced. I waved at friends and family as we continued, grinning like a loon.

The music still beat on and Liam continued to dance when I saw a flash of gray as I looked out into the crowd. I sucked in a sharp breath as piercing blue eyes met mine. His hair was still just as dark with the thick speckling of gray at his temples. His well-manicured goatee was now grown out into the sexiest short beard. My fingers itched to feel the roughness of that hair. He had ditched the lab coat and was now in a suit that looked specifically tailored for him. The black-on-black suit with his blue tie that matched his eyes only added to the masculine beauty that was him. I could see his lean muscle definition from here and it made my mouth water. The smile on his lips as he watched me, awoke some unknown feeling inside my core. I felt the urge to clench my thighs together as his gaze ate me up like a tiger stalking its prey.

Dr. Ian Young was here.

End of sample chapter
****

Lindsey and Ian will return in my next book, *Wickedly Innocent*.

Keep reading for a look into my new series coming later this year, *The Insidious Seven MC*.
****

After checking one last time to see if Lindsey was

doing okay after the incident, I walked over to the open bar to get a drink. I wasn't joking when I told my brother I needed a stiff one tonight. Don't get me wrong, I was happy for Damon and Jill. It was just a little unnerving I was officially the last Santos brother to get hitched. Sure, my sister, Sofee, was just as single as I was, but she was also the baby of the family. Nobody expected her to get married anytime soon.

Nothing would make *mi madre* happier than if I were to quit my "little biker club," as she called it, and settle down. She didn't understand that the MC had been the only thing keeping me sane these last ten years. I loved my family but I was ready to head back home to New Orleans.

I approached the bartender and held up a single finger and gave my order of a whiskey. I knew it wasn't everyone's drink of choice but I was craving the burn it would give me as I drank down the rich liquor.

I watched as a tall man slid up to the bar next to me and ordered a tonic water with extra lime. I eyed him carefully as he played with a coin between his fingers while he waited on his drink. He had an athletic build but from the looks of him, he been through the wringer. He had dark circles under his eyes as if he didn't sleep much.

Even though I was completely hetero, I could still appreciate the fact that he was attractive. His facial hair was on the scruffy side but looked to be that way on purpose. His hair was up in a stylish bun some men wore these days. Something about his reddish-blond hair and hazel eyes rang a familiar bell in my mind. *Did I know this guy?*

The bartender placed my drink in front of me and I downed it in one big gulp before tapping the glass. I would drink the next one slower, but right now I needed the instant relief a fast chug offered.

"Oh, shit, man. Please tell me it tasted as good as it looked."

I turned toward the newcomer and quickly decided he was a decent enough guy. His easy smile told me he never met a stranger he couldn't win over.

"Better than what that's going to taste like." I returned his smile as I pointed at the tonic in front of him.

He rolled his eyes and grabbed his glass before making his way toward me. I thanked the bartender for round two and met him halfway. He took a sip from his glass and the look he gave it after was one of disgust.

"Yuck," he spat. "I always heard that this is the drink you get if you're recovering in a bar, but that's fucking nasty." He put the glass back down on the bar and pushed it away from himself like a toddler would with broccoli.

I couldn't help the chuckle that escaped as I watched him. He held out the coin he had been playing with and I realized it was a sobriety chip.

"Ah, you see, a wedding usually isn't the first place one goes when they are trying to be sober," I said.

He grinned down at the coin before looking out across the room as if searching for someone. "Yeah, my sister's friend is the one that got married today and for some reason, she wanted to drag me along. I promised I'd be good and not drink." He picked up his tonic again. He held the drink up in the air and waved at someone while pointing at his drink like it was show-and-tell. I followed his line of view.

Emily was across the room sitting beside her date waving in our direction. Realization dawned on me then. The reason he seemed familiar was that he was Emily's brother. Those genes must run strong in that family because they really did look like twins.

He chuckled as he glanced back my way. "Even though I never had any problems with alcohol, my fucking *therapist* says I need to try and refrain while recovering."

I nodded as I took another sip from my drink. I welcomed the burn that came after. "So, what was your drug of choice then?" I asked.

The guy stood up straight and tugged on his tie. I laughed as he made a big show of becoming serious. He held out his hand and I gripped it before shaking it firmly.

"Hi, my name is Tanner and I love cocaine," he said and I laughed even harder.

"Nice to meet you, Tanner. My name is Liam," I said before releasing his hand.

Tanner grinned at me as though he finally recognized me. "That's right, you're Damon's brother. You're the one that showed my sister the inside of your mouth a couple months ago," he grinned.

Just like that, the smile was wiped from my face and I stood a little taller. Emily and I had never been a thing, we had only shared one kiss and nothing more. If Tanner was going to start shit with me, then I was fully prepared to defend myself.

"Relax, dude," he snorted. "What my sister does and with who is her business. Though I'm sorry if you didn't realize this, she's totally into Leo."

I huffed a laugh before relaxing. "I know that. No hard feelings there. I think she's an awesome person and deserves to be happy. Even if it's not with me," I said and then chuckled. "I don't think she would be able to handle the MC life anyway." I'd only ever met one woman that would be able to put up with the life I led. But I'd fucked that up years ago.

I winced as images of Tatem splayed under me as I sank deep into her flashed behind my eyes. *Dangerous territory, Santos. Move on.*

Tanner nodded. "That's true." He tried to take another sip of his tonic water and cringed again. "So, that must be your chopper out front then?" he asked as he pushed the glass back away from him.

His question pulled me back to the present. I didn't know whether to be concerned that this guy already knew so much about me or not. Either way, I pushed it aside for now and nodded. "You ride?" I asked

Tanner snorted and shook his head. "I rode my buddy's bike back in high school a couple times. It was nothing like the beauty you have, though. I always wanted one but never really had the chance."

I nodded and we both fell silent then. We looked out over the party and I caught my gaze coming back to him again. His eyes followed his sister as she sat with the rest of the wedding party, drinking and having a good time. I watched his features slump slightly as though the thought of his sister being happy saddened him.

"You good?" I asked as I leaned against the bar.

Tanner leaned with me and nodded again before shaking his head. It was like he was trying to convince himself he was all right.

"It's just," he stared off into space as he spoke. "I have this second chance, you know? I'm finally away from my shitty parents and I'm sober for the first time since I can remember. But it all feels … I don't know … fake."

Tanner ran his hand up the top of his head, smoothing the hair down below its restraint. "This,"—he spread his arms out, indicating the party going on around us—"this isn't me. This is Emily. And that's fine, great even." He sighed. "For her,"—he looked at me then—

"but I don't belong here."

I nodded. I knew the feeling. One of my brothers was a detective, the other a lawyer. Hell, even Sofee was a damn nurse. My whole family was full of good people who did good things. I was the black sheep. I was the one who chose a life with the MC and everything that came along with it. We were a group of guys that never really fit in anywhere before and that's why we worked so well together. We may be known around New Orleans for our sometimes less-than-legal activities, but we always had a common purpose. We always did what was best for the MC, what was best for the brotherhood.

As I watched the sadness consume Tanner's eyes, I had the overwhelming urge to welcome him into the fold. I knew this was crazy, I had just met this guy. I didn't know anything about him besides what I could guess. He was a mistake, a fuckup. So much like the rest of us. Something about him called to me with a brotherly intuition.

Whether he knew it or not, Tanner would fit in perfectly with the rest of The Insidious Seven. There would have to be a vote, of course. I didn't know what was telling me to offer this to him but I had an innate need to see it through.

"Tanner," I said and waited for him to meet my eyes. What I was about to ask required his full attention before continuing.

"Have you ever been to New Orleans?"

End of sample chapter

A.E. NALLE

EVERNIGHT PUBLISHING ®

www.evernightpublishing.com